ATLANTIS

GOLD

AN OMEGA FILES ADVENTURE

RICK CHESLER

10 9 8 7 6 5 4 3 2 1

PROLOGUE

Great Pyramid of Giza, 1938

Selam Hasim was lost.

He knelt on the stone floor of the chamber, somewhere deep within the great pyramid, and smoothed out a map on his knee while aiming a flashlight with his other hand. Drops of perspiration fell from his forehead onto the paper, pattering softly in the near silent space. The confusing array of mapped passages, rooms and chambers made his head spin as he tried to reconcile where he presently found himself with the hand-drawn diagram.

The room he thought he must be in had two exits, while the space he actually found himself in clearly only had one. So that must not be it, he thought, wiping the sweat from his forehead with a shirtsleeve. *Unless Hamar made a mistake with the map.* He shoved aside the grim thought and glanced at his wristwatch. The time of day meant little to him, for down here in the depths of the fantastic Egyptian structure, it was always dark. But the fact that nearly two hours had elapsed since he'd left his expedition's camp was most disconcerting indeed. He needed to get back before his associates noticed he was gone.

As an archeologist on a large, well-outfitted expedition from the University of Cairo, Selam was part of a professional team devoted to thorough, methodical study of the ancient wonder. Not all of the pyramid had been mapped yet, since new areas were still being discovered, and those lesser known sections were strictly off-limits to everyone. Selam was well aware of this rule, but had deliberately strayed from the authorized dig areas nonetheless. One major reason for this policy was safety; many of the pyramid's passageways had to be buttressed with contemporary building techniques to brace the walls, ceilings and floors against collapses and cave-ins. Another reason, Selam knew, was that disturbing a new area without observing proper archaeological technique would compromise the integrity of the site. One wouldn't know whether items had been laying as they were for millennia, or if their positioning was due to the recent disturbances.

He looked around the space again, to see if he had missed something. Sometimes new passageways were discovered, but then blocked off by moving stones back into place to prevent unauthorized persons from exploring them. But aside from the engineered tunnel that had led him to this room—what he thought had to be a subterranean space, beneath the actual ground the pyramid sat on—he saw only four walls, a floor and a ceiling, all constructed from the same solid stone blocks as the rest of the pyramid. It was of course a marvel of human engineering that the Egyptians had been able to cut, transport and move all of these blocks into place to build such a lasting structure, but Selam was currently concerned with much more pressing matters.

He stared down at the map once again, panic beginning to well in his gut. *If I'm not in this room here, then where the hell am I?* He traced the tip of a finger along the solid lines indicating horizontal passages, the dotted lines representing the vertical. And then it hit him-- hard.

You're in a new chamber.

He'd been looking for a room that was known to contain artifacts that had not yet been catalogued. The pyramids and other ancient sacred sites had long been the target of looters, and truth be told, Selam was not above making a an extra buck or two. If he could get to the off-the-books artifacts quickly enough, they were ripe for the taking and would fetch him a pretty penny in the black market antiquities trade. But his interest here today was something special. Even so, he had ended up in a different area altogether, an uncharted space. He was about to retreat back into the passageway that led him here when his gaze lit on a wall-mounted figurine of a pharaoh's bust.

These were not uncommon throughout the pyramid, but still, it could be worth something. Since he'd likely never get another chance to be in this chamber again, at least not alone, he crossed the room to take a closer look. Carved from a single block of quartz, the bust was about eight inches high by four wide. It protruded out from the wall by several inches.

Salem directed the beam of his flashlight all around the statuette where it contacted the wall. He did not want to break it or even chip it. The less marred it was as a result of being extracted from its original location, the more money it would be worth. Still, he had not the time to be as thorough as he knew he should be. He thought something looked a little odd about how it was set into the wall, something about the groove thickness. Usually the joints were tight enough not to permit a human hair inside, but these were much wider.

With a shrug, Selam put a hand on the figurine's head. He pulled it gently to the left, and then right, feeling no play whatsoever. Wide grooves or not, he surmised, the construction--even after the passing millennia--was robust, holding up as well as the rest of the impressive pyramid.

You've no time for this, you need to get back to camp. It kept running through his head like a mantra, but something about the symbolic head transfixed him. He repositioned his grip on the ornament and pulled it upward. Nothing. *I'll try one more thing.* Selam pushed down on the figurine's head.

The barest puff of stone dust drifted down from behind the ancient wall fixture. Then the stone figure began to slide down along the wall. The sound of stone grating on stone reached Selam's ears, lighting a smile on his face. It was coming loose. The artifact would be his for the taking.

The mounted figure came to a sudden hard stop when it reached the bottom of its groove in the wall, and Selam yanked it outward, expecting the object to pull free from the wall. But instead he felt the floor begin to shake.

Selam whirled around and looked at the rest of the room. The stone tiles were in upheaval, undulating all the way from where he stood to the chamber entrance. He felt the figurine come loose in his hand but he let it drop, no longer caring what the historical bauble might be worth.

Curious to see if a new doorway had opened up in front of him, he looked back to where the figurine had pulled away. Nothing new, except for the deep crack where it had been. He mentally kicked himself for triggering what appeared to be some sort of trap. *I have to get out of here right now!*

But when he spun back around his heart sank. Getting out of here wasn't going to be a given. The first row of large square floor blocks had...disappeared! But not disappeared, Selam could see. There was now water in their place. They had sunk. As he watched, more water flooded into the chamber, and the next row of floor tiles dropped beneath the raging waters.

Even as he stepped out onto the tiles that still remained, he had trouble maintaining his balance, as they were all in motion. He went down hard on one knee before regaining his balance in time to see another row of tiles sink away. The last remaining row was the one on which he stood, and that was much too far from the passageway to jump to it. At least the passage was still dry, he could see, since it angled up and away from this underground chamber. But how to get to it? He glanced around at the walls and ceiling. They hadn't changed, but they also offered no obvious means of escape. Comprised entirely of smooth stone with no cracks, hand- or footholds of any kind, they offered zero hope of climbing.

But there was plenty of water, which meant that he was going to have to swim. Selam shuddered at the thought. Growing up in Egypt, surrounded by desert sands, swimming was not something he had done a lot of. He had distant boyhood memories of splashing around in the shallow waters of the Nile, but the chaotic turbulence of rising floodwaters in the chamber was not something he was prepared to deal with.

He would have to cope with it, though, if he was to live, so he steeled himself for the jump into the liquid maelstrom, pulling his backpack straps tighter. As he was about to take the plunge, he caught sight of something in the waters below. They were clear, although moving fast, and when the waves subsided and the physics of the water and his light were just right, he could see down into the depths of the pyramid's watery base.

Something was down there, something large, protruding from the bottom. Then the stone on which he stood fell away and he was in the water, with whatever it was, literally forced to sink or swim. Right away he regretted not having ditched his pack. It weighed him down terribly, and what did it even contain that was worth dying for? A few run of the mill Egyptian antiquities that would probably keep him in extra wine for a few weeks, but little else, and some ordinary archaeology dig tools. But it was too late to remove it now. He had to keep kicking, keep flailing his arms, if he didn't want to drown in this godforsaken pyramid.

Drown in a pyramid? Even as his life was in imminent danger, Selam couldn't help but wonder how this was possible. Where did all this water come from so close to the Sahara desert? *It's a trap!* His desperate mind screamed out. *You unleashed it when you pulled the figurine.*

He kept swimming toward the exit, but water continued to rush in. He wasn't getting any closer. He began to panic. Great waves washed all around him and he looked back to see that the last floor stones had slipped below the water.

He swallowed water and began to cough. The water rose rapidly now in the chamber. Recognizing he was only burning his remaining energy by trying to get closer to the exit, he stuck his head underwater and opened his eyes. He still saw something down there, something that looked distinctly manmade. Taking a massive breath, he dove beneath the water and swam toward it. Maybe it somehow offered a way out?

The form was blurry without the aid of a diver's mask, but still recognizable enough. It was a stone head, a large one, much bigger than the figurine. A human head; even with his blurry underwater vision he could tell that much. The head was toppled over on one side, staring at him unblinking. Salem knew he was staring back it for too long, that he had not a second to spare. But something about the thing transfixed him. He could tell it was special, knew that it was something truly unique and rare.

5

Only the urge to breathe tore him from his reverie. He kicked his way toward the surface, one hand held up as he went, anticipating breaking through to air so he could breathe, breathe, breathe.

The panic he felt when his fist smashed into stone without leaving the water was all-encompassing.

He was still underwater even though he'd reached the chamber ceiling. He felt the weight of his backpack dragging him back down. He stared across the chamber to the tunnel exit. It sloped upwards, so if he could swim into that, he might have a chance. But it was too far away.

He stopped flailing and looked back down at the body-less head and accepted his fate while making eye contact with the unknown artifact.

Selam Hasim was going to die here.

CHAPTER 1

Carter Hunt turned a skeptical gaze from behind blue polarized sunglasses to the submersible craft bobbing in the water next to the work barge. A two-person affair with an acrylic dome propped open, looking at it now didn't exactly fill him with confidence.

"You sure this contraption keeps water out?"

Hunt's friend, Jayden Takada, stepped up to the rail next to Hunt. "As long as we remember to close the hatch, we'll stay dry, I promise. Over a thousand dives in these things and the only time I've gotten wet is when I spilled my beer."

"You really have found a way to stay busy after life in the navy, haven't you?"

Jayden grinned broadly. "Kidding about the beer," he said, casting a glance about the deck to make sure no one overheard that and took it seriously. "But really, being a submersible pilot's a good job if you have to work. Not all of us had a rich grandfather who left us a fortune. This is a vacation for you, trust fund baby, but I've got a job to do here first before I can have some fun."

Hunt laughed good-naturedly at the jab. After serving alongside each other in the U.S. Navy for ten years, the two friends could get away with that kind of ribbing. Hunt couldn't deny Jayden's point, however. At the age of thirty-two, the ten-year veteran, eight of which were spent as a commissioned officer, suddenly found himself with a whole lot of free time stretching out in front of him. Instead of re-upping after ten years as was expected, he left the service in good standing, disillusioned with some of what he had seen. This action was made possible due to his grandfather's sudden passing and leaving him a sizable inheritance, a fortune by most people's standards.

Hunt didn't intend to idle away his life in a haze of mindless leisure, though. He just didn't know exactly what he was going to do yet. This trip to Egypt to visit Jayden was intended to be the tail end of his break after leaving the military. When he got back home to the states he was going to set his mind to starting a business of some kind that would help others while allowing him to stay productive. With a college degree in history, he wasn't sure exactly what that would entail, but in the navy he'd been involved with safeguarding artifacts and historical treasures that had been looted during times of civil upheaval. He had been disgusted at how museums in Iraq and other middle eastern locations had been ransacked of their cultural artifacts. It saddened him that people would place their own interests above others, that they would deprive everyone of being able to see their cultural heritage in order to make a quick buck.

Hunt clapped Jayden on the back. "So, you have room for one more in that thing?"

Jayden nodded. "It's a two-seater and I don't need any technical specialists on this dive, so I can take you along as ballast."

"I knew I was good for something. Run the objective by me again?"

Jayden pointed to the coast of Egypt in the distance, where a city skyline and suburban sprawl were visible on the shoreline. "There's been a disruption of Internet service, and they suspect it has to do with the submarine cable a couple of thousand feet down here." He looked down into the water beneath the floating submersible. "So we're just going to dive down there and take a look, see if we can find a break in the cable."

Hunt grinned. "Sounds like fun!"

#

"Remember, Carter, this sub isn't mine—it's owned by International Telecom, the ones who contracted me to investigate the cable problem."

"Okay, so?"

"So don't mess it up. Don't touch anything—I mean *anything*—without asking first. Heads up, here comes the hatch."

Hunt looked up in time to see a crew member lowering the clear plastic dome onto the sub. He felt a slight pressure in his ears as the latches were fastened in place. "Don't worry, old friend, the last time I touched a control I wasn't sure about—"

"Yeah, the C130 over Tikrit. Don't remind me, okay? The guys were pissed at you for weeks after that, and I told you not to—"

Jayden was interrupted by a voice coming over the sub's radio speaker. "Topside to *Deep Challenger*, do you copy, over?"

Hunt eyed Jayden as Hunt moved his hand halfway to the receiver, as if asking permission to pick it up. Jayden shook his head and grabbed it himself. "Topside, this is *Deep Challenger*, we read you loud and clear. Standing by for the drop, over."

"Roger that. Support divers are in the water now."

Outside the dome window, a pair of scuba divers waved at Jayden and Hunt. Each swam up to the submersible and unclipped the lines that tethered it to the ship. They gave Jayden an okay sign, thumb and forefinger in a circle, indicating they were clear to begin their dive.

"Here we go, Carter." Jayden then flipped a switch on the control panel and they heard the hiss of air escaping. "Don't worry, it's just the air bladders in the buoyancy tubes." Water sluiced over the acrylic bubble dome as the craft lowered itself into the sea.

"Gravity will take us down until we get near the bottom," Jayden explained to Hunt as they sank below the waves. The pair of support divers stayed with them until they reached a depth of 100 feet, then they waved goodbye and began their slow ascent back to the ship while the sub continued on its way down into the ocean depths.

"Only nineteen hundred feet to go," Hunt said. "You got an in-flight movie in this thing?"

"Even better." Jayden pointed out the front of the window, where a large sea turtle glided past, chasing a school of silvery fish. The two friends passed the next few minutes in silence while they drifted deeper into the sea. The surrounding light changed color, the reds and yellows filtering out first, until gradually only blue was left, then even that faded to black around the 1,000-foot mark.

Jayden flipped on the sub's external halogen lights and the powerful beams stabbed through the inky darkness. Tiny particles floated in the light, and there was less life down here; no more large schools of fish or large animals. Still, there was life. A jellyfish with long, flowing tentacles drifted past them. Soon after that the brown mud of the sea bottom came into view.

"If you were wondering what the bottom of the Mediterranean looked like at 2,000 feet, now you know." Jayden gripped a joystick to level the sub out just above the bottom.

"Pretty boring," Hunt said, looking out to his right.

"Good thing we're not here for sightseeing, then, " Jayden said, activating the sub's thrusters to glide over the bottom. "We've got a submarine cable to inspect, but first we've got to find it. Should be right around here somewhere, the ship is anchored over the spot."

Hunt pointed off to his right. "I see something over there." Jayden looked over and nodded. A section of black pipe was visible on the bottom of the ocean, stretching out of sight in both directions.

"That's it, all right." He guided the sub over to it, until they hovered directly over the pipe.

"I don't see anything wrong with it," Hunt said.

"Based on where the signal loss is happening, we know there's about a two-mile section where some kind of malfunction occurred. We just need a direction to go in first. Right or left?"

Hunt looked both ways before answering. "Water clarity looks a little crappier off to the right, so maybe we should try that way first. It could mean something happened to disturb the sediments on the bottom."

"I knew there was a reason to bring you along." Jayden picked up the radio transmitter. "*Deep Challenger* to Topside: "We're at the pipe almost directly underneath the ship. It looks fine right here, so we're going to head along the pipe to the northeast and take a look, over."

The radio reply was immediate. "Copy that, *Deep Challenger*. We're standing by if you need us."

Jayden eyed his intended course along the pipe for a moment before putting his hands into motion on the controls. The submersible followed the pipe about five feet above it. In addition to Jayden and Hunt watching from the sub, cameras mounted outside the sub provided a live video feed to the ship's control room, so that even more eyeballs were on the pipe.

Hunt watched the black metal tube pass by beneath them. "So the pipe is just the outer covering, and the actual cables are inside that, right?"

"That's correct," Jayden said. "Fiber optics. The metal pipe is just to protect them from the elements."

"Or maybe a curious shark that has the munchies."

"That too."

They continued to follow the cable pipe as it snaked off into the gloom. Occasionally a crab or small fish would scuttle out from beneath the pipe, but mostly they saw a hard-packed mud bottom. The electric whir of the sub's thrusters was the only sound while the two men concentrated on visually scouring the pipe for breaks or anomalies. As they progressed, the water grew increasingly cloudy, but they were still able to see the pipe as long as Jayden slowed the sub to stay close to it.

Jayden was about to suggest they turn around and try in the other direction when Hunt tapped on the bubble dome in front of him. "Hold up, got something here."

"Hold up?"

"Yeah, careful, it's real silted up, but there's something different going on there."

Jayden slowed the sub to a crawl, inching them toward the anomaly. Clouds of brown silt swirled around their little craft as they crept along the bottom, just over the pipe.

"Right there, see that?" Hunt pointed into the gloom in front of them. Jayden put the craft into a hover and looked out along the pipe.

"There's the break! What happened to that thing?"

Hunt shook his head as he looked at the mangled section of pipe. A section was completely missing, but they couldn't see how much because the water wasn't clear enough. Bits of metal lay on the seafloor nearby, and a protruding snarl of cabling was visible from the wrecked end of the pipe they could see. "No shark did that."

Jayden picked up the radio transmitter and informed the ship that they had located a break and were conducting an inspection.

"Let's see if we can find the other side of the pipe, see how much has been taken out," Hunt suggested. Jayden agreed and put the sub's forward thrusters into low power so as not to stir up the silt on the bottom and reduce their visibility even further. They passed over the broken end of pipe and then scuttled over the muddy bottom, looking for the pipe's other end.

After a couple of minutes, they had still not found it. "I hope we haven't drifted off of the pipeline," Jayden said. Hunt pointed to the compass on the instrument console. "No, you're good. I took note of our heading. Stay on 210 degrees and we should hit the other side of that pipe."

Jayden looked over at his acting co-pilot. "Once again, Carter, you're proving yourself worthy of that seat. Will miracles never—"

"Whoa! Right there!"

Jayden turned off the thrusters, putting the sub into a controlled hover. "What is it?" Unlike Hunt, who had no piloting duties to occupy his attention, Jayden's focus was divided between driving the sub and also looking at what was outside. But before Hunt could answer, the radio crackled on the sub's console.

"Topside to *Deep Challenger*: we have a visual on the other end of pipe. Almost an eighth of a mile of destroyed cable...."

The radio operator continued to transmit, but Hunt pointed ahead, to where the other side of the pipe lay in ruin. "Jayden. Hey Jayden, we've got something up here that I don't like the looks of. Out to the right from the pipe. Be careful, slow down!"

Jayden looked out at the mangled pipe, then to the right on the mud plain, he saw what Hunt was talking about. "What is that?" Even as he asked the question, the sub pilot put the craft into reverse.

At the same time the radio chatter grew more urgent, with the topside crew also commenting on the object Hunt had pointed out, the speculation running rampant.

"Shipping container that fell overboard off a cargo ship and knocked out the pipe?"

"Is it a repeater or some kind of infrastructure? Where's our rep from Telecom? Get her on the horn."

But Hunt shook his head, his simple sentence drowning out all of Jayden's other thoughts the moment it reached his ears. "It's C4."

Jayden's hands froze on the controls as he stared at the boxy, gray object. "What?"

"I think it's a block of C4 that didn't trigger for some reason when the rest of it took out this pipe. Look at the blast pattern. This didn't happen from some kind of natural wave action or even a subsea earthquake. Certainly not an animal, even a very large one. This pipe was blasted apart, and for whatever reason, those bricks there were never triggered."

The radio boomed again with the voice of a topside crewman. "Jayden, we need some better images of that breakage. Can you get closer? The footage you got of the other end is good, we know what needs to be done there, but now we need to see how we're going to fix this side of things."

Hunt shook his head slowly back and forth, not liking the proximity to the explosives.

Jayden eyeballed the distance from the C4 to the pipe and then spoke into his transmitter. "A little bit, but not much. Little bit of a tricky cross-current down here, but I'll see what I can do, over."

Hunt looked over at Jayden. "Be careful. We don't need to bump into that C4 and maybe nudge the trigger the rest of the way."

Jayden got an odd look on his face and then picked up the radio transmitter again. "Topside, who would put C4 down here, anyway? Was that left over from of the installation process?"

There was a few second delay before a reply came back from a senior crewman. "It was not part of the installation. We don't know where it came from. Proceed with extreme caution, over."

Jayden put his hand back on the joystick and inched the stick forward. The sub inched toward the broken pipe. When he eased back on the thruster, the sub would drift immediately with the current toward the stack of C4.

"Watch it, watch it!" Hunt warned.

Perspiration rolled down Jayden's forehead despite the cool temperature in the sub's cabin. His hands worked the controls as the sub neared the shattered pipe that spewed severed cables out of its end.

"Just a little closer should do it," came the crewman over the radio, indicating that the video feed was not quite clear and close enough.

But Hunt shook his head as the sub started to wobble, buffeted by currents. "I don't like it, Jayden. We don't want to bump that thing."

"Right. We're outta here." Jayden accelerated the sub while turning left, hoping to bring them closer to the broken pipe as they passed by it in a wide U-turn that would take them away from the C4. But as he swung into the turn, the voice on the radio telling them the video was great quality, a sudden downwelling of water slammed them into the bottom. As soon as they hit, billowing clouds of mud were stirred up into the water by the sub, even though Jayden turned off the thrusters so as not to make it worse.

They flipped over and around before coming to rest in a total brownout.

"Not sure which way to go!" Jayden watched the compass spin wildly from the craft's gyrations.

"Take us straight up," Hunt advised.

Nodding, Jayden hit the button that activated the sub's airbags, one in each side pontoon, for sudden lift. But as he did, the sub was hit by a cross-current that turned it sideways, rocketing into the block of C4.

Hunt's warning was drowned out by the dull boom of the detonation.

The sub's floodlights suddenly went dark. Two seconds after that, the control panel indicator lights also blinked out. Hunt and Jayden both braced themselves by gripping the frames of their seats.

"We've lost power! I've got no control," Jayden yelled.

"Let's hope those airbags stay inflated and we're rising." Hunt squinted out the dome into the swirling blackness. He couldn't tell which way was up. All they could do was to sit and wait.

"Spam in a can," Hunt said.

"What?"

"We're like spam in a can right now. It's what test pilot Chuck Yeager said about the first astronaut to orbit the Earth. That he wasn't a real pilot, just meat in a can."

"Thanks, Carter."

"Hey, you know what else pilots say?"

"I'm afraid to ask."

"Any landing you can walk away from is a good one."

"We'll find out soon enough. Because if this can plops back to the bottom…" He left the sobering thought unfinished. To be powerless 2,000 feet down without even a communications link to the ship would mean a slow death by suffocation as their oxygen ran out.

But Hunt's next words buoyed their spirits. "It's getting lighter."

Indeed, looking at what they now knew to be up, through the dome, they could see the barest lightening of the water, meaning they were looking towards the distant sun. It meant that the buoyancy airbags were doing their job, lifting the sub through the water toward the surface. The ride seemed to take forever, but gradually it grew brighter and brighter until it was obviously daylight, meaning they were definitely rocketing towards the surface.

A few minutes later the powerless submersible was close enough to the surface for Hunt to make out the underside of their support vessel. It occurred to him that should they come up directly beneath it, striking it, there would be nothing they could do. Without power, they had no steering, nor could they communicate with the ship to tell them to move it out of the way. But they came up almost a football field away from it, bobbing like a cork in the sunny Mediterranean. It had become stiflingly hot in the cabin and Jayden and Hunt wasted no time in popping the hatch to rejoice in the cool sea breeze. Upon spotting the bright yellow vessel, the ship's crew deployed a tender vessel to retrieve the submersible and its crew. Knowing they had been out of contact, they wasted no time reaching them.

As the sub was tied to the tender, Jayden and Hunt were helped into the support boat. One of the boat crewman remarked how they'd seen the video feed of the broken pipe before it was disrupted. "Big section of pipe missing. We've got our work cut out for us to replace it, but thanks to your surveillance, we know what to expect."

Hunt agreed before adding, "I'll say one thing. Taking out those cables was no accident. Somebody sure wanted to knock out communications between Egypt and the rest of the world."

CHAPTER 2

Great Pyramid of Giza

"According to the LiDAR scans, it should be right here." Dr. Madison Chambers directed the beam of her flashlight to the far corner of a room that once housed a mummy and accompanying treasures meant to see it into the afterlife. LiDAR, or Light Detection And Ranging, was laser-based technology that had recently allowed archaeological discoveries to be made from air-based platforms such as planes. Once an anomaly was detected, field teams would zero in on what was found via imaging for some boots-on-the-ground investigation.

That investigation was here and now, and Dr. Chambers was its leader. A respected archaeologist and tenured professor at a major American research university, Madison found herself in charge of a thirty-person team of scientists, technicians and research assistants, most of whom were now above ground in the camp tents or at ground-level excavation sites. The LiDAR imaging had led her to this place at the very bottom of the pyramid, and she suspected a subterranean chamber of some sort lay not too far away.

Short of stature at just over five foot tall, but long on bravery, Dr. Chambers, long chestnut hair in a ponytail beneath a ball cap, walked across the stone floor to a caved-in section of wall. Crumbling sections weren't uncommon in the pyramid, but as one of the newly discovered rooms at the base of the pyramid, the exciting thing about it was that it could perhaps act as a doorway to somewhere new.

Madison stepped around the mummified Egyptian, already thoroughly photographed and catalogued by her team, although left in place by agreement with authorities at the Egyptian Ministry of Cultural Affairs. The smaller artifacts had been crated and removed to prevent looting. Reaching the crumbled section of wall, Madison aimed her flashlight—it would be pitch black in here without it—over the heap of fractured stone blocks.

They were densely piled, still forming what looked to be an impenetrable wall. Tentatively, the archaeologist stepped one foot onto a fallen block. She breathed deeply, knowing that this was a potentially foolhardy act. The blocks may not be in a stable enough configuration to withstand sudden weight after who knows how long. And here she was by herself, to boot. Yet, the lure of the unknown and the potential promise of publication-worthy discovery was too alluring.

Reasonably satisfied that the blocks were not about to move, Madison stepped up onto another displaced slab a few feet higher. *Should have worn a headlamp*, she chided herself. Holding the flashlight with one hand did not safe climbing make. Still, a few tantalizing glimpses through the cracks of stone convinced her there was some kind of opening on the other side; a passageway, perhaps, although she couldn't be sure yet.

She continued to climb, proceeding higher before moving laterally to her right. She caught herself looking down at one point, and although she was only ten feet above the floor—probably about halfway to the vaulted ceiling—she felt a rush of panic at the realization she could fall and be hurt. But that would only mean starting over from the bottom, Madison told herself. She relaxed her stance and loosened her grip a little on the rocky holds she had chosen to support her weight. She needed to loosen up; staying tense was counter-productive.

Only a few more feet to her right was a massive slab of rock that jutted out into the room that she didn't have any hope of getting around, not from this height at any rate. But the space in front of it looked promising, so she picked her way carefully across the jumbled wall until she reached a blessed sight: a nearly flat rock she could actually stand on. She was grateful for the chance to rest.

Madison took a bandana from her back jeans pocket and wiped the sweat from her forehead. This was hard work, but it wasn't everyday one got to explore a new area of the great pyramid, so she could work through the pain and discomfort. Careful to set her footing before turning around to look through the cracks in the broken wall, Madison took a couple of deep breaths before proceeding. Ever so slowly, she spun around in place on her little pedestal of rock.

Raising her flashlight to shoulder level where one of the larger openings was—large enough to permit her head and one hand holding the flashlight to peek through—Madison aimed her beam of artificial light into a space that hadn't seen human presence for a preponderance of years. She sucked in her breath with the startling realization that she was looking into a downward sloping passageway of some kind. Rock walls, floor, ceiling.

I've got to find a way in there. Her fears now abandoned, she now lamented the fact that she wouldn't be able to fit through the opening in front of her. If she was going to investigate this new passage, she would have to find another way in, which meant that she would have to climb around some more. She couldn't see any obvious places to make it through, so she climbed a bit higher and then started moving out to her left, away from the big slab that blocked the way further out to her right.

The archaeologist found what she was looking for about halfway across the jumbled wall, and very near the ceiling. Just my luck, she thought. It would have to be the hardest part of this collapsed wall to reach. There was no way she was going to let an irrational fear of heights or closed spaces, or anything else, for that matter, stand in her way. Madison methodically sought out hand-and footholds that took her up the wall to the rock she had seen there.

A huge stone, precariously balanced. It looked like it was about to tip over, like it could fall into the newly discovered space at any moment, and that's what she wanted. Perhaps with a little help, she could get it out of the way? Madison made extra sure her footing was solid before putting both hands on the elongated boulder. She felt it wobble back and forth. She began to rock it like a cradle, pushing a little harder each time it swung out into the exposed passageway.

She let out a yelp as the big stone slid off into the unknown space beyond, landing with a thud. She flailed her arms once but recovered quickly. She smiled upon seeing the open space the missing rock had left behind. Large enough for her to fit through, things were now only a matter of careful foot and hand positioning to be able to work herself through the gap and then carefully let herself down on the other side. None of this proved too much to overcome, and within a few minutes the archaeologist was stepping onto the stone floor of a passageway she was certain had not seen human traffic in a long, long time.

Madison aimed the beam of her flashlight around the passage walls and ceiling. Carved entirely out of stone, she saw no writings or artifacts of any kind. The entire tunnel sloped gently downward where she could see an opening and…a shimmering floor? Unsure of what she was looking at, she walked slowly toward it. An internal voice told her that she was acting recklessly now, that she should have other team members with her in case something went wrong—what if there was a tunnel collapse, she had moved rocks around, after all—but it was a long trek back up through the pyramid and then to the camp. Better just to take a look at where this led now, then she would have something to report.

Halfway down the passageway she paused to listen. It had been quiet down here in the chamber that led to this passage—literally a tomb-like, pervasive silence—other than the sounds of her own actions. But now she could hear something. It was soft, coming from the end of the passage. She started walking again but shone her light into the opening at the end of the tunnel. Whatever was there shimmered and moved.

Madison recoiled in fright. *What is that?* She stood there trying to process it, to make sense of it while at the same time debating whether it would be better to retreat back to camp and return with a crew. But in the end she decided that whatever it was wasn't threatening and her curiosity won out. She continued down the rest of the passageway, pausing once to feel one of the walls, to see if she could flake away a small protuberance of rock, but it was solid.

Upon reaching the end of the tunnel she sucked in her breath as she looked out over the newly revealed space.

Water!

The entire room, or chamber, or whatever enclosed space this was, was filled with water that lapped gently against the pyramid walls. Or stone walls, anyway, Madison reflected to herself. Based on the LiDAR scans, she knew that this subterranean space was actually out to the side of the pyramid itself, rather than part of it. It was connected by the tunnel she had just traversed. She walked right to the edge of the water, knelt down and touched it. Cool, not extremely cold, but definitely much cooler than it would be up on the surface of the desert. Which got her to thinking...Where did this water come from?

This was the Sahara Desert; there were very, very few lakes, ponds and rivers here. Annual rainfall was less than two inches. She stared down into the water as she thought about it some more, angling her flashlight different ways to try to get the beam to penetrate farther. The water was clear, but the overall darkness made it difficult to see into its depths; the light reflected off the water's surface making it difficult to see with any detail. It was deep, though. She could see that much. She could make outlines of submerged objects—probably large stones, or building blocks much like the ones she had just climbed over and displaced in order to reach this place.

She looked around the area some more, directing her light to the ceiling and walls above the water. If the entire chamber was dry, she noted, it would have been a very high ceiling indeed. It would have been a lot of trouble to have excavated such a large space beneath the pyramid and then to line it with stone blocks. She knelt on the edge of the flooded chamber, staring absent-mindedly into its depths while she thought about it. Why would the Egyptians have gone to so much trouble to build a tomb or chamber around an existing aquifer? Or even to import water into the chamber, to flood it intentionally? *Why would they flood it on purpose?*

Staring down into the depths of the watery chamber, she knew the answer had to lie with whatever waited down there. Although she was a certified recreational SCUBA diver, this kind of specialty dive was far beyond her abilities, as well as those of the rest of her team. She would have to recruit some outside help. She thought about this for a moment. The list of scuba-diving archaeologists in her contacts was a short one. But she was the archaeologist, after all, she only needed someone who could dive in a tricky environment, could follow basic direction, and who happened to be somewhere relatively nearby with a willingness to help out. A smile crossed her lips as she recalled an email she'd received from a friend a few days earlier.

She knew exactly who to call.

CHAPTER 3

Great Pyramid of Giza

Carter Hunt dismounted the camel and looked around at the excavation site. A small tent city had been erected a stone's throw from the pyramid, and now at mid-day under blistering desert sun, there was no one to be seen walking around.

"So where's your *friend?*" Jayden asked, placing special emphasis on the word as he climbed down from his own dromedary. As if in response to the question, one of the tents suddenly opened and a short, attractive woman with long hair tied in a ponytail, wearing a khaki outfit, immediately made eye contact with them. She raised a hand and waved as she strode toward them.

"Carter! So glad you could make it!" She trotted up to them and gave Hunt a big hug while Jayden made suggestive expressions over her shoulder. Both men were single and he knew that Hunt had dated Madison in the past.

"Anything for a friend. Not going to lie, though, it helped that we were already in country. Flying out here for a scuba dive from the states might have been a bit more problematic."

She smiled while shaking hands with Jayden. "Of course, that's why when I remembered you said you were going to be here with Jayden, I called you straight away." She looked over at the pyramid before looking back to Hunt. "This is so exciting! I can't wait to show you what I found." She waved toward the tent she'd emerged from. "Come on, let's get you out of the sun."

Hunt paid the man with the camels, who had also towed a cart behind one of the dromedaries with their scuba gear. Then they walked over to the tent, where Madison pulled the entrance flap aside, ushering them in.

Hunt gave her a lopsided grin while looking around at the tables stacked with computer gear and video monitors. "Wow, impressive setup. You really bring a lot of stuff when you go camping." A ham radio station occupied one table, while the LiDAR equipment was laid out on another.

Madison laughed good naturedly. "You make it sound like we sleep in and have s'mores every night around a campfire singing *Kumbaya*."

Hunt smiled in return. "I'm sure you manage to get some work done. You always were a workaholic. After all, that's how you got to be a tenured professor and world-class researcher at the tender age of...what are you now, thirty?"

Jayden nodded, acknowledging Madison's accomplishments while admiring the technical setup in the tent.

"Carter, really, a woman doesn't discuss her age!" Madison said with mock indignation, moving to a laptop open on a table. "Thanks again for stopping by. The number of people willing to cart scuba gear across the desert by camel to help me on my dig was pretty small, so I'm very glad you're here. Now take a look at this."

Hunt and Jayden stood next to the archaeologist in front of the computer. On the screen was the LiDAR image depicting the previously undetected subterranean chambers off to one side of the pyramid.

She pointed to the space between the chambers and the pyramid. "These are connected by a series of multiple passageways, or tunnels, of which I explored one."

"And you just found these yesterday?" Hunt asked.

Madison pointed to one of the chambers outlined in the LiDAR image.

"Not the first two chambers—here—which we found last week, but this new one, here." Her finger stabbed the screen over the chamber that was farthest from the pyramid itself. "It's flooded with water."

Hunt and Jayden exchanged puzzled glances. Hunt put it into words. "Water in a sealed Egyptian pyramid chamber?"

Jayden pointed to the image. "Could it be the result of some kind of excavation technique, where it was deliberately flooded with hoses for some reason?"

Madison shook her head firmly. "No. That's not a technique I've ever heard of and I don't see what good it would do anyway."

Jayden shrugged. "I guess that's why I'm not an archeologist."

"So you want us to scuba dive in that flooded chamber and tell you what's down there, is that about the gist of it?" Hunt asked, steering the conversation back on track.

Madison nodded enthusiastically. "That's essentially it. Are there artifacts or hieroglyphics down there or is it just an empty chamber? How deep is it?"

"What's the water temperature?" Jayden wanted to know.

"It was cool to the touch, but not cold. At the edge anyway. I didn't go for a dip."

Hunt looked to Jayden. "We should wear exposure suits. There could be an inversion layer, a thermocline, where it's cold at the bottom."

"Or who knows, even really hot!" Jayden said with a laugh.

Hunt made eye contact with Madison. "You want us to get wet today, then?"

Madison grinned broadly. "I thought you'd never ask. Let me get some of my team together to help with the gear and setting up some portable lights, and we'll get underway right after lunch."

#

Two hours later, Hunt, Jayden, Madison and half a dozen members of her archaeology team reached the chamber Madison had climbed through in order to access the flooded chamber. Battery powered utility lights were set up to light the space without the need for flashlights. Hunt and Jayden looked around, duly impressed by their new surroundings.

Jayden wore a mystified expression as he asked Madison, "So we're like some of the first people to be in this room for thousands of years?"

The archaeologist nodded. "That's right. This chamber was discovered only a few days ago, and is off limits to the public—to anyone without a permit from the Egyptian authorities, which I was lucky enough to have been granted."

"It's not luck, Maddy, it's hard work." Hunt pointed out.

"Speaking of hard work," she replied, "there's a fair bit of that in our future before we can get that scuba gear through to the new passage." She nodded to the wall of jumbled stones she had climbed up and through in order to access the flooded chamber.

The team set to work displacing stones to allow enough space for them to transport gear through safely. When that was done, Hunt wheeled the cart full of scuba gear into the new passageway while Madison led the way toward the watery room. The rest of the team again set up utility lights in the new space. The light reflected off the water and cast moving shadows about the walls and ceiling.

"Kinda spooky in here," Jayden said.

"Can't wait to see what it looks like down there!" Hunt picked up a scuba tank and began setting it up. "Let's do this."

A few minutes later he and Jayden stood on the edge of the indoor body of water—what could be called either a large pool or a small artificial lake—adjusting their face masks.

Hunt looked to Jayden. "Would have been nice to have the full face masks with integrated intercoms like we had in the navy, right?"

"It's okay, I can go without hearing your sweet voice for an hour or so."

The laughter from the crew echoed throughout the chamber as the pair of divers walked out from the edge of the shore and then slipped beneath the water. They paused just beneath the surface, marveling at the crystal clear visibility. After a minute Hunt poked his head back above the surface and lifted his mask up on his forehead so he could talk to Madison and the crew.

"Even though the water's super-clear, we still can't see the bottom—it slopes down out of sight into what looks like a jumble of stone blocks. That's all I can tell for sure from here. We'll go down there and check it out."

"Be careful, you two!" Maddy said.

Hunt gave her the okay sign before slipping back beneath the water. He caught up with Jayden, who was about ten feet below him, sinking slowly into the crystal grotto. So far it reminded him of a cavern dive—an enclosed space that was more wide open than a true cave, which tended to be narrower with branching passages. Without daylight deep inside the pyramid, it was nearly dark already even though they were still in shallow water. Hunt switched on his dive light and Jayden did the same. The two divers continued their descent into the flooded chamber. They went slowly, since it was so clear as to be vertigo-inducing—the sensation that they were suspended in air over a jumble of boulders was a strange one. Hunt kept a close eye on his depth gauge. When it indicated that there was 100 feet of water over their heads, he tapped Jayden on the shoulder and indicated they should pause and have a look around.

The deeper they went, the less the compressed air in the tanks on their backs would last, and so Hunt wanted to take stock of their surroundings and make sure that if they went deeper, that there was a reason to do so. Swimming around blindly was not the prudent thing to do.

So he and Jayden planted their fins on two flat slabs of rock. The entire way down was lined with them, like a never-ending hill comprised of massive rock slabs strewn about. Hunt could see nothing particularly interesting among them, though—no artifacts or anything, for that matter, other than the slabs themselves. To his untrained eye they looked like the same stone that was used to construct the rest of the great pyramid, and he supposed that's what they were. Perhaps this was a quarry or dumping ground of some sort for extra rock when they were building the legendary tomb? He made a mental note to ask Madison. He took a few snapshots of the scene with an underwater camera so that Madison and her team would have a firsthand look later.

He suggested to Jayden that they swim laterally across the room at this same depth, but while looking down to see if they could spot anything of interest. Jayden gave him the okay sign and the two kicked off the slab and finned their way out toward the middle of the chamber. While not cold, Hunt was beginning to feel the chill of the water at this depth, and was glad to get moving again for the warmth his muscles would generate. The scenery was much the same as they swam across: a sloping pile of large rock slabs and boulders, stretching down to some unknown depth. They had almost reached the other side of the chamber when something far below caught Hunt's eye.

He stopped kicking along and rested on one of the slabs while focusing his attention on what lay below. It was the color that had caught his attention. Brown or maybe tan. Either way, it stood in sharp contrast to the sandy shade of the building rocks. Hunt glanced at his air pressure gauge and indicated for Jayden to do the same. They both still had enough for a swim down to the mystery object. Hunt pointed down to it and watched Jayden raise his eyebrows.

Then Hunt released some air from his buoyancy vest so that he would sink, and started to swim down toward the object.

CHAPTER 4

The unusual object looked a lot closer than it was. That's what ran through Hunt's mind as he and Jayden dropped down into the flooded chamber. The jumble of stone slabs and boulders became more complex as they dropped, forming small hillocks they had to swim either over or around, and large caves they had to swim through in order to continue downward.

But the sight of the object quickened his pulse and led him down further. He glanced at his depth gauge while passing over a concave block section: 125 feet. Too deep to stay down much longer, but the object—now it looked like it could be something interesting, since he saw what appeared to be sculpted detail—still lay some distance down the flooded slope. The extreme water clarity made it difficult to accurately gauge distance. Jayden tapped his shoulder and showed him his air gauge. He, too, was concerned about the depth. Hunt pointed to his watch and held up five fingers, indicating how many more minutes they would spend down here before beginning their return to the surface.

Then they kicked their way toward the light brown object. Hunt's curiosity grew with every fin stroke as they neared the unknown curiosity. So far, anyway, it appeared to be the only thing in here that wasn't a building rock. So what was it?

Hunt swept his light beam left to right and back again, scanning the area for anything that might be either noteworthy from an archaeological standpoint, or else a potential danger to themselves. So far he saw neither except for the brownish object, a little lighter in tone than the surrounding rock, which he now guessed was some sort of statue. He and Jayden stopped a few feet from it so as not to disturb it. Both of them played their light beams across the strange find.

Within a few seconds, Hunt was pretty sure he knew what it was, but he wanted to look at it from another angle to be sure, so he swam around the object to his right until he could see another side of it. His suspicion was confirmed.

He was looking at a life-size head, made of what looked to him to be bronze. The head was detached from whatever it had been attached to, whether a full body statue or some kind of pedestal base for the bust alone. Aware that they were rapidly running out of time down here, Hunt quickly snapped off a couple of pictures of the object so that Madison and her team could see it exactly as they had found it.

Then Hunt moved to the statue. He pointed to it and, after making eye contact with Jayden, pointed to the surface. He was going to try and bring it back up. Jayden shrugged and pointed to his watch, the meaning clear to Hunt: *Okay, if you can do it, but better hurry up about it.*

Hunt eyeballed the way the bronze head lay amidst the crux of stone blocks. It was situated such that it lay over a foot-wide gap; were it to drop into that after being dislodged, it would be unrecoverable. So Hunt made sure to place one hand firmly beneath the head before attempting to lift it out. Then he tried to lift, grunting with the exertion. He made eye contact with Jayden after not having immediate success. *This thing is heavy!* Then he redoubled his efforts and tried again, this time able to anticipate what he was up against. Bracing a knee against a stone slab, and an elbow against another, he put the muscles of his entire body into wedging the heavy statue head up and out of the crevice it had rested in for untold years.

Slowly and surely, Hunt lifted the artifact from the rocky wedge until it was cradled only in his arms. As he prepared to turn toward Jayden so as to get some support from him, he glanced down through the crack now that it was easier to see down into it without the bronze head being there.

A human skeleton lay sprawled out on a stone slab about twenty feet down. He put his face mask as far as he dared into the crevice and peered down into the crevasse, but he saw nothing else besides the skeleton. He held the statue head in the crook of one elbow while grabbing his camera and holding it up to Jayden. They would definitely want a snapshot of that skeleton. Jayden took the camera and then looked down into the opening. He looked back up once at Hunt, eyes wide, and then snapped off a photograph.

That done, Jayden pushed himself up away from the crevasse and helped Hunt hold the stone head while Hunt added air to his buoyancy vest to overcome the additional weight. Both divers knew that another option would be to ditch his weight belt, with the head itself more than replacing that, but should he then drop the head, he would rocket to the surface with disastrous ill-effects to his health. So that would remain a last resort.

Hunt inflated his vest almost to full capacity before he was able to tread water without sinking while holding the head. Then he and Jayden began a slow and cautious ascent to the surface, which shimmered and sparkled far above their heads when they aimed their dive lights at it. They skirted their way around an overhang of pyramid slabs before resuming their vertical ascent. Jayden stared at his air pressure gauge a lot. It was in the red. He hated to think where Hunt's was, burdened as he was with the heavy stone, causing him to breathe even heavier and faster.

The thing that kept both of them going was seeing the work lights set up on the edge of the water up above. They seemed so close, like they were within reach, and watching them grow larger was a great comfort. Hunt focused on them so much that he almost didn't notice the cone of light coming from below.

When he glanced down to make sure he wasn't too close to the jumble of rock slabs, he saw it. Without a doubt. A piercing cone of light barreling up from the depths, seemingly out of nowhere.

What was *that*? He almost dropped the stone head out of surprise, and then also out of the urge to have more bodily freedom, but he had the discipline not to do that. He looked over at Jayden and saw his dive buddy staring up toward the work lights. He kicked his right leg out and knocked him in the leg with a fin tip. Jayden looked over at him immediately. Hunt jerked his head downward until Jayden directed his gaze into the deep.

Hunt could tell from his friend's reaction alone, by simply watching his face, that something was going on. He looked back down again, even though it was difficult to do while carrying the artifact, but the light, whatever it was, was moving fast, It had already travelled beyond his field of vision so that he had to spin around in order to see it. When he did, he felt a pang of adrenaline assault his guts.

An underwater scooter.

The torpedo-shaped vehicle featured, in addition to a nose-mounted halogen light, a single propeller used to drag a diver through the water. Hunt couldn't see the diver since the headlight blinded him, but he could tell by the speed and sharp upward trajectory of the scooter that this was not a research diver, even if Madison had neglected to mention that she already had divers with equipment on site. And she hadn't mentioned that, Hunt thought, so then who was this guy?

Make that guys, plural, he thought, as a second scooter-diver rocketed into view from behind a mound of stacked boulders. *And how did they get in here?* There's no way they'd entered after them, they would have heard the splashes as they entered the water, and seen the lights as they made their descent. No, they must have come in another way. He tried to visualize the LiDAR imagery he'd seen back in the tent, but with everything going on he couldn't conjure a detailed enough image to be useful.

And right now, anyway, he supposed it didn't much matter, because both scooters were heading right for them at what had to be at or near their maximum speed, about five knots. Who were they and what did they want? Hunt had no idea, but underwater in an Egyptian pyramid with a tank running dry of air was no time to stop and chat, so he continued his ascent.

Fortunately, Hunt thought, a decompression stop wasn't needed on this dive or he'd have to stop at ten or fifteen feet and breathe air for a few minutes before completing the ascent in order to avoid the bends, so he was clear to ascend. Which was a good thing, since his air already seemed like it was getting harder to pull. *Probably a good thing my hands are occupied with holding the head or else I'd be staring at the needle on my air gauge drop*, Hunt thought.

But as he eyed the surface, which looked to be about thirty feet or so away, Hunt saw that there was something to keep him from getting there after all. The two scooter-divers zoomed in on his position without slowing until one of them stopped a couple of feet above Hunt's head. But the other wasn't stopping. Its nose cone was pointed right at Hunt's midsection. It was going to ram him.

Hunt wanted to stiff-arm the scooter away but knew if he took one arm off of the bronze head that he'd risk losing it to depths of piled slabs. So did the best thing he could come up with and turned sideways to the scooter, presenting his right elbow while still cradling the head.

In spite of Hunt's readiness, Jayden was the one who thwarted the underwater scooter. The ex-navy man bashed the nose of the underwater vehicle with the closed fist of his right hand, sending it off course to the right, where it glanced off Hunt's body without serious impact. Hunt still had possession of the metal head while the diver brought the scooter around in an arc to come back again.

Hunt continued his ascent while Jayden continued to fend off the marauding craft. But soon Hunt was butting his head into the bottom the other diver's legs. That man—and Hunt could tell it was in fact a man by the strength in the legs when he kicked him—ditched his scooter in favor of hand-to-hand combat with Hunt. He swiped a gloved hand at Hunt's regulator hose in an attempt to dislodge his mouthpiece, but Hunt's quick head movement caused the assailant to swipe at nothing but water.

Taking a chance on dropping the precious artifact, Hunt gripped the bronze head with both hands and shoved the heavy weight into his opponent's side. He felt ribs crack and took great satisfaction in the grunt of pain that reached his ears through the water.

He also got the first look at the attacker's face as he whipped his head to the side in pain. White male, mustache, approximately forty years of age,

Hunt ascertained. That's all he could tell through the face mask. He noted it was the full facemask variety with embedded electronics that allowed him to communicate underwater with his dive partner. As if in confirmation of this fact, Hunt saw the man's lips moving behind his mask, and then the second scooter's nose cone was ramming into Hunt's back.

He bobbled the bronze head but regained control of it before losing his grip on it completely.

But then the gleam of a dive light reflecting off of metal temporarily blinded Hunt as a serrated dive knife was plunged at his neck from above. Hunt dodged the blade and then he saw Jayden's wetsuit-clad arm gripping the gloved hand holding the knife. No longer could Hunt pass this off as a case of mistaken identity, or losing control of the scooters, or anything like that at all. This was a deliberate attempt to kill them.

But why? The question danced around in his mind even as he fought the underwater battle, double-teaming the knife-man with Jayden, again using the bronze head as an instrument of blunt force trauma, ramming it into the interloper's back. Hunt heard the piercing snap of bone as Jayden bent the knife-wielder's hand back until the wrist broke and the blade dropped from his hand.

That assailant went limp and drifted away from the melee while his scooter sank slowly to the bottom. Hunt saw an opportunity and snagged the machine with a fin tip. Maybe it could be his ticket out of here. After the exertion of the fight, he was glad he didn't have a free hand to look at his air gauge, since he probably had almost none left. In fact, wasn't it getting harder to pull a breath even now?

Hunt hooked a leg around the battery-powered propulsion device and pulled it to his body. He positioned his midsection over it so that it supported the weight of the artifact head. Above him he could make out a flurry of arms and legs as Jayden grappled with the remaining aquatic assailant, but since he carried the heavy artifact, he decided he should make his exit stage left while he could and let Jayden only have to worry about himself. He found the trigger on the scooter's hand grip and pressed it all the way down. He was rewarded with the instant purr of the electric motor as the diver propulsion vehicle pulled him away from the fight and towards the surface.

Hunt aimed the nose of the scooter toward the blurry utility lights that were rapidly becoming larger. When he could distinguish individual ripples of water on the surface, meaning he was very close to it, he went to pull his next breath of air, but there was nothing there. He tried once more breath, but still nothing. Eyeballing the distance to the surface, he decided he could make it without ditching the heavy head. The last thing he wanted to do was lose the object of all their effort after everything they'd been through, so close to the archaeology team.

Hunt saw outstretched arms on the shore of the subterranean artificial lake; the sense of having help standing by boosted his confidence and he kicked harder, knowing he was almost there. He rode the scooter up onto the rocks, gripping the artifact with both hands lest it fall back into the water, while one of Madison's field techs pulled the scooter from the water.

Madison was there, leaning over, her soft features etched with concern. Hunt raised the ancient head up to her. "Take this. Keep it safe and get back. The men down there are dangerous."

Madison took the head, clearly not expecting the weight. Hunt held it for her while she adjusted to its mass. Hunt stripped off his empty scuba tank and dropped it on the rocks. Then, before Madison could ask him what he was doing, he dove back into the water.

Jayden grappled with the other enemy diver about twenty feet below. The other scooter was nowhere in sight, probably having sank to the bottom after being abandoned by its rider to fight, Hunt surmised. He scissor kicked the remaining distance to the aquatic melee, where he was unable to tell who had the upper hand. Both divers fought like Tasmanian Devils, whirling and flailing in a chaotic blur of arms, legs, fins and bubbles.

He looked around for the second diver, the one whose ribs he'd cracked with the artifact, but saw no sign of him.

Hunt reached down and unsheathed the titanium dive knife strapped to his calf. While operating the scooter and carrying the head, he'd been unable to make use of it, but now he relished the chance. Jayden had to be about to be out of air at any second. He had to end this fight right now. Hunt moved in with is blade at the ready, eyeing the thrashing limbs, looking for an opportunity. Fortunately, the intruder's tank was painted black, while Jayden's was yellow, and it was that difference that allowed Hunt to distinguish his target from his friend.

Hunt had no desire to maim or kill another human being, but he would do what he had to in order to protect his friend and himself. He moved in with the knife, grabbing the regulator hose attached to the black tank. He gripped the rubber with his left hand and then sliced it through with a his right. A thick stream of bubbles—the diver's remaining air supply— immediately poured from the severed hose, making it difficult to see around the white jet of air.

As expected, their foe immediately switched gears from offensive fighting tactics to self-preservation. He twisted and writhed, attempting to get away from his opponents so that he could swim to the surface to breathe. Jayden was still holding onto him but Hunt pulled him away shaking his head. *Let him go.* He was no threat to them anymore.

Jayden relinquished his grip on the mystery diver and he swam away from them, first laterally, and then vertically toward the air that awaited him above.

Jayden handed Hunt the mouthpiece of his "octopus," a second regulator scuba divers use in emergency situations. It allowed both of them to breathe out of the same tank, but from different mouthpieces.

With the bubbles out of the way, Hunt took a look around to see if the other diver still lingered, but he saw nothing other than the disorganized pile of stone slabs. Not even a scooter was visible.

When he went to pull a breath from the tank and got nothing, no air, he knew they had extinguished Jayden's tank, too. The two ex-navy men looked at one another and swam the few remaining feet to the surface.

CHAPTER 5

A member of Madison's archaeology team was waiting to assist Hunt and Jayden onto the dry pyramid rocks. Madison herself glanced over at them, but didn't come to greet them this time herself. She was too busy staring at the bronze head Hunt had given her.

Hunt and Jayden clamored up onto the dry part of the subterranean chamber and shrugged out of their scuba gear, handing it off to members of the team. As soon as he was free of his gear, Hunt stood and aimed the beam of his dive light around the dry part of the big room.

"You didn't see anyone up here? No one else who's not part of your team?" he asked Madison. The archaeologist looked up from the bronze artifact and shook her head.

"No. Either they were already in this chamber before we got here— which I think is unlikely—or else they swam in underwater from a connecting passage. Also, up top here as you can see, there are many nooks and crannies in the shadows a person could disappear into without being seen."

As Hunt replied, Jayden added his light to the first and began to slowly walk around, also looking for signs that the intruders had lingered. "So they may have discovered an alternate way into the this same chamber?"

Maddy nodded. "The LiDAR images showed a lot of detail, many possible passages. I just happened to come from this way…" She jerked her thumb back at the wall of slabs they'd cleared an opening through. "…but that doesn't mean there aren't other ways."

Hunt walked over to Maddy so that he could lower his voice, no longer exactly sure who might be within earshot. "Why would there be so much interest in this particular chamber? Because it's flooded?"

Madison shrugged. "Certainly the water makes it unusual. And of course it's been sitting here for thousands of years, so it is odd that it should attract such interest now."

Hunt nodded to the bronze head cradled in Madison's arms. "Odd unless there are artifacts in here that might be worth something?"

Maddy looked back down at the bronze head. "You know, this head is most unusual indeed. I need to get it back to my field lab so I can run some more tests."

Hunt looked around the chamber. "Make sure you don't walk around in here by yourself anymore. Jayden and I will stay here a little while longer to make sure those divers don't return, then we'll meet you at your tent. Your team will go back with you, right?"

Maddy nodded. "See you in a few."

#

"Cold beers in the cooler over there if you want." Madison spoke without looking up from the bronze head that she had placed on a folding table. She, Hunt and Jayden were the only three in the lab tent, while the rest of their team continued with the excavation work. Some of them had been left in the flooded chamber with two-way radios to report any suspicious activity if seen, but so far they had seen nothing out of the ordinary. Madison had sheepishly explained that she did not want to call authorities to the site if no one was in danger because it would place her dig on hold, something her career could not afford at the moment.

Hunt and Jayden each cracked open a Sakara beer. "Congrats, you're a certified Pyramid Diver," Hunt told Jayden, who nodded with a smile.

"Never thought I'd get that certification."

"Come on, let's see what we brought up from that crazy dive." Hunt moved to the table where Maddy was examining the bronze head. She indicated the neck portion, where it head been broken away from the rest of the piece.

"So here we see where the head was separated from the base. From the way it flares out here, it kind of looks to me like it might have been part of a full body statue, as opposed to just a bust. I've already taken some pictures of it and so now I'll run an image database search to see if we can find a match."

Hunt and Jayden moved in for a closer look at the artifact that they'd gone through so much trouble to obtain while Maddy typed on a laptop. "Can I touch it?" Hunt asked the archaeologist, fingers poised over the rough edges where it had separated from the rest of it.

"Bet that's not the first time you've asked her that," Jayden quipped. Maddy swatted at him with an aerial photo printout of the dig site, which he deftly avoided.

"You can lightly touch it, but not hard enough to move it around, okay? We don't want to chip it."

Hunt said he understood and proceeded to run his fingers over the artifact. Not that he didn't know what bronze felt like, but he liked to think about the history of the piece while touching it, to feel the connection between himself and some distant past. He closed his eyes and tried to imagine this statue in its former setting, people admiring it, walking by it, going about their daily lives....

"Carter, maybe you should switch to coffee, you falling asleep on the job?"

Hunt opened his eyes and looked to Maddy. "Do we have an idea of the age of this thing yet?"

She paused to look up from the computer. "I think it's very old. But we'll know for sure soon enough. They're running a sample over in the lab tent. We sacrifice a little accuracy for the speed, but it'll date it to within thousand years or so."

Hunt looked at the statue in surprise. "So you took a piece off of it?"

Maddy shrugged and gave him a sheepish grin. "There's no other way to age it. It's a tiny chip that I'm sure more than came off incidentally during your careful excavation of it." She gave extra inflection to the last part of the sentence, eliciting bashful looks from the two divers.

A tone sounded from the laptop and Maddy's expression brightened. "Got match on the image search!"

All three of them crowded around the screen, where a picture of a statue took their breath away. There were two images, one a painting and one a photograph. Both statues appeared to be bronze, but one of them—the one in the actual photograph—was missing its head. Madison pointed to the other one, the painting, before enlarging the image to show more detail on the head. The figure was an adult male with a classic Roman nose and short but wavy hair, sitting atop a horse. His expression was mildly stern.

"I'd say that's our friend, here." She looked over to the bronze head on the table, while Hunt and Jayden also made comparisons.

"The features and proportions look to be an exact match," Hunt said.

"So what happened to the one in the photo?" Jayden wanted to know.

"Lost his head," Hunt joked.

Maddy leaned in and squinted to read some text on the screen. "It says here that this statue used to be in the Azores, pointing west with, oddly enough, an *Incan* language inscription, *cati,* which roughly translates to 'go that way.'" She paused to gauge the reactions of her audience, but Hunt and Carter appeared lost in thought. After a pause, Maddy went on.

"The full statue of horse and rider was discovered when the Portuguese discovered the Azores islands, in 1427. They took it back to the king of Portugal, but it was broken and the pieces were lost sometime after that." She looked over at them and smiled ."So there's also an Incan connection here, which is strange."

Hunt was the first to voice the thoughts swirling in their heads. "So how does the head of a statue that was in the Azores end up in a flooded subterranean chamber of the Great Pyramid of Giza?"

Before anyone could answer, a voice came at the entrance to the tent.

"Dr. Chambers, test results here, may I come in?"

Maddy turned around in her chair and called over to the tent entrance, "Yes, please do," before saying in a hushed tone to Hunt and Jayden, "Looks like we're about to find out how old this thing is."

"What's your guess?" Hunt asked, as a young man carrying a small plastic box and a computer printout of multiple pages.

Maddy shrugged. "Looks vaguely Roman. If so, around 2,000 years ago isn't a bad guess."

Jayden's eyes widened. "That thing we found is 2,000 years old?!"

Maddy made a dismissive gesture, but before she could reply the lab tech said, "Guess again." He pointed to the bronze head. "The metal alloy from that piece is approximately 11,000 years old, give or take 1,000. We'll have more accurate results later, but this quickly, that's the best we can do."

"That's great, thanks!" Maddy dismissed the lab tech and he left the tent. Her mouth dropped open in surprise. "Eleven thousand years old?" All of them stared at the bronze head.

"Pre-dates the Romans by a good ten thousand years at least," Hunt said.

"Isn't that a little weird, though?" Jayden cut in. "I mean, when was the Bronze Age?"

Maddy thought for a second before answering. "From about 2,000 BC to maybe 800 BC, so this artifact of ours pre-dates that, too. And by at least 9,000 years."

"What ancient civilizations lived 1,000 years ago?" Hunt pondered aloud. He looked to Maddy, but to his surprise it was Jayden who answered.

"I know of one. Kind of silly, though. But it fits the timeframe."

"Spill the beans. Which one is it?" Maddy asked, intrigued.

Jayden shrugged as he answered, as if surprised he was the only one who knew. "Guess you two don't watch much Discovery Channel."

Hunt's eyes widened, "Uh-oh. I know where you're going with this. And it does fit." He nodded sagely.

Maddy crossed her arms. "Will you two gentlemen please clue me in?"

Hunt and Jayden both remained silent for a few seconds, as if neither wanted to be the one to put forth the name. At length, Hunt uttered it.

"Atlantis."

CHAPTER 6

Madison's laughter echoed around the research tent. "Atlantis? How many beers have you had?"

Jayden shrugged. "It fits the myth. That's all I'm saying."

Hunt held up a finger. "Let's forget about Atlantis for a second, and look at what we know." He pointed to the bronze head. "That piece, recovered from a flooded chamber that was recently discovered in this pyramid, is about eleven thousand years old."

Maddy nodded, picking up the thread. She pointed to the laptop screen. "And, it's possible that this is the missing head from a full body statue of rider and horse that was in the Azores, pointing west, when the Portuguese first discovered it."

"With an inscription reading 'go that way'," Jayden added.

Maddy thought about this before replying. "Let's see what's west of the Azores…" She brought up a world map on laptop's web browser. "Across the Atlantic Ocean from the Azores, the next major island group we come to is the Bahamas."

"So," Hunt said, sipping from his beer, "pretending for a second that one believed in the Atlantis myth—a myth that was started by Plato in ancient Greece, does the inscription suppose that the Portuguese, or whoever was to get there first, was looking for the lost city?"

"I'd say it does," Madison said, and Jayden nodded his agreement.

"So if we visited the Azores," Hunt continued, we could try to find the site of the statue and see if we come across additional clues there. Or, we follow the pointing statue directly to the Bahamas, where—"

The sound of nearby gunfire drowned out the rest of Hunt's words. Instantly, he and Jayden dropped to the ground, and Hunt swept an arm out to grab Maddy's ankle, reminding her to get low also. They heard shouts coming from not too far away, although the words were indistinguishable over the gunfire. Hunt turned his face sideways to the ground and looked over at Maddy. Her eyes were wide with fear.

"Does this mean anything to you? Local police, maybe?"

"No. I've been on dozens of digs here over the years, and I've never had gunfire."

"Then we better get ready." Hunt moved to the tent entrance and zipped it shut. He looked at Jayden. Neither of them carried firearms. He addressed Maddy. "Do you have any guns?"

She laughed and shook her head. "Guns on an archaeology expedition?"

Hunt shrugged. "You're a female working in some remote locations. They'd come in handy now, that's for sure."

"It would make the permitting that much more difficult…" While she elaborated, Jayden moved to the bronze head they'd already risked their lives for. He placed a hand on it where it rested on the table.

"What if they're coming for this?"

Maddy stopped talking and eyed the artifact.

"Hide it," Hunt suggested.

"Where?" Jayden looked around the research tent as the sound of gunfire and shouting drew nearer. Maddy pointed to a small wheeled cart used for hauling dig equipment. "We can hide it in there, I guess. Help me clear it out." She and Jayden ran to the cart while Hunt roved rapidly around the tent.

"Where are your tools? Hammers, prybars, anything like that?"

Maddy pointed through the walls of the tent. "That stuff is in a different tent, or just outside laying around if it's being used."

"I guess we'll just have to improvise." Hunt stopped at a pile of computer cables and picked through some of them. He quickly unraveled a few of them and selected one. By the time Maddy and Jayden had emptied out the cart, Hunt had wrapped one end of the cable around a support pole at the tent's entrance. By the time the statue head had been placed in the cart, Hunt had the other end of the cable tied to a pole on the opposite side of the doorway, about a foot off the ground, just inside the flap.

More gunfire erupted and a wall of sand sprayed against the wall of the tent. Hunt backed up and waved Jayden and Maddy to the middle of the space where they knelt among stacks of gear crates. As they hid, Hunt picked up a battery backup unit used to temporarily power the computers in the event the generator lost power. Wordlessly, he hefted it and practiced the motion he would used to throw it as a deadly missile should it come to that. Jayden also rooted through a crate and came up with another unit with which to do the same.

But then the gun blasts ceased and they heard a voice, in English, speaking through a megaphone. "Everyone outside lay down on the ground. Now! Anyone inside the tents: come out now with your hands up. Anyone found inside a tent will be shot on sight." To prove the statement was not an empty threat, a burst of automatic weapons fire shredded through the upper part of the research tent, opening it to the dry air and bright blue sky.

The megaphone voice boomed again. "You there, slowly get up and begin piling all recovered artifacts on the ground right here. Go! Go now!"

A sharp exhalation escaped Maddy's mouth as she made eye contact with Hunt, who made a placating gesture with his hands. *Stay put.* But inwardly, Hunt was worried. He'd seen plenty of artifact theft, especially in Iraq during his service for Operation Bulldog Mammoth, but that was more like looting unattended valuables, not an armed robbery like this. It bothered him because it reminded him of something.

Outside, the amplified voice came again. "This cannot be everything. If you are lying to us you will pay the ultimate price!"

All eyes in the research tent went to the wheeled cart that now contained the bronze head. "That's what they really want," Hunt said.

"How do you know?" Maddy whispered back.

"They had divers in the flooded room. They somehow knew there was a flooded chamber there. They've done their homework on this site enough to know to bring dive gear. It stands to reason they also looked into whatever it is that might be down there." Hunt glanced to the cart concealing the bronze head.

Suddenly they heard footsteps approach the tent. Two voice began talking just outside, not through a megaphone but in private conversation. "They say that is everything, yet it is not there."

Another voice, this one lower and gruffer than the first, responded. "Then we must search the tents."

A pause, and then: "There are many, it will take time."

"We have waited eleven thousand years already. What is a few more hours? Tell the men to turn each tent inside out. Orders are to kill anyone hiding inside."

"Yes, sir!"

The sound of booted feet tromping across the sand away from the research tent indicated that the conversation was over.

Hunt turned to Maddy and whispered. "I suppose there's no trap door in this tent that leads into the pyramid, is there?" She smiled but shook her head. "Sorry, it's just a tent over the sand."

Jayden's eyes lit up. "Over the *sand*. Quick, find me something to dig with." Although not like fine beach sand, the ground beneath their feet was soft and crumbly, essentially hard-packed sand.

Maddy's reply was urgent. "Like I said, all the digging tools are in another tent. This one just has computers and electronics."

"We'll have to improvise." Hunt began looking around. Seeing nothing obvious from which to fashion a digging implement, he then turned to the crates they hid amongst and began opening the lids, rummaging around inside each one, tossing out items that were of no use. After a few more seconds he withdrew his hands from a crate. In each he held an electrical power strip, an elongated plastic strip with power outlets at the end of a long cord. He took one and began wedging one end of it into the ground, testing its feasibility as a digging implement.

"Poor man's shovel," he whispered after wedging out a hole a foot deep without too much effort. He tossed one strip to Jayden, the other to Maddy, before pulling out a third for himself. Then all three of them set to enlarging the hole he had started. He cautioned them to dig quietly, as the sounds of occasional megaphone-shouted commands punctuated with gunshots rent the air outside the tent.

After a few minutes Hunt threw down his power strip. "I think that should do it." He went to the wheeled cart and removed the bronze head. Carrying it to the hole they had dug, he gently rolled it to the bottom.

"Now we cover it back up." The three of them used their hands to fill back in the hole, covering the artifact. Then they smoothed out the sandy dirt, making sure it was even with the rest of the ground, and finally walked around on top of the patch of dirt so that it didn't look too obviously smoothed over.

No sooner had they finished than they heard footsteps walking rapidly towards their tent. Hunt pointed to the entrance. Jayden moved silently to one side of it while Hunt told Maddy to lay on the ground. He found a tarp and covered her with it. Then he ran to the opposite side of the door as Jayden and waited, catching his breath, willing himself to be silent as the footsteps approached the research tent.

Hunt hand-signaled to Jayden to wait for whoever entered next to trip over the wire before making a move.

A voice said, "You get that one, I'll check this one, here." Then a set of footfalls receded in the opposite direction while another continued toward the research tent entrance. Hunt braced, preparing to spring. The footsteps stopped just outside the tent and Hunt saw the shadow of a pair of hands reach for the tent zipper. Jayden tensed as the unknown individual unzipped the entrance flap. When it had been opened, the first part of the intruder to enter the tent was the muzzle of an assault rifle.

Hunt made eye contact with Jayden and held a hand out. *Wait.*

But the intruder was being cautious, too. No one immediately rushed into the tent. Hunt watched the muzzle of the weapon swing left to right and back again, no doubt a tell as to the wielder's gaze. Hunt could only hope he didn't look down. But the intruder's next steps gave him his answer.

The gunman walked straight into the tent at a brisk pace, tripping over the cord Hunt had tied at shin-height. He and Jayden sprung on their foe instantly, with Hunt grabbing the barrel of the rifle with both hands and swinging it away from them while Jayden actually fought the would-be treasure looter.

Jayden landed a right cross to the criminal's left cheekbone, knocking him into a daze that rendered him all but harmless. But as Hunt wrestled the gun away from him, the assailant's finger curled around the trigger, squeezing off a short burst. It shot harmlessly through the roof of the tent, but Hunt knew it would likely draw reinforcements.

He wondered how many thugs they were up against. He got low to the ground and peeked out through the tent entrance. He counted four looters—enemy combatants, as he thought of them—moving about the dig site. But he knew there were more. Some had to be inside the tents, or out of his field of vision. He checked the weapon's magazine—it was loaded, but he preferred to have more ammo—a lot more—if he was going to go up against at least four armed criminals. So he moved to the fallen robber and searched his body while Jayden held his arms back even though he appeared to be unconscious. It could be an act.

Hunt felt the shape of ammo clips on a belt beneath the man's shirt. He removed the belt and put it around his own waist. Now he felt better, more prepared, but still--he knew they would have to be extremely careful. These men clearly had no scruples. The penalties for artifact theft in Egypt were severe. They were risking death or life in prison in order to steal these artifacts.

His subconscious shouted the question yet again: *what could be so important to make them want to do that, to give them that kind of motivation?*

Hunt had no idea, but he intended to find out. But first, he and his friends had a little jam to get out of. He almost walked away from the looter after grabbing his ammo, but on second thought, decided to search the rest of his body. He was rewarded with a 9mm pistol worn on an ankle holster beneath the man's black pants. Hunt removed that, too, and handed it to Jayden.

"How come you get the automatic?"

Hunt frowned in his direction. "Seriously?"

"Ro-sham-bo you for it."

Hunt knew his friend was prone to moments of levity in the midst of a tense situation to break up the tension. His humor had served them well during their time in the navy, both in and out of combat zones, particularly on long transport runs to break up the monotony. But Hunt wasn't in the mood to laugh, there was no time for that. He racked his brain for a solution to the pickle they were in. He believed the man who had said they would be shot if found inside a tent. These looters would not be prone to reason, but would be highly reactionary, far more likely to pull a trigger than to reason things out.

He considered taking the incapacitated adversary as a hostage. They could walk him at gunpoint outside of the tent and into the open, then demand their release. But Hunt couldn't be sure they wouldn't kill them anyway. Not every criminal organization placed a high value on the lives of their own when backed into a corner. No, it was too risky. But it was also too much of a risk to stay in the research tent. When this man didn't come out, more would be sent to investigate, and they would be wary.

Hunt was still deliberating over these options when the amplified voice roared once again, this time from what sounded like the middle of the dig site. Hunt guessed it was about fifty feet in front of their tent entrance.

"We will give you *one final warning*. Step out of the tents. Anyone found inside a tent will be shot on sight. Your life is not worth protecting some old objects. Give them to us and go home to your families. Do the sensible thing."

Hunt froze as he heard the last phrase. *Do the sensible thing.* Not only the words themselves, but the exact phrase in combination with that voice. He was certain he'd heard it before.

"Daedalus, is that you?" Hunt's shouting startled Jayden, whose facial expression quickly transformed from one of shocked alarm to surprised recognition.

"Who speaks? Come forth!" Came the voice from the megaphone.

To Jayden, Hunt said in a low voice, "Looks like our old friend is back up to his old tricks."

CHAPTER 7

Hunt dropped his appropriated automatic weapon just inside the tent and then raised his hands before stepping outside. Jayden's voice trailed after him in a hushed, anxiety-ridden rasp.

"You crazy, Carter?"

But Hunt 's voice exuded confidence as he addressed the lead interloper. "Long time, Daedalus. What's it been, fifteen years?"

The man Hunt addressed lowered his megaphone and spoke directly to him. "Not long enough, Carter Hunt. Not long enough."

Hunt shook his head in a slow and exaggerated fashion. "You still at the helm of your despicable organization, the one that stole priceless artifacts from Iraqi museums during the chaos of the Iraq War?"

Daedalus nodded. "Treasure, Inc. has all the necessary permits to operate here, as we did in the middle east. Do not concern yourself with matters that do not pertain you." He stroked the thick black stubble on his beard as he studied Hunt's reaction, one of revulsion and disgust.

"Not only are you a thief and a criminal, Daedalus, but you're a liar, too. You've never had a permit in your life. You have no respect for others and think that you're above needing to go through any kind of permission process. You don't fool me."

"I guess you've never checked the public records at the Egyptian

Ministry of Cultural Affairs."

Hunt laughed aloud while unseen behind him, Jayden picked up the dropped automatic weapon. "Yes, applying for permits to obtain a few clay pots or amphora and then running around stealing anything in sight while claiming to be legally permitted really fools people, Daedalus."

"Why don't you come to work for me, Carter Hunt? You seem to have a knack for knowing where to find precious artifacts. A real history buff, yes?"

"I'd rather collect unemployment."

Daedalus' eyes narrowed a bit but he soon returned his expression to its normal, haughty look. For a man of indeterminate age, he was in excellent physical shape, Hunt cold see. He knew him to be of Greek heritage, but not a lot else, not that he cared. As far as he was concerned, he knew all he needed to about the man. He stole precious artifacts around the world for personal gain, under the guise of a legitimate international import-export company called Treasure, Incorporated. He'd been at it for at least twenty years, and now, with this most brazen job at the venerable great pyramid of Giza, showed no signs of letting up.

"Suit yourself, Mr. Hunt. I will simply allow you to leave, after you show me what you found in the pyramid, that is."

"We didn't find anything."

Daedalus' eyes narrowed. "That's not what my divers said. Where is the bronze head?"

Hunt's heart sank. His information was solid. He had to buy some more time until...until what, he wasn't even sure—until the police showed up? Until he thought of a plan? "We dropped it during a fight with your divers. It fell back into the pit. I'm sure you could find it if you dive it a few times."

Again, Daedalus stroked the stubble on his chin while thinking, this time with an amused expression. "I'm sure we could find it if we turn a few tents upside-down. Something tells me I should start with the one you just came out of." He brought the megaphone to his lips and shouted into it, in Greek, his native language. A few seconds later, two men trotted over with automatic rifles aimed at Hunt.

"Search this tent," Daedalus commanded. His two armed henchmen nodded and advanced toward the research tent, one of them with the muzzle of his weapon trained on Hunt while the other swept his gun back and forth while approaching the tent.

#

Jayden tensed as he lay in a prone position on the side of the tent entrance with the automatic weapon aimed at the door. He could only imagine Maddy was going crazy with not knowing what was happening—he doubted she could even hear the exchange outside—but he applauded her patience, for she had been quiet so far. But then he began to worry that she didn't have enough air underneath the tarp. What if she had passed out from lack of oxygen?

Keeping the muzzle of his weapon trained on the tent entrance, he backpedaled carefully to her, extra-wary not to trip over a crate or computer cable. He could hear multiple sets of footsteps nearing the tent.

"Maddy! You okay?" He whispered the question sharply, hoping to indicate that it was urgent while also reminding her to answer in a whisper as well. They did not need to give away their presence.

"I'm okay! What's happening?" The breathy response lifted Jayden's spirits.

"Bad guys with guns are coming into the tent. Stay put, Don't move until we tell you to."

"Roger that."

Jayden then moved away from the tarp, passing the patch of dirt where they'd buried the bronze head, and over to the side of the tent behind a pile of crates containing computer networking equipment.

Hunt's voice sounded at the entrance to the tent. "I'm telling you, there's no bronze head in here, or any other artifacts for that matter. This is the computer tent. It's where the eggheads do their research, which means Googling stuff online and applying for more grants so they can keep coming out here to do more digs. Super-boring."

"Shut up and get inside," came the gruff, megaphone-boosted reply. Hunt came stumbling into the tent, hands above his head. He looked straight ahead but his eyes darted about until he fixed on Jayden's inert form off to his left, firearm at the ready. He made sure not to show a reaction and kept walking until he was fully inside the tent, then stood in place with his hands still up. Behind him, a gunman of Mideastern descent followed in his footsteps, his eyes darting about the tent but failing to notice Jayden, who had flattened himself behind a stack of crates.

He made a quick visual assessment of the room and then whirled around and shouted to his boss. "Lot of stuff in here. Send in two more men to search."

Staring straight ahead, Hunt winced. With at least three of them searching, it was certain they'd find Jayden and Maddy. And possibly even the bronze head. From outside the tent, Hunt heard Daedalus call out two names through his megaphone. Seconds later, additional footsteps ran toward the research tent.

Two more men, also of Mideastern descent, entered the tent. Although armed with pistols, their weapons were holstered. Immediately they began opening crates and rooting through them, looking for artifacts, in particular the bronze head. Meanwhile, the Treasure, Inc. member with the assault rifle kept it trained on Hunt's back while standing just inside the tent entrance.

As the search proceeded, the two men grew increasingly frustrated, overturning boxes and dumping out equipment, kicking it over and cursing as they moved from crate to box to crate. One of the men tipped over a table of computer gear, and a printer landed on the blue tarp on the ground. A sharp female cry emanated from beneath it.

Hunt sucked in his breath. Maddy! He watched as the two searchers froze and their hands went to their holstered pistols, drawing them.

"Hold your fire!" Hunt shouted. "She's unarmed. Hold your fire!"

He heard rapid footsteps behind him and then felt a booted foot impact hard against the small of his back, sending him flying into the upturned table. He flopped over it in a heap, landing on the blue tarp. He considered using the momentum to roll away and make a stand, but his better judgement overcame the impulse. That was the kind of reckless action that got people killed. He wasn't Rambo, he knew that.

Hunt lay still after landing, stretching his arms out and splaying his hands to show he was still unarmed. The man with the submachine gun moved around the mess until he was aiming his weapon at the tarp. He growled menacingly. "You under the tarpaulin, come out from under there, slowly. Any funny business and you die."

"Listen to him, Maddy," Hunt said. He knew she had no experience in combat or adversarial situations such as this and was afraid she might try something he wouldn't be able to get her out of. He didn't like using her real name, either, but decided it was worth it under the circumstances.

The tarp rippled and a white arm crept out from beneath it, followed by Maddy's shoulder and head. She pulled herself out until only her feet were still beneath the tarp and lay there unmoving, face down on the ground.

"Dr. Chambers, I presume?" The voice of Daedalus, unamplified, emanated from the tent door.

"Yes, it's me. This is my dig. Who are you and what do you want?"

"I'm looking for a bronze artifact, the head of a statue. Have you seen it?"

Maddy replied without hesitation. "I have not."

"Do you understand the consequences to yourself and your team should I discover that you are lying to me?"

"What makes you think you are above the law here?" Open defiance crept into Maddy's voice.

Hunt interjected. "He makes a living stealing artifacts that belong in museums—that belong to the public at large—and selling them on the black market instead to wealthy private collectors with no scruples."

"Ah, Mr. Hunt, but Treasure, Inc. is so much more than that. A pity you do not understand." The voice of Daedalus was even and without emotion.

Hunt persisted. "I understand that you have been looting priceless treasures for over two decades now, Daedalus. It must be an addiction for you."

Daedalus appeared unfazed. "At its heart, Treasure, Inc. is an import-export business. I simply match commodities with prospective buyers. But yes, I do take a certain satisfaction in a job well done, like any business owner, I suppose. So if you consider that an addiction, please sign me up for your twelve-step program, Mr. Hunt."

"You and Pablo Escobar must have graduated from the same business school," Hunt sneered.

While the exchange went on, Daedalus' men continued to root through the tent, overturning crates, equipment and tables, ransacking the place. Daedalus folded his arms and watched over it all with a smug expression. Hunt mustered all the strength he had to contain his nervousness as his men walked back and forth over the area where the head had been buried. They didn't pause there, though, and no sooner had he gotten over that fear than a new one cropped up.

Jayden.

He was still hunkered down on the far side of the tent, but one of the treasure, Inc. henchmen approached his position now. Hunt silently willed his associate not to do anything rash, especially not to fire his appropriated automatic weapon. Site-wide, they were far out-gunned. But just as the man was about to reach Jayden, and doubtless discover him, Daedalus issued another command.

"We've wasted enough time here. Riaz, Binra, both of you: grab the girl. Now!"

CHAPTER 8

On the ground in the tent, Maddy turned her head to look toward Daedalus, but her view of him was blocked by a pair of boots coming her way.

"Daedalus, what are you doing?" Hunt demanded.

"A little insurance policy," Daedalus answered, raising his voice above the scuffle that ensued when first Riaz, and then Binra, grabbed Maddy and hauled her roughly to her feet. "Perhaps Dr. Chambers can lead us to what we seek, even without the bronze artifact."

"What do you seek?" Hunt shouted. He forced himself not to lose his temper. If Daedalus was to lose his, he could gun them all down in a fit of rage. He'd seen despicable behavior from the man and his employees before. Hunt pushed aside flashbacks from Iraq, almost smelling the scent of burning museums and treasures lost forever because if Treasure, Inc. couldn't have them, no one could.

Daedalus took on a look of amusement as he answered Hunt. "Why, you don't know? I suppose I should leave you to stew in your ignorance, then. You have no idea what the bronze head you found means, do you?"

"Why don't you tell me? Maybe we can help you find what you're looking for without all the violence."

Daedalus glared for a moment while staring at Hunt. "Ah yes, you are a student of history, are you not Mr. Hunt? Very well..." He paused to watch his two henchmen drag Maddy toward the tent entrance, on the side away from where Jayden still lay in hiding.

"I think that all of us in this room—including your assistant on the floor over there with one of my submachine guns, who won't dare use it because if he does the girl dies—know that we're looking for the lost city of Atlantis."

Hunt felt the wind empty out of him as he processed the double bombshell. They had lost their element of surprise, and the bronze head he and Jayden had risked their lives to obtain was connected to Atlantis after all. It took everything Hunt had not to let the defeatism creep into his voice. "Jayden, don't try anything. Stand up slow, hands in the air."

Daedalus beamed. "Sounds like you're already working for me! Maybe you have a future with Treasure, Inc. after all."

Hunt's eyes brimmed with fire. "The only future I have with your company is to put it out of business for good. If I have to make that my life's work, Daedalus, that's what I'm going to do. Mark my words."

Daedalus stiffened but had no reply for Hunt. Instead, he turned to watch Jayden rise to his feet, empty hands in the air. "Now, step over here...Jayden, is it? Surely your ancestors would not approve of that name," he added, attempting to insult Jayden's Asian-American heritage.

Jayden wisely said nothing but complied with the order, shuffling slowly over to the center of the tent, eyes downcast, hands up. Meanwhile, Maddy was screaming.

"You can't do this! You don't even have permission to be on this site. Are you crazy? Police will be here. This is a state-sponsored archaeological dig site!"

The smug grin on Daedalus' face made Hunt want to knock his teeth out, but he restrained himself while his nemesis replied. "I have several close friends in the Cairo Police Department. I can assure you that my presence here would not be taken negatively." Then to his associates he said, "Take her to the compound without delay. No stops on the way. I will meet you there."

The Treasure, Inc. workers nodded and began dragging Maddy kicking and screaming out of the tent.

"What's going on, Daedalus?" Hunt said. "All the artifacts she collected are here on site. Why do you need her?"

"All the artifacts minus one. The bronze head," Daedalus said. "So she's our little insurance policy. If you have the head but are lying about it, you can feel free to change your mind at any time—including right now-- and you will get your friend back. No doubt you will miss her," he said with a sneer while gawking at her lithe form being manhandled through the tent door. She pleaded with Hunt using only her eyes.

"But on the other hand," Daedalus continued, "if you truly don't know where the bronze head is, then Dr. Chambers will no doubt prove most valuable in our search."

"Don't worry, Maddy, we'll find you!" Hunt called as she was led from the tent by Daedalus' two goons. But deep inside he had no idea how he would find her. Daedalus was from Egypt, No doubt it was where his affliction for historical artifacts had been nurtured. He knew this country infinitely better than did he and Jayden combined. What to do?

But Daedalus had one last question for him. The Treasure, Inc. leader held his hands up in a mock what-now gesture. "As they say in your laughable country, the ball is in your court, Mr. Hunt. My team will continue to research this site and comb it for the bronze artifact I believe you salvaged from the flooded chamber today. Meanwhile, we will, ahem...*work with*...Dr. Chambers toward that end. Good day, sir. If we meet again, hopefully it will be because you have something for us. Because otherwise, you will not like the outcome, I can assure you of that."

Daedalus calmly walked over and picked up the assault rifle Jayden had left behind. Leveling it at Hunt and Jayden, Daedalus then proceeded to stroll out of the research tent.

Hunt and Jayden stared at each other, alone in the research tent. "Maybe we should call the police," Jayden suggested.

"Maddy's team saw her get carried off, not to mention all their artifacts were robbed at gunpoint. They'll handle that."

"So what's our plan?"

Hunt pondered the question while he looked around at the ransacked research tent. Equipment that had been procured and setup at great expense to uncover the lost lessons of history now lay in ruin. He couldn't stand it, it made him so angry, and yet he knew it was the modus operandi of his foes.

At length, he replied, "Treasure, Inc. is looking for Atlantis." He paused, as if to consider this.

"Yes, Daedalus said as much," Jayden pointed out.

Hunt went on. "The way I see it, we have two options: One, we try and act locally to first locate where Maddy is being held, and then conduct a raid to bust her out alive."

Jayden slowly shook his head. "I don't much like the sound of that."

"Me neither. Or..." Hunt held up a finger. "We find what Treasure, Inc. is after before they do. Then we offer it to them in exchange for Maddy."

"What, Atlantis? You're saying we find the lost city of Atlantis and then give it to the very people we despise?"

"We don't have to give them the actual city, which may not even exist. But we have the bronze head. We could give them that."

Again, Jayden shook his head, but faster this time. "I still don't like it. Once they have what they want, we'll have zero leverage on them. What's to stop them from killing Maddy at that point?"

Hunt shrugged. "You're right, There's nothing to stop them from doing that, and in fact, their past actions suggest that there's a distinct possibility they *will* do that."

"So then we're back to finding Atlantis?"

"We don't really have to find it, Jayden. We only need to follow in Treasure Inc.'s footsteps. I think there's a good possibility they're going to bring Maddy with them, since she's an expert archaeologist. We only need to figure out where they're going to go."

Jayden nodded. "Maddy was talking about how the statue—when the head was on the full horse and rider statue in the Azores—pointed west."

"Yes!" Hunt's eyes had an unmistakable gleam in them now, a

combination of excitement and determination. "And we thought it likely the 'west' the statue pointed to was the islands of the Bahamas. So that leaves us with either…"

"The Azores or the Bahamas are the most likely places Daedalus is going to take Maddy to," Jayden finished for him. Hunt nodded in agreement.

"We're closer to the Azores from here."

"Azores it is," Jayden said. "Let's go before our friends decide to come back."

"We need to grab something first." Hunt glanced at the patch of dirt where they'd hidden the bronze head.

Jayden's eyes widened. "Now? What if Daedalus left guards posted out there?"

"I'm guessing that within two hours, this entire site will be crawling with local police. I'm sure Daedalus got his people out of here. And with the leader of the expedition kidnapped and missing, it could be quite some time before we're allowed access on site ourselves. So I'd say that now is our best chance if we want it with us when we take our little extended vacation to the Azores."

Jayden moved back over to the area where they'd buried the artifact, grabbing a power strip along the way. "Let's grab our trusty digging tools and get to work, then, shall we?" They did, and a few minutes later, between frenzied bouts of digging punctuated by frequent glances to the doorway, they caught sight of the precious artifact once again. Hunt emptied a duffel bag of its tangled nest of cabling and loaded the bronze head into it.

"Now what?" Jayden asked, dusting off his pants. "We're just going to stroll on out of here?"

Hunt frowned. "We were supposed to call the camel guy an hour before we're ready for him to pick us up."

"We can't wait around that long, so what are our options?"

Hunt thought for a bit before answering. "Maybe we can hitch a ride with somebody. Come on, we'll just have to wing it." He grabbed the duffel bag containing the bronze head and moved to the doorway. He peered out while Jayden walked over. "I don't' see any of Daedalus' men. Let's move out. Walk casually, don't move too fast."

Hunt and Jayden exited the tent and made their way across the open dig site grounds, the great pyramid looming ahead of them. Hunt couldn't help but think what other secrets it contained, about the strange chambers concealed beneath the actual structure. It helped to keep his mind off of the reality that he carried in his hands what was essentially a priceless artifact made even more so by the fact that it could potentially lead to the lost city of Atlantis.

Hunt actually found himself smiling a little as he crossed the site, which was now empty, all of the personnel having taken cover inside the tents or having left the site already. He was smack dab in the middle of a historical mystery, and now saving his friend would depend on how well he utilized his skills and knowledge. Not a situation he would have asked for, certainly, but having to chase down the myth of Atlantis in order to save Maddy was something he was prepared—and felt able—to do.

Jayden's voice broke him from his thoughts. "Hey, isn't that Maddy's ride over there?" He pointed to a silver Mercedes SUV parked in what was designated as the car lot, in a line of about a dozen other vehicles.

"That's it. Hopefully she left the keys in it." Hunt and Jayden walked to the SUV and Hunt pulled on the driver's side door handle. It opened. "So far so good." But then his mouth turned down at the corners as he failed to spot the keys lying on the seat or in the ignition or on top of the visor. After a little more searching he concluded she had taken them with her.

Jayden quickly looked around at the site and then turned to Hunt. "I can get it started without the keys, but I'll need some wire strippers."

Hunt raised his eyebrows but reached to his waistband where the Leatherman multi-tool he usually carried was clipped to his belt. He unfolded a pair of pliers from the folding tool and handed them to Jayden. "I'll keep watch."

Jayden got into the driver's seat and closed the door, while Hunt tried to appear as casual as possible leaning against the car while his gaze scanned in all directions. Again, his mind turned to the mystery at hand, to the scant clues the bronze head that now lay in a bag at his feet might provide to the whereabouts of the lost city…and the vast treasure that legends held it contained.

Not five minutes later, his reverie was interrupted by the smooth roar of the SUV's engine coming to life as Jayden worked the gas pedal. The tinted automatic window rolled silently down to reveal Jayden's grinning face. "Hop in!"

Hunt picked up the bag. "I'll get in as long as you promise never to tell me where you learned how to do that."

Jayden beamed. "Deal!"

Police sirens pierced the air as Hunt ran around to the passenger side and got in with the bag.

Jayden put the SUV in gear as he looked over at Hunt while he got in. "Where to?"

With a mischievous grin on his face, Hunt said, "The Azores."

CHAPTER 9

The Azores, Island of São Miguel

"Atlantis Rent-A-Car, isn't that appropriate?" Jayden remarked as they walked up to a booth in the Ponta Delgada Airport. Officially part of Portugal but operating as its own autonomous province, the nine-island chain of the Azores are about a four-hour flight from Boston, but closer to twelve from Egypt.

"I guess it's no secret that the Azores is one of the most commonly suggested final resting places for Atlantis," Hunt said, stretching his legs after the long flight. "Not to mention the Portuguese government recognizes these islands as 'the remains of Atlantis'. They say that the Azores are actually the mountain peaks of what used to be Atlantis, all the rest of which was flooded."

"You rent the car," Jayden said, "and I'll get us espressos."

"Deal." Neither of them had slept much on the flight over. Both had read up on the Azores and the Atlantis myth, as well as making in-flight phone-calls to Maddy's friends and associates to make sure they knew she'd been kidnapped and that the local authorities had been alerted, which they had. Still, there had been no sign of the archaeologist since she was forcibly dragged from her research tent. Nor had there been any word from

Treasure, Inc., or any news stories about the dig site raid.

A few minutes later, a caffeinated Hunt sat behind the wheel of a rented Jeep Compass SUV, with Jayden in the passenger seat and the duffel containing the bronze head at his feet. "Motor's so quiet I can barely tell its running," Hunt quipped as he rolled off the lot onto the street.

"Good, you never know if we might need the element of surprise." Jayden smiled as he took in the busy airport surroundings. They now drove through the hub of the Azores, but knew from their research that much of the island chain was idyllic and remote. He glanced at his smartphone's navigation app. "Make a right up here and then we get on a highway for a while."

"Copy that." Hunt followed the directions and after he had merged onto the busy highway, lapsed into thought again. He was under no illusions that their mission was an easy one. In fact, it was all he could do to keep from letting on to Jayden that he thought they were likely on a wild goose chase. But at the same time, he could think of no other actionable alternatives.

"So we're diving right into the heart of it, right?" Jayden said, referencing the most highly associated region of the Azores that their research told them was associated with Atlantis.

Hunt agreed. "Lagoon of the Seven Cities, here we come." After a long drive during which Jayden made a couple of more unsuccessful attempts to track down information about Maddy's whereabouts by phone, they turned off onto a smaller, single lane paved road that wound up a mountain. Traffic thinned, and the view grew more impressive with each passing mile.

Far below, two lakes came into view. They were nestled in the crater of a dormant volcano, with verdant mountains forming a high rim around them. One was larger and blue in color, while the other was smaller and greenish. They were connected by a thin river. Hunt parked the SUV and both men got out to have a look at the view.

"So I know this site is supposed to be one of the more popular sites for Atlantis, but there's a legend associated with it. How does that go?"

Hunt replied while looking out across the lakes. "The story I read has it that in ancient times—don't ask me exactly how long ago that was—a king lived here with his daughter. He loved her but was way over-protective, you know, like one of those modern-day Dads who answers the door holding a shotgun when he knows it's his teen daughters' date."

Jayden laughed. "Yeah, I've met a few of those. Go on..."

"So he lived happily with her until, predictably enough, she became a teenager. Then she started to sneak out of the house..."

"Uh-oh, I see where you're going with this..." Jayden stared down at the lakes from behind his Oakley sunglasses.

"Yeah, she started taking walks out into the woods surrounding the house, until one day she came across this dude playing the flute. She watched him for a while and before too long, she introduced herself and one thing led to another and before you know it they were dating."

"Nature takes its course. But something tells me this isn't a happily-ever-after story."

"Well, after a while she couldn't stand being exiled from her home anymore and thought that her father would understand, so she showed up at the front door with her new friend."

"Uh-oh."

"As you can probably guess, he wasn't quite as understanding as she had hoped for, and even though the young man politely asked the king for his daughter's hand in marriage, his reaction was to turn the boy away and forbid the two from seeing each other again."

"Saw that coming a mile away."

'Right, so the girl snuck out one last time to say a final goodbye to her boyfriend."

"Awwwww."

"Yeah, they hugged and cried, and two lakes were formed from their tears." Hunt pointed down at the two lakes. "One blue, because the princess' eyes were blue, and one green because her lover's eyes were green. The green lake is shallower, I guess because he didn't cry as much as her."

Jayden shook his head. "Wow. It makes so much sense. But tell me Hunt," he said, turning to look at his friend. "How does any of that get us any closer to solving the mystery of Atlantis?"

"I've been thinking about that." Hunt stroked the thin layer of black stubble on his face. "It has to do with the statue that our head came from. At least I hope it does."

Jayden appeared lost in thought for a few moments before speaking. "So the statue was of a horse and rider, correct?"

"Right."

"But when the Portuguese first got here, they tried to take it back to their king, but screwed up and broke it into a bunch of pieces..."

"Which is how we ended up with the head," Hunt said.

Jayden looked around at the deep volcanic crater and the lakes below. "So even though the statue isn't here anymore, where *was* it?"

"That's exactly what I was hoping the old story would help us figure out. According to the accounts I read, the statue was on top of a mountain on this very island of San Miguel. Now, if the two lovers cried twin rivers of tears that ran *downhill* to form those two lakes, then they must have been up high to start out with, right?"

Jayden shrugged. "Makes sense."

Hunt looked around in a circle. "I don't see any higher points than where we're at right now, do you?"

Jayden also had a look around before shaking his head. Hunt continued. "So this must be it."

Jayden furrowed his brow. "*Where?*"

"Right around here, somewhere. Let's have a look around, shall we?"

"Jayden appeared dumbfounded. "What, you mean randomly just start looking around? You've got to be kidding me."

Hunt said, "We're at the highest point of this crater. It might make sense that a statue—what would have been a prominent landmark for the time—would be placed as high up as possible for maximum visibility and impact. Plus, it goes with the fable." Hunt could read the disbelief on Jayden's face, so he added, "I don't really expect to find anything after so much time has passed. But we've got a commanding view up here of the surrounding countryside. If Daedalus brings Maddy here—and we know she knows about this place—we'll see them coming."

That seemed to snap Jayden out of his funk. "Let's get to work, then. You want to start on foot or by driving around real slow?"

"Let's scour this area right here by foot first and take it from there. Hold on, I picked up something that might make our search go a little easier. It's in the back of the SUV." Hunt walked over to the vehicle and opened the tailgate. He pulled out two machines, each consisting of a plastic disc at the end of a metal pole with an electronic box and a handle grip at the other end, along with a pair of headphones attached by a coiled wire.

"Metal detectors, cool!" Jayden said.

"The statue was bronze, so..." Hunt explained. He also took out a couple of folding shovels and tossed one to Jayden. "In case we get a signal. Doesn't look like there's a lot of trash up here like bottlecaps and old cans and stuff, so we should have a nice clean search. Let's make sure they work, though, by testing it on something metal."

Jayden took out a set of keys but Hunt waved him down. "Actually, we should use something more like the metal we're trying to find." He looked to the SUV.

Jayden smiled. "Ah, like the head. Makes sense. I'll get it." He got the bronze head from the car and removed it from the bag. Then he set it down on the ground and passed his detector over it. "Yep, nice signal," he confirmed to Hunt, who also came over with his device.

"So take a mental note of what it sounds like, but keep in mind that buried a couple feet down—that's about the limit of these detectors—it'll sound a little different. But we'll probably dig up any signals we get anyway. Just wanted to take a baseline. Let's do this."

The two ex-navy men agreed on how to divide the area up into two sections; Hunt took one and Jayden took the other. They began walking back and forth in a grid pattern. They wore headphones to hear when the detector found a signal, so talk was kept to a minimum. Ten minutes of sweeping the detectors back and forth later and neither of them had received any kind of signal.

"Like I thought," Hunt said, "it's a clean area. Let's keep searching."

A few minutes later, Hunt paused when he heard the shrill beep in his ears. "Got something," he said to Jayden, taking off his headphones. He put the business end of the shovel on the spot and began to dig. By the time Jayden walked over to see what he had found, a disappointed Hunt pulled an old *Especial* beer can out of the ground.

"Guess it's not all that pristine after all," Jayden said.

"Much better than when I tried this on Santa Monica Beach, back in the day."

"I've been there. You probably dug up some of my old cans! Hey, maybe we should break for lunch," Jayden suggested. "I saw a little seafood place down in town that looked pretty decent. Maybe we could—"

"Hold up. Somebody's coming." Hunt's gaze was directed down at the single road which had led them up here. A vehicle of some kind was on its way up.

"Let's put the gear away." Hunt moved to the SUV and stashed his detector and shovel inside while Jayden did the same. Then he closed the hatchback and took out a point-and-shoot digital camera and began taking shots of the scenery. Jayden hammed it up, backing up against the view.

"Get a couple of shots for my Mom, would you? I am on vacation, after all."

Hunt laughed while clicking off a couple shots as the vehicle—they could now see it was a station wagon-SUV hybrid—drove up to them. But as he watched, he saw Jayden's face transform into a mask of fright.

"What's wrong? Who are they? Is it Daedalus?"

"No. I mean, I don't know who it is. But look!" He pointed past Hunt, who turned around and looked. There, lying on the ground, was the bronze head.

"Crap!" Hunt moved to it, but the SUV's tires were already crunching over loose rock as it drove onto the site. There was no time to pick up the artifact and carry it back to their vehicle without being seen.

"Do something, Carter. They're here."

Hunt eyed the bronze head as it sat on the ground, about ten feet from the edge of the crater's hill. Having a feeling he would regret the action, but not knowing what else to do, Hunt gave the heavy head a hard soccer kick, which sent it rolling toward the edge. It came to rest a couple of feet away.

"Keep going," Jayden called, "I don't think whoever it is paying attention yet."

Hunt walked over to the head with as casual a gait as he could muster in case he was being observed. Then he booted the bronze head one more time, this time sending it rolling down the side of the crater. He did his best to take note of where exactly it had gone over the side, so that they could track it down after they were alone once more. At the same time, he didn't want to attract suspicion or even interest by appearing overly fixated on one particular spot, so he didn't linger long. Keeping the camera in front of his face, Hunt turned around and began ambling back over to Jayden.

"It's a rental," Jayden said in a low voice.

"Does that mean anything?" Hunt continued to make a show of snapping off touristy pictures.

"Only that it's probably not a local."

The vehicle pulled to a stop such that Hunt had his back to it and Jayden was eyes on. "Family of four, two kids in the backseat, I think we're safe."

The front doors opened and a tall man with a jovial demeanor got out along with a woman wearing a loud sundress. Both of them were sunburned a rosy pink. The woman told the kids to wait inside, no doubt to make sure these strangers atop the volcanic crater were not bad people.

Hunt put down the camera and he and Jayden walked over and introduced themselves with fake, though American-sounding, names. The couple introduced themselves as the Willinsons, from St. Louis, Missouri, and immediately put Hunt at ease that they were not related to Treasure, Inc. or Maddy's disappearance. The mother opened the rear doors and soon the kids were running around the site, exploring loudly.

"So this is the highest point of the island, according to my travel guide," the woman said, taking in the majestic view. Hunt said that's why he and Jayden had come here, too.

"You can really see the difference between the green and blue lakes from up here," the husband said. Then he added, "There's the bridge, honey—see?--dividing the two lakes."

"Bridge?" Hunt asked, squinting below.

The family man turned to him. "Yeah, there's a bridge right between the two lakes. We drove across it earlier. Even down there you can see the difference in the water color, green on one side, blue on the other, Pretty striking. Can see clear down to the bottom, lot of big boulders down there, it looks like."

Hunt and Jayden exchanged glances. "Interesting," Hunt said, "maybe we'll check that out."

"You should," the wife chimed in. "You'll get some great pictures. Nice to meet you fellas, I'm going to set up for our little picnic." She excused herself and went to her rental car. After a little more small talk that centered around the best places to eat what kind of food in town, the husband did the same and then Hunt and Jayden were left standing together, looking down on the legendary lakes.

"Looks like metal detecting is out until these guys leave. Should we check out the bridge?" Jayden asked.

"What for?" Hunt was irritated that their search was cut short, for one thing. And for another, the bronze head now lay somewhere down the mountainside.

"I don't know, the guy said he could see boulders down there in the water, kind of reminds me of the flooded pyramid chamber we dove."

Hunt thought about this for a few moments but appeared unmoved. "I think the first thing we should do, as soon as we have the chance," he said, glancing over to the picnicking family, "is to climb down that hill and get the head back."

The urge to walk to the edge and look down was difficult for Jayden to suppress, but Hunt convinced him to wait it out while they pretended to take more tourist pictures. The time seemed to pass very slowly, but not half an hour later, the family packed their belongings back into their rental car and said loud goodbyes before driving back down the mountain.

As soon as their vehicle was no longer in sight, Hunt and Jayden walked to the edge of the crater.

CHAPTER 10

"I don't see it." Jayden walked up to the edge of the drop-off and stood next to Hunt.

"Me neither."

"You sure this is where you kicked it off?" Jayden's gaze swept the steep hillside below. Scrubby vegetation covered the mountain, with a few small evergreen trees here and there dotting the inclined landscape.

"Yeah, see there's where my foot came into contact with the dirt. He indicated a scuff mark made by his shoe.

Jayden eyed the spot, then stepped a little closer to the edge and continued looking for signs of the bronze head. "We're going to have to go down there, then, because I don't see it."

Hunt concurred before adding, "See that plant there? Looks like it got recently crushed, so it could be that the head rolled down that way."

"Might as well start there, " Jayden agreed. The pair of ex-military men began picking their way down the steep hill. As far as they could tell there were no vertical sections, and they could face downward while they moved, not needing to face the cliff as with rock climbing. Still, it was no walk in the park; hands were needed to steady themselves, and twisting an ankle was a constant threat.

"Watch for snakes," Hunt said.

"What? Are there snakes here?" Jayden looked around nervously.

"I don't know. Seems like there could be."

Jayden made a spitting noise. "Geez, Hunt, I'm supposed to be looking for a bronze head, now you want me to keep an eye out for snakes, too?"

"Well you'll be of no use if you get bitten by a poisonous snake."

They continued their slow and cautious descent down the hill. About two-thirds of the way down the terrain became less steep, making the going easier, but at the same time more overgrown with thorny scrub brush, making it harder to see the ground.

"Ouch, damn! These brambles hurt." Jayden paused to pull a thorn from his arm, leaving a speck of blood.

"I think you'll live," Hunt said, kicking some brush out of the way. He eyed the remaining slope down to the lakes. "I don't think it could have rolled all the way down to the water."

"That's good. Because I don't think it'd be good luck to have to scuba dive twice for the same head."

"Down there it changes. See those rocks?"

Jayden followed to where Hunt pointed. A low, crumbling rock formation, overgrown with vegetation, formed a break in the hillside before it sloped the rest of the way down to the water. "That should form a nice little backstop for our rolling head, I would think."

Hunt and Jayden slid the rest of the way down to the lip or rocks and began looking around. There was still a lot of plant life that had to be kicked out of the way, but after seeing the rock wall, Hunt became more convinced that the rolling head couldn't possibly have made it over, unless it had rolled far off course to either side, a prospect he didn't want to think about as he eyed the lake below.

"It's got to be around here somewhere," Hunt said, eyes to the ground.

"Uh, yeah, about that. Half of it's around here, anyway." Jayden pointed, and Hunt gasped.

The head had broken on the way down when it impacted a rock, and half of it—the top half—lay at Jayden's feet. Hunt picked up the empty bronze shell. A puzzled expression overtook his features as he examined what remained of the artifact. "Funny, but it seems awfully light, even just for half of it."

"Let's find the other half, It's got to be around here somewhere." Hunt held onto the broken half and resumed searching the ground along with Jayden, who couldn't help but needle his friend while they looked.

"So how do you feel about busting up an ancient artifact? Nice going, really."

Hunt shook his head. "It's not like I meant for it to break. I thought it would just roll down a ways and stop in the grass. In fact, it's just my luck these seem to be the only rocks anywhere—whoa!"

"What?"

"I found it. But look at it!" He knelt and picked up the other half of the statue, extricating it from a stand of weeds.

"What's that inside it? That greenish blue stuff?" Jayden asked, voice barely above a whisper.

Hunt dropped the empty broken half he'd already found in order to concentrate on the new one. He ran his fingers over the bluish-green substance that had been revealed inside the head. "It looks like an amethyst crystal. The whole head looks like it was filled with some kind of fancy crystal, the kind that would go for thousands at a gem show."

"Let's see..." Jayden bent down and picked up the hollow half of the head. Then he fit it over the protruding amethyst on the half Hunt held.

"Perfect fit," Hunt observed. "Definitely had to have been inside the head already. Not some kind of freak accident, like it just rolled down the hill into the gemstone or amethyst or whatever it is. Quartz, maybe."

Jayden rolled his eyes. "Ya think?"

"The question is," Hunt said, ignoring the sarcastic jab, "why was it inside the statue head in the first place? What does it mean? Back in the days when it was made, no one would have known, except perhaps expert sculptors who could tell by the weight, that there was anything unusual inside it."

Both of them paused to look around. Were they being observed? But there were no people within sight or even earshot. No boats on the lakes, no traffic of any kind on the bridge. *The bridge,* Hunt thought. He recalled the tourists talking about it, how it exactly divides the two lakes. He looked over at it now. *Divides the two lakes. One green, one blue...one green one blue...*

"Earth to Carter, what's up?"

He stared into the crystal-filled head as he responded. "This head is filled with blue-green rock."

"Yeah. I can see that."

"One lake is green. One is blue."

Jayden looked briefly to the lakes, then back to Hunt. "Carter, did you hit your head on the way down here? You feeling okay?"

"Just bear with me. When you mix green and blue together, what do you get?"

Jayden shrugged. "Some kind of blue-green."

Hunt pointed at the mineral inside the statue head. "Kind of like this, right?"

"Yeah. So?"

"Don't you think it's too much of a coincidence that this statue head, that used to be here on this very island, is filled with a rock the exact color of the two lakes where they come together?"

Jayden looked to the two lakes, focusing under the bridge where a bright blue-green line demarcated one lake from the other. "Like whoever made this statue put the rock in there as a color coded clue?"

Hunt held his hands up in a why-not gesture. "Even after all these years, the color is remarkably similar." He looked to the water beneath the bridge.

But Jayden was still unconvinced. "Or it's the same color now but it didn't used to be. How do we know?"

"The legend of the tears is pretty old."

"How old? Eleven thousand years?" Jayden crossed his arms.

"I don't know. It's a legend. But this place—the Seven Cities lakes, is often mentioned as a possible resting place of Atlantis."

"And with all that attention you think no one's ever had a peak down there under the bridge? I mean c'mon, Carter, what are the chances?"

But Hunt was undeterred. "It won't take much effort to have a look down there for ourselves. First of all, let's just walk the bridge and see what it looks like. We're pretty close to it from here."

Jayden agreed to that and they made their way the rest of the way down the slope to the lake itself, to the deeper blue one. They were able to follow its shoreline along the water's edge toward the bridge without major difficulties. Parts of the shoreline were grassy while others had stands of pine trees to thread their way between.

No one was on the bridge when they got to it. Hunt felt a little conspicuous walking around with a broken bronze head filled with some kind of gemstone or mineral, but he had no bag in which to put it. As they reached the bridge, the water depth and color changed immediately. Deep and blue became shallower and bluish green, or cyan. Looking out onto the green lake, they could see that it was shallower with a little more wave action.

Hunt and Jayden walked out onto the arching wooden bridge, which was low to the water, until they were about halfway across at its highest point. They looked down into the crystal clear waters.

"It's like that guy said," Jayden admitted. Formations of large boulders sprawled out in the shallow depths below.

"Must be lots of caves and caverns down there," Hunt observed. "But let's think about this for a minute: Whoever it was who made that statue for the Portuguese explorers to find here in the Azores all those years ago, they went through the trouble of embedding a mineral gemstone of some type into the statue's head, which was attached to the body of a man who was riding a horse."

"And the whole thing was fixed to a base with an inscription reading 'go that way'." Jayden recapped.

"Some say that inscription was written in Incan. I read that on the plane."

"So what do the Azores have to do with the Incas?"

Hunt stared into the water while he answered. "Hate to say it, but maybe we should drive back into town, rent some scuba gear, and come back here to find out."

#

Two hours later

"I'm so worn out from our little shopping spree and the hike back here, that I don't even feel like diving," Jayden huffed as he shrugged out of a large backpack.

"Think about how refreshing it'll be once we hit this cool, crisp mountain lake water," Hunt said, attaching a breathing regulator onto a scuba tank.

"I thought tears are supposed to be warm."

"Wow, I'm impressed. I didn't think you paid that much attention to the legend."

"I like to surprise people now and then."

The two finished setting up their gear and took a look around. The tranquil scene was just that; they were the only two people in sight for miles. During the hike from the nearest available parking spot to the bridge, they'd worried that there would be tourists here and they would draw too much attention. But right now, anyway, they were the only ones here.

"Let's just drop down and have a look-see. Doesn't have to take long," Hunt said, climbing onto the bridge railing. He sat on the rail so that his back faced the water.

"Just like a backwards roll entry off a boat?" Jayden clarified.

"You got it. Put a little air in your vest so you don't sink too fast, wouldn't want to hit one of those rocks."

"Got it." Hunt heard the hiss of air as Jayden pressed a button to put air from his tank into his buoyancy compensator vest, inflating it.

Hunt flopped over backwards into the lake with a splash, and Jayden followed suit a minute later.

"So clear it makes me dizzy," Jayden commented after lifting his face from the water.

"Let's drop down," Hunt said, releasing air from his vest with an escaping hiss. The pair began their descent into the lake. It was hard to say how deep it actually was since the bottom was a disorganized pile of boulders, sort of like the pyramid chamber, but on a flat plane rather than a steep incline.

The descent took only a few seconds before they reached the smooth tops of the highest-reaching boulders. A thin layer of green, slimy algae covered them, causing Hunt to lose his footing when trying to stand on one. Looking up, he could see the underside of the bridge in a distorted, watery view. He felt a tap on his leg and looked over to see Jayden pointing down at a gap between two large boulders.

Hunt nodded and he followed Jayden as they finned head first into the crevice. It opened into a small cavern. Jayden stopped a few feet inside the entrance, waiting for Hunt to catch up. A few startled fish darted out the way they came in. Aware that they were now in an overhead environment, where there was no direct access to the surface, Hunt checked his gauges, which told him he had plenty of air left and that they were only twenty feet underwater. Looking around the enclosed space, Hunt saw light streaming in from the opposite side of the cavern.

He and Jayden moved across the boulder cavern side by side, observing the floor and walls of the space as they passed. Nothing out of the ordinary was visible, only natural rock, and some leaf litter and tree branches from the surrounding lake vegetation. They emerged from the cavern only to see another opening between a group of boulders a few feet deeper.

Hunt pointed down to it and Jayden nodded before finning toward it. Again, they entered a cavern and swam through it. Like the last one, it also held nothing unusual. They continued to poke around the boulders, swimming over and through them for the next hour, without finding anything noteworthy. Hunt had begun to feel the chill of the mountain lake when he checked his air gauge and saw that he was getting low; it was time to head back up.

He flashed the face of his gauge to Jayden and jerked a thumb towards the surface, the signal to ascend. Jayden nodded and the two divers slowly made their way back up to the surface of the lake. Hunt immediately checked the bridge for signs of people but was relieved to see that it was empty. He'd periodically glanced up at it while underwater, since the water was clear enough to see people on it, but he hadn't seen any. He and Jayden quietly made their way to the bridge on the shore closest to them, careful not to make loud splashes, which might carry far across the lake and draw attention.

"No sign of Atlantis," Jayden quipped.

Hunt flipped over onto his back for the semi-long swim to shore. "Sure was a lot easier getting in than it is getting out, isn't it?"

"Yeah, it's nice when gravity's on your side."

Hunt agreed as he stared up at the mountainside that towered above the lake while he kicked backwards toward shore. He admired the green vegetation lower down on the crater wall, and then a few bursts of color where wildflowers grew higher up—reds, yellow…and at the rim, near to where they had parked the car earlier—an explosion of cyan.

"Hey Jayden, how much do you think this place has changed since whoever it was put that statue here?"

"What do you mean, like this lake?"

"The lake, the crater, the wildlife—the trees and plants—you think they're still the same kind, in about the same places?"

"You sure do wonder about some weird stuff. I suppose it's mostly the same though, why?"

"On the way back into town to return the dive gear, I think we should stop off at the top of the crater one more time."

CHAPTER 11

"You just like metal detecting, don't you?" Jayden said as he pulled the two shovels from the rental SUV while Hunt took out the detectors.

"There are worse things to be doing, but I really think this is worth a try."

Jayden wore a skeptical look. "So let me get this straight: you think there's something up with the color blue-green, or cyan or whatever? Because the statue head contained a cyan rock, and these are cyan flowers…" He waved an arm at the riotous bush with its bluish-green blossoms a few feet away. "…that it means whoever planted that statue had some kind of color-coded secret message?"

Hunt put the metal detector headphones on. "It sounds pretty wild when you put it like that, I admit, but basically, yeah. And and kind of blue is extremely rare in plants, expecially flowers."

"But these bushes might not have even been here back then."

"But they might have. We don't know, so we may as well take a few minutes and see if we get a signal."

For the second time that day they set out with the metal detectors on the crater summit. Together they walked the perimeter of the large flowering bush without obtaining a signal. As they made their way around they suddenly heard light footsteps, and then breathing. Hunt tensed, but relaxed when he saw a mangy wild dog trot around the bush.

"Looks like a coyote," Jayden assessed.

"Could be," Hunt said, "because coyotes are pack animals, and here comes another one." A second canine ran up to them, nose to the ground. It did not have a threatening demeanor, nor did it appear cagey or wary of the humans. Both animals sniffed around in the bushes, always maintaining a few feet distance from the humans without seeming to put too much effort into that positional awareness.

They stood and watched for a minute to see if more dogs were coming. When a third showed up but mimicked the behavior of the first, Hunt told Jayden they should get to work. "Maybe we should get this done before too many of them get here." Jayden agreed.

Then Hunt made his way into the brambles, determined to cover the ground it hid beneath its thorny vines.

"You're loony-tunes, Carter, you know that, right?" Jayden taunted from somewhere unseen inside the sprawling, cyan foliage. "I mean really, is this your idea of a vacation, because—"

But Hunt interrupted him with an excited shout. "Hey! I got something!"

"Yeah, I know, you got a case of the crazies, Hunt, because—"

"No, I'm serious. I've got a signal. Get over here and help me dig."

By the time Jayden was able to hack his way through the bush to Hunt's position, he'd already dug a six-inch deep hole, careful not to be too reckless about it lest he destroy something delicate if it was there.

"Probably just an old beer can," Jayden said as he helped to dig, clearing dirt out of the hole after Hunt excavated.

"Ever the optimist, aren't you?" Hunt said.

"Realist."

"Who would drink beer in this thorny bush like this?"

"You probably would. But I don't know, maybe this hedge is new, or—
"

"Whoa, hold up! Here it is." Hunt moved his shovel away from the now two-foot deep pit they'd dug. "What have we here?"

Something solid lay in the dry dirt. A pointed object, protruding up from below. Hunt reached into the hole and brushed some of the dirt away, revealing a glint of gold-colored metal, roughly in the shape of a finger. Around them they could hear the wild dogs shuffling around but they continued to work on extricating the item from the earth.

"There's more to it than just this," Hunt said, excitement creeping into his voice. At the same time as Hunt worked, Jayden began digging carefully with a hand trowel a couple of feet away from the golden finger, looking to see how far whatever the object was might extend.

"Got something here, too," he said, dropping the trowel to hand-wipe dirt away from whatever it was he'd uncovered. "Same color." They continued to sweep away the dirt, digging carefully with hand trowels where necessary. As they worked, more and more of the golden object was uncovered, as well as some black color.

"Seems pretty solid, whatever it is," Hunt said. After continuing their efforts for several more minutes, Hunt was finally able to lift the find out of the hole.

"Wow!" Jayden exclaimed as Hunt cradled the object like a baby.

"Look familiar?" Hunt asked.

Jayden appeared confused. "Wait a minute, we're not in Egypt anymore, right? We're in the Azores?"

"Last I checked," Hunt joked, looking around. The dogs still lurked nearby but he saw no signs of people. "So do you recognize this thing?"

It was a statuette of a man with a dog's head. Around his neck, but affixed to the statuette itself, was an ahnk made of black onyx.

"It's Anubis," Jayden said. "The Egyptian god of the dead, right?"

Hunt nodded as he turned the work of art over in his hands. "Yeah. Some called him 'The Guardian of the Scales,' and claim that his main function was to watch over the dead. It has to do with the belief that after death, a person meets the gods who would place his or her heart on a scale. Ceremonial acts of weighing the heart from the Book of the Dead depict Anubis judging whether the person deserved to live an eternal life."

"So basically, this guy right here decided every soul's fate."

"Correct. But I wonder is....what's he doing here, an Egyptian god, in the Azores, a Portuguese island chain?"

"It wasn't always Portuguese."

Hunt thought about this for a moment while he eyed the statuette of Anubis. "True. It was the Portuguese who took the statue of the horse and rider, though, so whoever put that there—maybe the Egyptians—left the Anubis here."

"The Egyptians do seem connected to Atlantis."

Hunt stood again and readied his metal detector. "Let's see if there are any other finds around here." With the golden statuette tucked under one arm, Hunt passed the detector's circular disc over the same hole the Anubis piece had come out of, but it gave no more signals. Then he and Jayden proceeded to cover more of the surrounding area, including deep into the thorny cyan bush, but again, the detectors were silent.

"Looks like Anubis is it for this site," Hunt concluded, hefting the golden statuette.

"Wonder if it's really gold, you think so?" Jayden wondered.

Hunt hefted the find in one hand, testing its weight. "Feels heavy enough, but we'll have to have it tested to say for sure. The black rock looks like onyx."

Jayden nodded as he eyed the decorative ahnk. "I wish Maddy could see this."

At the mention of their friend, Hunt became somber. "Me too. We need to find her. I really wonder where she is now."

Jayden looked up from the statuette. "I wish there was some way to find out."

Hunt held up the statuette. "I have a feeling this might lead us to her."

CHAPTER 12

The room was dark and cold. That's all Dr. Madison Chambers knew. She had no idea where she was. Groggy and with a lingering headache, she found herself tied to a chair that seemed to be bolted to a concrete floor. She supposed she was in a cell of some sort, but she couldn't be sure, so complete was the darkness.

Although her hands were bound behind the chair, and her legs were tied to the chair's legs, she was not blindfolded, so she knew the room must really be dark. She had no idea what time—or even what day—it was. Everything after being in the research tent with Carter and Jayden was a frenetic blur to her. She remembered being dragged out of the tent by Daedalus' thugs at gunpoint. She recalled a couple of her colleagues on site approaching her to ask if she was all right before being turned away with warning shots fired into the dirt near their feet.

And then she was roughly shoved into the back of a Suburban, the two thugs climbing in on either side of her, while a driver of Arab descent she'd never seen before raced away from her dig site onto a lonely desert highway.

But that was how long ago? A few hours? A few days? She tried moving her body to the extent her bonds would allow. She didn't seem to be physically injured. No major wounds or any broken bones as far as she could tell. That was something, but overall she felt dehydrated, fatigued and had a headache. She needed water, Tylenol, information…These needs overwhelmed her and she called out in the darkness.

"Hello? Hello, is anyone here, please? I need help!"

No voice came in response. She did her best to calm her breathing while listening for any sounds at all, but she heard only the repetitive buzz of what she thought might be a ceiling fan or some kind of electrical hum. She cried out again for help, even louder this time, as loud as she could. She'd seen television shows about kidnapped people who were kept in suburban neighborhoods in close proximity to other people for years, and had they only called more attention to themselves….She tried not to let dark thoughts like these invade her mind but trapped in the darkness alone, after the terrible events that had unfolded at her dig site—at a place that for her had always represented normalcy and a sense of professional advancement—she began to tremble with fear.

Suddenly she heard a *click* and a bank of ceiling-mounted fluorescent light bars flickered to life. The brightness was blinding after the time in the dark and she looked down with half-closed eyes to try and preserve her sight in order to assess whatever threat might be coming her way next.

But she heard the voice before she saw the man from who it came. "Dr. Chambers, I have something to show you."

Daedalus.

She would never forget that voice as long as she lived. She wanted to, though, Oh, how she wanted to. She looked up at her kidnapper.

"What do you *want* from me?"

"Nothing a world-class archaeologist such as yourself should have any trouble giving me. A lost city. Atlantis."

In spite of herself and the horrid situation in which she found herself, Maddy threw her head back and laughed aloud, long and hard. Daedalus closed the door to the room and stood a few feet away from her, his arms crossed. "I'll wait. I know this must be an emotional experience for you. I find it regrettable, but unfortunately I see no other way. So please, whenever you are ready…"

Maddy laughed some more until she started sniffling. Then she leveled her head and fully opened her eyes. She stared directly at Daedalus, who still wore the same outfit she had seen him in at the dig site. She hoped this meant that not that much time had passed. She knew that the more time that went by after a kidnapping the less likely it became the victim would be found unharmed. Then the anger set in and she glared at the Treasure, Inc. leader.

"Seriously? That's what this is about? Atlantis? It's a *myth*, for Christ's sake, Daedalus. Fiction created by Plato to create a learning parable. It's not real."

Daedalus took on a contemplative expression. "There are those who maintain that, yes. But it's also true that there are stories with elements of falsehood that happen to be true on the whole."

"I'm not really in the mood for an academic discussion."

"That's too bad. Perhaps once you realize that your freedom depends on it, you'll change your mind." Daedalus turned on a heel on began to walk toward the door.

"Where are you going?"

"To find more stimulating conversation. Maybe I'll check back on you in a few days to see if you're more amenable."

Maddy froze in her bonds. She simply could not imagine being left alone here for days, even with food and water, and she had no idea whether that would be available. She was about to say something that would let him know, okay, she would cooperate, when another man walked into the room. He glanced quickly at her, avoiding eye contact, before addressing Daedalus and then handing him a tablet with something on the screen that was obviously of pressing concern.

Daedalus nodded and the messenger left, leaving the tablet with his boss. Daedalus walked over to Maddy and showed her the screen. "What does this mean to you?" he asked without preamble.

Maddy caught her breath upon looking at the photograph. It was Hunt and Jayden in an outdoor setting in front of a bush. But it was what Hunt held in his hands that was undoubtedly the centerpiece of the image.

"Carter's holding Anubis," Maddy said. "The Egyptian god of the underworld."

Daedalus nodded. "Yes, I am familiar with the basic mythology behind Anubis. But tell me, Dr. Chambers, what does Anubis mean in the context of Atlantis? And more importantly, where are your friends?"

Maddy did not hesitate with her answer. "I don't know where they are. But I can speak to your first question."

"Let's start with that."

Maddy forced herself to maintain her composure and not lose her temper with this career criminal mastermind. "Atlantis itself, as recorded by Plato, was a drowned city. Its citizens were supposedly punished for allowing their avarice to get the better of them, for letting their morals slip. So God flooded the city. The ancient Egyptians might have regarded the entire city—if they knew where it was or thought they did—as one giant submerged tomb. Therefore, there would be a lot of dead people to guard. So Anubis could be associated with Atlantis in that way."

Maddy held Daedalus' gaze to indicate she had finished making her point.

At length, Daedalus nodded slowly. "Yes, I had considered that. But assuming you don't actually know where your friends are..." He looked at her skeptically as he said this. "...where might you expect to find Anubis artifacts related to Atlantis—in what part of the world? Egypt, I suppose?"

Maddy gave what passed for a shrug in her binds. "That's the obvious one, both symbolically and because that's where they just were—by the way, where am I? Am I still in Egypt?"

Daedalus nodded but didn't elaborate. She went on.

"But we didn't find any Anubis artifacts at the great pyramid, not to mention I have to say, what I can see of that photograph doesn't really look like Egypt." She stared again at the image on the tablet, the rangy cyan bush and scrubby, sloping terrain visible in what little background there was to see behind Hunt and Jayden.

Daedalus took on a contemplative face, an expression that put out an aura of reasonableness that Maddy knew was as fake as a curio shop mummy in Cairo that lured customers in the door. "Where does it look like to you that could also be a resting place for Atlantis-related Anubis artifacts?"

Maddy's voice hardened. "I don't know off the top of my head. I would need to do some research, with an Internet-connected computer."

Daedalus nodded very slowly "Perhaps that might be arranged. For I am somewhat puzzled as to how your friends were able to locate what appears to be a genuine artifact—of course, it does not escape me that it could be a fake in an attempt to gain my attention—related to Atlantis in so short a time. Actually," he added before Maddy could say anything, "this would be the *second* Atlantis-related artifact those two have recovered, after the bronze head in the pyramid."

"Carter has a history degree and has always taken an interest in archaeology and historical items. Not to mention that it was *my* team and LiDAR research that led to the discovery of the bronze head, *if* in fact it is related to Atlantis."

Daedalus shot her a thin smile. "Yes, I suppose you are due credit as well. That is after all, why I had your dig site under surveillance and why I want you here with me, by my side." Maddy visibly cringed at the mention of being at the egomaniac's side, but he continued on unfazed. "Nevertheless, Mr. Hunt's lucky streak seems to go beyond what most men are blessed with. Perhaps he should try his luck in Vegas. At any rate, I would be amenable to providing you with more comfortable working conditions in return for your cooperation. Is that something you would agree to?"

"Yes." Not much of a decision to make there, Maddy thought.

Daedalus grinned broadly, though the smile did not reach his dark brown eyes. "Excellent. I shall prepare your work area. My associate will be down shortly to escort you." He turned on a heel and began walking out the door.

"Daedalus?" Maddy called. He stopped and turned around.

"Yes, Dr. Chambers?"

"Do you plan to kill me after I help you?"

The founder of Treasure, Inc. stared at her, his eyes boring into hers until she wanted to look away. She held his gaze, though, demanding an answer while showing him that she was no fool. Then he broke into what he no doubt hoped was a convincing smile, but in fact Maddy found it otherwise.

"Of course not, doctor. Is that any way to do business? I think you will find that I am a reasonable man. Perhaps, after we complete our job here, you would even consider coming to work for my organization. You would have unparalleled resources and access to technology to aid in your research and excavations."

"Let's not get crazy. One thing at a time, Daedalus. But above all I would need to feel like I'm not working for a hardened criminal. Right now, you're asking me to give up the location of my friends. If I do that, and then anything bad happens to them, I would of course never dream of cooperating with you."

Daedalus made a clucking sound while shaking his head. "I can assure you that no harm will come to them. My interest in them extends only as far as the trail of artifacts that leads to Atlantis. That is all. For now, I must go. I will see you soon."

Then he turned and walked away into a dimly lit hallway, disappearing from sight.

CHAPTER 13

Sao Miguel, Azores

Hunt and Jayden occupied a table with an umbrella over it in the middle of a busy outdoor café.

"Any message yet?" Jayden asked as Hunt checked his smartphone for the tenth time in as many minutes.

Hunt shook his head. "Seems Daedalus isn't taking the bait yet."

Jayden set his Super Bock beer down on the table with a clack. "Maybe he's not into dog-men. Just doesn't do it for him."

Hunt picked at his churrascaria meat. "Anubis is very well known in historical circles. He'd be well aware that any antiquities trader would be more than interested in it. Add to that the Atlantis connection, and I'd bet dollars to donuts that—"

He was interrupted by his smartphone chirping on the table. He glanced at the screen. "Unknown number, originating outside of the US, is all I can tell." He picked up the phone and glanced at Jayden, who nodded. "Could be you just forgot to pay your phone bill, but may as well check it out."

Hunt put the phone to his ear, opting not to have the call on speaker mode since they were in the middle of a crowded café. "Hello," he said, offering no de facto information.

"Mr. Hunt, how is your old friend, Anubis?"

Although no name was given, the voice was unmistakable. *Daedalus*.

"Speaking of old friends, Daedalus, how is Madison?"

"Dr. Chambers is doing well, I can assure you. She is even entertaining an offer of employment from my esteemed organization."

"Put her on, let me talk to her now."

"First things first, Mr. Hunt. Before we get serious, let ask you point blank: is the Anubis statuette a genuine artifact and not a fake?"

Hunt looked at Jayden and said in a low voice he wants to know if it's real. Jayden nodded calmly while sipping his brew, before saying, "Real as it gets, baby!"

"How do you know?" Daedalus asked Hunt.

Hunt spoke into the phone. "We actually don't know for certain, but it was found in the ground using professional equipment based on professional research. It appears to be made of solid gold with onyx overlays."

Hunt steeled himself for a barrage of skepticism from the black market antiquities dealer, but instead he was confronted with a new direction. "Do me a favor and take something like a screwdriver or a knife blade and chip off a little piece of the gold. Then take a closeup picture of the interior metal and send it to me."

Hunt muted the phone and relayed the odd request to Jayden, who responded by guzzling the rest of his beer with a shrug and saying, "If it'll get Maddy back."

Hunt reached down to the backpack he'd acquired to put the artifact in, not feeling safe leaving it in the rental car. He looked around quickly before opening the pack on the table. "I guess one little chip won't make much difference." He unmuted the phone and spoke into it.

"All right, Daedalus, I'll do that for you. But in return you're going to let me speak with her, correct?"

"Once I get the picture, yes. You have a deal."

Hunt removed his Leatherman multitool and pried open one of its blades. "Give me a minute to find the best place on the artifact to take a piece out," he said into the phone. Jayden flipped over the statuette and together they examined it carefully. The backside of the figure was adorned with black onyx as well, in the form of the chain or rope that held the ahnk necklace, as well as some kind of robe-like garment.

Jayden shook his head as they looked at it. He turned the mini-statue toward him and nodded as he stared at the soles of the feet. "These are the same golden metal, but when he's standing up, the chunk we take out won't be visible."

Hunt nodded and said into his phone, "All right Daedalus, we're going to take a small piece out of the bottom of the thing's foot. Going to place you on hold. Give us a couple of minutes."

"Should I hum some elevator music for him?" Jayden joked. But Hunt was already busy with his tool, testing the hardness of the metal while gripping the statuette. "Careful, don't shatter the whole leg off."

"I'd say I know what I'm doing, but I don't want to hex myself."

"Just needle out a little piece, you can do it."

Hunt bent to the task. "Thanks for the vote of confidence. Gold is a pretty soft metal, so if it is real gold…" Hunt paused while he dug the tip of his blade into the bottom of Anubis' left foot. "…it should be easy to…"

Hunt frowned as the tip of his blade skidded off the sole of the dog-man's foot. "…gouge."

"Let me give it a go." Jayden held a hand out and Hunt handed him the multitool. Jayden turned the figure his way and then tried his luck. The blade also slipped away from the surface. "Huh. No go." He handed the tool back to Hunt, who folded the blade away and selected a different implement,, this one more like a bottle opener. Then he put it to the bottom of the foot again and applied pressure.

"Okay, I've made a scratch." He pulled the tool back while admiring his handiwork.

"Keep going. I'm curious to see what it looks like inside there, now. This can't be gold."

"Yeah, strange. It's heavy like gold, though. Just harder. Not impervious, though. I scratched it, so…Here we go." Again he applied the tool to the figurine, this time gripping it harder with one hand to steady it, while applying a lot of force with the hand holding the multitool.

Suddenly a chip of metal went flying form the statuette, clattering on the table. Jayden picked it up while Hunt eyeballed the small gouge left in the sole of Anubis. He squinted as he stared into the metal foot. "It's still mostly gold, but not solid gold. Its peppered with little flakes of silver."

"Maybe it's some kind of alloy?" Jayden ventured. "Gold mixed with some other metal?"

Hunt reached for his smartphone and activated its camera. "Whatever it is, let's get a snapshot of it and give Daedalus a look."

He took the best close-up photograph he could with his phone, as well as a wider shot that showed the chip missing from the foot, and then texted the images to the number Daedalus called from. He resumed his voice call. "Check your messages, Daedalus. Photos sent."

"Taking a look," came the terse reply. Minutes passed, during which Hunt and Jayden stared at the phone between gulps of beer and bites of *churrascaria*. Hunt was about to ask Daedalus if he was still on the line when a voice sounded through the device's speaker. It wasn't Daedalus' though. That much was obvious because the voice was female. Hunt snatched up the phone.

"Maddy!"

"It's me, Carter."

"Hi Maddy!" Jayden leaned across the table to chime in.

"Are you okay?" Hunt asked.

"I'm physically okay, yes." Her voice sounded stressed, though, there was no doubt about it.

Realizing Daedalus would likely cut the conversation short at any moment, he got right down to business. "Where are you?"

"I don't know. I—" Sure enough, the voice of Treasure, Inc. was back on the line.

"You have your proof of life, Mr. Hunt. Now I'm going to have to ask that you stick to business." Before Hunt could reply, Maddy's voice came back over the line.

"I looked at your photos, Carter. Nice find, by the way. It looks genuine. Neolithic period. Now give me an estimate of the dimensions and weight."

Carter did so and then she continued. "Right, so since it's not one solid metal, but also mixed with onyx, we can't calculate what the weight should be if it were solid gold. However, it does seem a little light to me, even allowing for the onyx. And then, coupling that with the photo, which shows the specks of silver-colored metal, I think it's safe to say that it's comprised of some kind of gold alloy. Possibly gold mixed with brass, or copper, or even pewter, or—"

"Or orichalcum. Thank you, Dr. Chambers, you may return to your workstation to await further orders."

Workstation? Jayden mouthed silently.

"What is orichalcum?" Hunt asked. He had an idea, but wanted to make sure Daedalus knew what he was talking about.

"Orichalcum is purported to be an ancient metal alloy used by the Atlanteans in the construction of their buildings, particularly for the interior of Poseidon's temple. It was mined on the island and considered almost as valuable as pure gold."

"Have you ever come across it before?"

A pause, then, "No. Its existence is widely considered to by rumor, much like the lost city itself. It seems you may have come across some. Tell me, this artifact: where did you find it?"

Jayden heard the question through the phone's tinny speaker and shook his head at Hunt. *Don't give him our location!* Hunt nodded. He reached into his backpack while speaking and pulled out some of his research notes.

"Daedalus, I'm no fool. If I tell you where we are, you'll just send in some strike team to take the Anubis statue from us by force. I'll make you a deal, though: I'll give you Anubis, and in return you give us Maddy—*alive and unharmed.*"

At length, Daedalus replied with, "Very well. Tell me where you are and I will bring her to you."

Hunt laughed into the phone. "No deal, Daedalus. You must really think I was held back a couple of grades in school. That's the same thing as giving you our location. So here's the deal, and it's a fair deal that will give both of us what we want without compromising either of our safety."

"I am all ears, Mr. Hunt."

Carter opened one of his books to a map and nodded slowly to himself. "I want to meet you in a crowded, popular place. How about the Bahamas?"

"The Bahamas? Where? Which island?"

"The island of New Providence, city of Nassau. Tomorrow. We will have Anubis for you."

"Nassau, okay. Where in Nassau?"

Hunt looked at Carter and smiled. "Meet me in Atlantis. By Poseidon."

CHAPTER 14

Nassau, Bahamas

The giant manta ray glided over Hunt's head, while a recorded male voice droned on about the people of Atlantis, Atlanteans, they were called, and how advanced their technology was for their time.

"I have to hand it to you, Hunt," Jayden said, stepping aside to allow a mother with a stroller to move past him up to the aquarium display in the crowded lobby area of the Atlantis Resort, "I'm really racking up my frequent flyer miles hanging out with you. My credit card perks are going ballistic."

Hunt tore his gaze from the majestic animal to glance around at the crowd ogling the over-the-top sprawling indoor architecture. A massive skylight let in streaming sunshine between huge pillars wrapped in ivy, while patrons looked down from the veranda seating of a seafood restaurant one floor up.

"As pressing as the situation with Maddy is, you have to admit, this place is pretty cool."

Jayden stared back into the giant aquarium, watching a school of thousands of silver fish swim through a carefully sculpted rock tunnel beneath a statue meant to resemble some mysterious ancient god. He sipped from the Bahama Mama concoction he purchased at a poolside bar a few minutes earlier ("Just to make sure I blend in with the tourists, you know"). "I could get used to it, I guess."

But then he saw Hunt shift the weight of his backpack on his shoulders and was reminded of the urgency of their mission here, the reason why they had come all this way on a moment's notice. To save the life of their friend, and as a bonus, to keep priceless artifacts out of the hands of a murderous black market antiquities dealer. He hadn't realized before how much he cared about preserving history for everyone to see. Maybe Hunt was on to something, he couldn't help but think.

Hunt glanced at his Omega dive watch, given to him as a special present from his grandfather when he'd graduated college. "We should start moving to the rendezvous point."

He and Jayden walked across the large marble tiled floor until they entered a mall-like area enshrouded with indoor trees and subdued LED lighting. High-end shops lined both sides of the enclosed avenue: jewelry, souvenirs, Bahamas-themed resort wear, scuba gear, activities booths encouraging guests to try parasailing, jet-skiing, snorkeling or deep sea fishing…There was certainly no shortage of things to do here if one was not short on money or time, Hunt thought. He entertained a fleeting notion of he and Maddy lying on a secluded beach in one of the island chain's outer isles….*Maybe, just maybe, when all this is over*, Hunt thought…

"There he is!" The no-nonsense urgency in Jayden's voice was unmistakable as he looked straight ahead into a large foyer. Hunt also directed his gaze that way. The ceiling was multiple stories tall here, again with a skylight, and an indoor waterfall cascaded down into a fountain luxuriously decorated with marble sculptures of mermaids and shipwrecked sailors. And there, against one wall, was a giant sculpture of Poseidon the sea god, seated in a massive chair while holding his iconic trident. A family of three stood in front of it while a man—Daedalus—took their picture.

"One more, just to make sure—say All Praises to the Mighty Poseidon!" The family laughed and he handed them back their camera as they sauntered away.

"I don't see Maddy with him," Hunt said under his breath.

"He sees us." Jayden nodded casually at Daedalus, who returned the gesture.

"Game on." Hunt and Jayden walked toward Daedalus. Contrasting to their own beach bum wear—surfer's board shorts and scuba shop tank tops with flip flops, towels around their shoulders—Daedalus wore expensive resort linens, leather loaders and a lot of gold jewelry, including a shipwreck coin from the famous Atocha wreck discovered by Mel Fisher off Key West in the 1980s, as a medallion that Hunt had no doubt was authentic and not one of the replicas most people wore.

Hunt and Jayden walked up to Daedalus at the foot of Poseidon. Daedalus handed Hunt a point-and-shoot digital camera. "If you would be so kind, sir!"

Hunt shot his friend's kidnapper a used car salesman smile and snapped off the obligatory tourist shot. He handed the device over to Daedalus while saying in a low voice, "Where is she?"

"She is enjoying herself at the bar in the company of two exciting gentlemen...not you two, I'm afraid, for the moment. But that is about to change, am I right?" Daedalus glanced kitty-corner across the space to an indoor establishment called The Sandbar that beckoned with a literal sand beach floor and tiki hut ambience. Hunt caught his breath as he saw Maddy there, wearing a black bikini top with a pink sarong, seated on a bamboo barstool at a table between two of Daedalus' Treasure, Inc. goons. Both of them wore khaki shorts with open button down aloha shirts to show off their hairy chests festooned in heavy gold chains.

"You have a thing for 1980s rap videos, Daedalus?" Jayden mocked.

But the black market mogul was unfazed. "Perhaps she will do the wild thing with you two later, yes?" He grinned lecherously until Hunt took off his backpack. The smile disappeared and Daedalus watched him intently.

"Here's what you came for. Tell your cretins to release her to us and it's yours."

Daedalus spread his hands in a gesture of reasonableness. "You can see that she is fine, Mr. Carter. I have brought her to you. Allow me to see the artifact, to verify its authenticity, and you may join her at her table…alone." A couple of twenty-something lovebirds walked up to Poseidon at that moment, the young woman, sapphire nose ring glinting in the overhead lights, climbing up onto the knee.

"You see," Daedalus said to Hunt and Jayden, "every woman loves a god. Now let me see the one you have brought me. Let me see Anubis." His gazed seemed to burn right through Hunt's backpack. The couple took their pictures and then bounced off, laughing, oblivious to the drama playing out before them.

Daedalus watched Hunt's hands carefully as he unzipped the pack and pulled from it a statuette wrapped in cloth. Daedalus extended his hands and Hunt passed him the object. All three men were silent as Daedalus unwrapped the item, its golden splendor soon peeking through the folds of the fabric.

"It does seem to have the proper weight, at least," Daedalus said as he unwrapped the figurine the rest of the way.

"Take it or leave it, Daedalus. We found what we found, okay? You said you wanted it, here it is. Now let Maddy go!"

Hunt expected some kind of acerbic retort, but instead, as the figure came free of its wraps, Daedalus was transfixed while he inspected it. He turned it over slowly in his hands, eyeing it reverently before holding it upside-down and looking at the bottom of the feet.

"So here is the chip from where you took the sample."

"Right," Hunt confirmed.

"Do you have it?"

"Have what? The little chip that came out?"

Daedalus looked up from the statue to make eye contact with Hunt. "Yes, the piece you gouged out—do you still have it? It can be used for chemical analysis of the material, and It could perhaps be reattached, making the piece whole again."

Hunt shook his head before looking to Jayden. "You didn't save that little piece, did you?"

"You kidding? I'm lucky if I can hold onto my wallet when I go on vacation, I'm not going to keep track of a little pebble. We might have used it as a paperweight to hold down the receipt on our table at that café in the Azores."

Daedalus pursed his lips for a second but then shrugged. Another group of people ambled up to the Poseidon display, and one of them politely asked Daedalus if he could move out of the way while they took a picture. Hunt did his best not to let his pleasure show while Daedalus stepped aside and sidled up to Hunt.

"Overall, good work, Mr. Hunt. Your artifact recovery skills are surprising even to me. If you—both of you," he added, also looking at Jayden, "would like a position in my organization as *professional* treasure hunters, do let me know." Hunt and Jayden scoffed at the sarcasm Daedalus injected into the word "professional." But the Treasure, Inc. founder was looking over to the table where Maddy sat with his two henchmen at the tiki bar. He raised a hand in the air and nodded.

"In the meantime, I hope you enjoy the rest of your stay on this beautiful island with your female friend. I do hope we meet again."

"That makes one of us," Jayden quipped. Daedalus glared at him ever so briefly before walking toward the bar.

"Come on!" Hunt saw Maddy step down from the bar stool and begin to walk away from the tiki area. She passed Daedalus on her way toward Hunt and Jayden. Hunt could see that Daedalus said something to her, and that she shot him a look to kill in response. Then she was running to Hunt, hugging him and then Jayden, tears brimming in her eyes.

"Maddy, are you okay—have you been hurt?"

She stared into Hunt's eyes. "I'm shaken up, but no, they didn't actually hurt me. Thank you so much, though—both of you. If it wasn't for you offering that Anubis artifact, I don't know what would have happened."

At the mention of Anubis, Hunt's expression became grim. "Speaking of that, we better get a move on before Daedalus gets a closer look at it."

Maddy's eyes widened. "You mean…it's not genuine? You found a fake?"

Hunt lowered his voice even more. "Let's just say that we found a genuine article, but what we gave Daedalus just now was not so genuine."

Jayden tapped both of them on the shoulder. "C'mon, we better make like a tree and leave."

The trio began to walk toward an exit door, a large archway overhung with vines with a sign above it reading, TO MYSTERIOUS GROTTO. As they were about to pass under the exit, Daedalus' enraged voice carried after them: This is fake! Mr. Hunt, wait right there!"

But Hunt had no intention of waiting. "Let's move!" As he ushered Maddy through the massive archway, with Jayden plowing on ahead of them, gunfire rang out behind them. Puffs of plaster dust billowed from the walls, and screams of terrified tourists erupted around them as the three of them ran outside of the building.

CHAPTER 15

The trio ran through an upward sloping tunnel with fake rock walls, irregularly shaped, dimly lit with concealed blue LEDs. Strategically placed ferns were implanted here and there into the walls and ground. Other people occupied the tunnel, some going toward the fleeing trio, some with them, but only Hunt, Jayden and Maddy ran, until the gunshots reached the entrance to the grotto tunnel.

Mass panic ensued, with everyone in the tunnel scattering in different directions, some simply dropping to the ground and covering their heads in blinding, deer-in-headlights fear.

Hunt, Jayden and Maddy kept moving fast, each of them pausing occasionally to help someone up or to offer words of encouragement. Then they saw daylight up ahead; the tunnel widened as it became steeper, until it transitioned into a stone stairway for the last few feet. Jayden marveled aloud at how much vertical distance they were travelling.

At the top of the stairs the tunnel opened up onto an outdoor area that was lushly landscaped to look like a tropical grotto. A series of pools with black bottoms and waterfalls draining from one to the next sprawled in every direction. Not sure of which way to go, Hunt knew they had to keep moving, so he pointed straight ahead to the largest pool.

Only a couple of feet deep and occupied by a dozen or so people lounging about, most with drinks in their hands, the artificial pond had a large waterfall draining into one end, on their right, and another spilling out of it at the other, to their left. The screams of those still in the tunnel leading out to the grotto echoed behind them as they waded out into the pool. Hunt glanced up ahead of them at a fake rock wall festooned with wet plants. It might be climbable, but it wouldn't be fast and they would be sitting ducks on the wall.

Hunt told them they needed to keep moving. "They're almost on us, keep going. Blend in with the crowd as much as you can." As if to demonstrate this point, he picked up a floating straw sun hat someone had lost, and put it on. Then he quickly realized it looked funny to be standing around in a pool with clothes on, so he took off his shirt before replacing the hat. Jayden also removed his shirt, then suggested to Maddy that she do the same.

"I'd be topless if I did that!"

He grinned at her mischievously. "They'll recognize that bikini top for sure."

"Here, put this on over your top.' Hunt handed her the T-shirt he'd just taken off. It was new, purchased in Nassau and read, "Visit the Bahamas and Forget the Dramas." Maddy quickly slipped into it, got it wet and then rolled it up and tied it off so that it exposed her midriff, appearing like a stylistic choice rather than a hurriedly donned last resort. Maddy was silent, but Hunt knew she had to be petrified.

They heard shouts of terrified bystanders over near the grotto entrance and knew the Treasure, Inc. team must be getting close. "Let's move, come on this way!" Hunt led them toward the left side of the pool. He wasn't sure why, just that it was farther away from where their pursuers would be emerging any second now. But as they threaded their way past the few remaining people at that end of the pool, he realized his mistake.

"We're really going to stand out here, two men and a woman, even with the change-up in outfits," Jayden pointed out.

Hunt looked around and realized he was right. All Daedalus and his goons would have to do is glance over this way and they would be outed.

But moving back to the right seemed suicidal, to head right toward them like that. And again, glancing up at the vertical rock wall of the grotto pool, it would be a tough climb and only make them stick out like sore thumbs. Behind them was a planter area abutting the side of a building, but it didn't have enough ground cover to really conceal them. Looking in the only way remaining, to the left, Hunt cursed softly while shaking his head.

A wooden wall, five feet tall, with a closed gate in the middle of it barred further progress in that direction. A sign above the wall on the rocks proclaimed in red block letters, DANGER: AREA OFF LIMITS! AUTHORIZED PERSONELL ONLY! in English and Spanish.

They heard screams from the grotto pool behind them. "Come on!" Hunt moved to the gate in the wall. It had no handle, only a round keyhole set flush into the door. He pushed and pulled on the gate but it was locked.

"Up and over, let's go," Jayden said, interlacing the fingers of his hands so that Hunt could use them as a step. He did and sprang up and over the wall.

"What's it like?" Jayden called as loudly as he dared through the fence.

"Who cares!" Maddy said, they're coming!"

"Here!" Jayden gave Maddy the same boost he'd done for Hunt, hoping it would be enough for her. Surprisingly, she was agile and quick about it, and was over the fence in no time.

"You work out or something?" Jayden asked through the fence.

"Climbing gym, once a month."

Jayden pulled himself up and over the fence and dropped into the other side with a splash. "Whoa!"

They still stood in the shallow grotto pool, but only ten feet in front of them, a rushing waterfall cascaded over the edge. They could hear water splashing into another pool far below. Hunt was ready to decide on a strategy as to what their next move would be, but the splinters of wood from the shredding fence following the burst of nearby gunfire put an end to that.

"Over we go, right now!" Hunt grabbed Maddy by the hand, knowing she might balk at the drop even with the specter of gunfire. He knew

Jayden could hold his own, and he was right. The wily Asian-American ex-Navy man leapt over the falls without even looking at what might lie below. He did have the presence of mind to lay his body more or less sideways, not knowing how deep the water would be below. In fact, if the other pools were any indication, they only had a right to expect a couple of feet of water when they landed.

Hunt and Maddy jumped a second after Jayden, holding hands, feet first and laying flat. "Keep your head up!" Hunt warned, not wanting her to hit the back of her skull when she landed. They heard the rush of water on the way down and felt the spray from the waterfall. It was over in a couple of seconds.

Hunt saw a flash of Jayden rolling over in the water, and then he was hitting, bracing himself for a hard impact that never came. He was pleasantly surprised to feel nothing but water. In fact, soon he had to tread water to stay afloat; it was that deep.

"Are you okay?" he asked Maddy. The archaeologist had also been totally submerged, and now she gasped for breath, confused and disoriented by the rapid, high-adrenaline experience. "Yeah, I think so."

"I'm okay, too, I know you were worried," Jayden sputtered from a few feet away. "Looks like we landed in the deep end of the pool."

Hunt looked around at their new surroundings, which were very different from the black-bottom grotto they'd just fell out of. He got the odd sense that there was a lot of water beneath him. He couldn't see the bottom, unless it was painted a certain way as to blend in. He ducked his head underwater and opened his eyes, but all he could see were blurry shapes far below.

"Jayden, this is weird. Looks like we're in at least forty, fifty feet of water."

With a confused look on his face, Jayden also dunked his head and took a look below. "I see fish down there!"

And then it dawned on Hunt, who opened his eyes underwater again to confirm what he already knew. "This is the giant aquarium we saw from below, with the manta ray!"

"Manta ray?" Maddy stammered. Can those hurt us?"

"No," Jayden said, "but the reef sharks they have in here might."

"I'll take a few reef sharks over bullets any day of the week," Hunt said, reminding them of their current predicament. He knew their bold move had bought them a little time, but not much. They still needed to move. But where? Looking up, Hunt saw the first hand reach up and over the wooden fence they'd climbed. In a few more seconds, they'd be sitting ducks for the Treasure, Inc. shooters.

Looking around at the tank they were in—and that's exactly what it was, Hunt saw—the perimeter was protected, walled off, by ten-foot high plexiglass siding. This was because the top of this pool was level with part of the grotto grounds, and Hunt saw a few tourists walking around the manicured paths outside the tank. Hunt heard the sound of feet thumping on the ground and looked up to see the first Treasure, Inc. hunter land on the other side of the fence. Spinning around and looking down the length of the tank, which was roughly oval shaped, with them having landed at one of the narrow ends, Hunt saw no other people inside the raised walls. He saw some kind of platform that extended a few feet out over the water of the pool about halfway across on their right side, and started swimming for that.

Jayden and Maddy kicked after him. Hunt worried that their splashing made for an easy target, but he didn't see what other choice they had. He could only hope they would reach the platform before their pursuers started firing. Or even better, that Daedalus called his dogs off, although that didn't seem likely. Hunt flashed on the Anubis statuette, the store-bought fake he'd gouged a chip out of on the foot, and the genuine article, now stashed away in his hotel room safe.

The work platform was a horseshoe -shaped catwalk of metal grating that extended out over the water, with an open drop into water inside the U-shaped walkway. Hunt recognized it as a diving platform, and recalled with a start the working scuba divers below who gave verbal presentations to tourists from inside the tank, talking about the sea life and archaeological replicas inside. Eyeing the work area now with diving in mind, Hunt thought he saw dive gear set up on the work platform.

He turned his attention to swimming the last few feet to the platform and locating the swim step that he knew should be there if in fact this platform was used for diving. He found it in the center of the structure, at the furthest point over the water. He tapped his friends on the arm and pointed to the steps. Jayden climbed up and out first, extending a hand to Maddy and assisting her. The first shot rang out as Hunt climbed up onto the metal grate-work. He heard police sirens now in the distance. He hoped that maybe the sound of them would scare Daedalus and his men off, but no such luck—a second shot rang out, and this time he saw a spark fly, accompanied with a loud *ping* as the bullet bounced off the metal and into the water.

Maddy put her hands in the air, convinced that they had failed to escape. The gunfire stopped. For how long, Hunt could only guess, but he wasn't taking any chances that their fate would be kind if they were taken back into Daedalus' custody after tricking him with a fake Anubis. He eyeballed the gray metal cylinder standing on the platform a few feet away. A scuba tank, already connected to a breathing regulator, he could see from the black hoses attached to the valve at the top of the tank, and a dive mask looped around the valve by the strap. Only one set of gear, but it would have to do.

He regretted not having the time to see if the tank was full of compressed air by reaching the submersible pressure gauge, but somehow he suspected there wouldn't be time for that. He was right.

Daedalus' voice boomed at him once again, this time from the top of the waterfall. It was somewhat hard to hear him because of the sound of the falling water—Hunt guessed he didn't want to attract too much attention with a bullhorn. Regardless of what the man was saying, Hunt knew they had no time left. He blocked out Daedalus' words and devoted all of his attention to his hastily forming plan of action.

The scuba tank. *Use it.* That's all he could think of—to get out of harm's way by going down into the tank itself. But there was only one tank and three of them. In a micro-flash of synaptic brain activity, Hunt considered leaving Jayden and Maddy here while he grabbed the tank and dove straight down. He could seek help down there, waving at people through the glass....But he dismissed the thought almost as soon as it had come to him. If he did that, then Maddy and Jayden—especially Maddy, since she was the expert on archaeology—would be used as bargaining chips by Treasure, Inc. They would be at his mercy. No, he had to take them with him somehow, there was no other alternative.

All of these thoughts transpired as Hunt's hands reached the scuba tank. As if in slow motion, he felt his mouth opening to yell to Maddy and Jayden—stealth no longer mattered—to grab onto him and hold on...and then his fingers were closing around the valve, turning it as he pulled it into the water with him, turning it on in order to make sure the air would flow.

He felt Maddy's hand slip off of his leg as he splashed into the water. He hoped Jayden would be able to grab a hold of her. He knew Maddy was a certified scuba diver at the recreational level, otherwise he never would have considered this plan. Hunt's hands traced the rubber hoses back to the valve as he sank upside-down into the water, tracing the separate regulators. He found the primary and handed it off to Jayden, who had a hand waiting to receive it. Good, that meant he's on board with the plan, Hunt thought. Now for the hard part...

He grabbed the second regulator mouthpiece—the one called the "octopus" that was designed as an emergency redundant backup with a longer hose—and pulled Maddy to his right side, so that Jayden was on his left and Maddy on his right. He felt her hand clawing his, scrambling for the mouthpiece. When he felt her take it from him, he slipped the mask strap off his wrist and put it over his head. He quickly exhaled forcefully though his nose to clear out the water inside the mask...and then he could see!

Unfortunately the first thing he noticed was a tracer stream of bubbles a few feet in front of them, slanting down into the water as a bullet was fired from somewhere above. Hunt pressed the button on the buoyancy compensator vest to make sure all the air was vented. Fortunately it was one of the style with integrated weights, so he began to sink, which was exactly what he needed.

Jayden got with the program, kicking down and paddling with the hand not holding on to Hunt. Hunt looked over at Maddy and saw her eyes wide open and full of panic as much as water; knowing she couldn't see anything more than blurry shapes made him nervous she would panic and not be able to function, but so far she was kicking down also, knowing they needed to go down under the water to be safe from the shooters' bullets.

After a few more kicks Hunt felt the strong urge to breathe, so he reached over to his left and tapped Jayden on the shoulder. Immediately his dive buddy passed him the regulator. It was awkward swimming tethered together by the regulator hose, but at least it kept them close together. Hunt greedily sucked four breaths of air from the mouthpiece before handing it back to Jayden. They would have to swap breaths like this the entire time they were underwater, while Maddy, being the more inexperienced diver, had her own regulator. Hunt hoped their was sufficient air left in the tank. There was a pressure gauge dangling down on its own hose somewhere, but he didn't have a free hand to be able to look for it and drag it up to his face to be able to read it. What difference did it make, anyway, Hunt thought. If they ran out of air they would have no choice but to swim up to the surface and take their chances with the madman Daedalus and his henchmen. Not much of a choice really, he thought.

After a few more kicks Hunt began to see fish swimming about—a school of silver, sardine-like species, as well as large groupers, some the size of VW Bugs, lazily finning about. He craned his neck so that he could see up, to make sure the Treasure, Inc. Men weren't entering the tank, or leaning right over the side for a better shot. But he saw no one up there. Turning his focus back to the bottom, he assessed the tank they now found themselves in. To their left, a pinnacle of a large, manufactured rock formation lay perhaps ten feet below. He tried to picture the tank from when he and Jayden had stood on the floor outside of it earlier with the rest of the tourists. He recalled a faux stone archway, some cheesy Aztec-type statues, and the giant manta ray, but not much else.

He looked the other way, to his right and down, and saw a stream of bubbles emanating from behind a synthetic shipwreck. That meant a scuba diver. But who? He fought back a surge of adrenaline as he imagined one of

Daedalus' men from the flooded pyramid about to attack them here. They wouldn't stand a chance, the three of them sharing one scuba rig. But on the other hand, unlike in the pyramid, here they were in full view of the public, with hundreds of tourists right outside the glass. Even so, that hadn't stopped them from shooting up the grotto.

But as hunt tapped Jayden on the shoulder and pointed, the diver came into view, swimming out thorough a hole in the side of the model wreck. He held his arms out while facing the people on the other side of the glass. Hunt knew he was speaking to them through a microphone in his special facemask, giving a narrated underwater tour of the tank, talking about the sea life and answering questions from the visitors.

Hunt knew that this person was their ticket to safety. He wasn't sure Jayden or Maddy would be able to tell they were looking at a diver without their masks on, so he herded them toward the man—he was pretty sure it was a man from the physique in the wetsuit.

Hunt watched the underwater tour guide delivering his spiel to the crowd of onlookers on the other side of the glass as the cumbersome trio made their slow, ungainly approach. Hunt hoped the man would turn around, because if he did he would see them; he didn't want to have to sneak up and tap him on the shoulder—that could really spook a person, Hunt knew, even though he would probably think he was a big fish at first. Hunt almost found himself chuckling at the thought, despite the seriousness of the situation.

A few frantic taps on his shoulder told Hunt that Jayden saw the diver. Hunt gave him the "okay" sign, thumb and forefinger in a circle, right in front of his mask, hoping he would recognize it. A few more kicks brought them to within a few feet of the aquarium diver, who Hunt could see was actively engaged with his audience outside the tank. Then the underwater presenter turned sideways while pointing at some feature of the exhibit, and did a double-take as he saw what had to be the strangest sight he'd ever seen while working in the exhibit: Three people breathing off of one scuba tank, only one of them wearing a mask.

Hunt watch the man's eyes widen like saucers. He saw he had a white writing slate dangling from his wrist. Hunt pointed to it, hoping that a concrete task would keep the individual from panicking. He got the message and passed Hunt the slate with its attached pencil.

The name of a fish was already written on the slate, but Hunt only needed to write five simple words, and he scribbled them out in a corner of the slate while a confused Jayden and Maddy looked on:

ACTIVE SHOOTERS ABOVE CALL 911

CHAPTER 16

Hunt watched the aquarium diver speak rapidly inside of his full face mask. From the reaction on the faces of the crowd outside the glass, Hunt could see that his message was being conveyed. Then the diver turned to Hunt, gripped him by the shoulder, and pointed up. Hunt reflexively looked that way, hoping it wasn't Daedalus' divers coming after them, but the employee was only pointing out the exit.

Hunt nodded and together, the four of them began their ascent, with the aquarium diver offering his second mouthpiece to Jayden, which freed Hunt considerably. About halfway up, Hunt could hear some kind of alarm braying somewhere outside in the aquarium building. Good, he thought, clear the place out. He didn't want to go through all of this in the tank only to come back up to be met with Daedalus' men again. They made the ascent smoothly and then approached the same platform from which Hunt had entered. He tensed, half expecting to see a bullet streaking through the water as a white bubble stream before impacting his flesh, but it didn't happen.

Breaking the surface, Hunt's gaze went up to the top of the waterfall from where they'd jumped. But that area was now free of shooters, of any people at all. Likewise, the dive platform from where they'd jumped into the tank. The aquarium diver pulled his mask up onto his head and spoke directly to Hunt, Jayden and Maddy, who spat their regulators out and took deep breaths of the outside air.

"You guys okay? Let's get you to this dive platform here and get you out."

He received no arguments, and together the four of them swam to the platform, where a multitude of aquarium staff were now gathering in order to render assistance. All four of the divers were quickly hauled out from the water onto the mesh grating. Hunt knew an explanation for their actions was about to be demanded in the next few seconds, as soon as it was clear none of them were injured.

But what to say?

He didn't want to tie their involvement to a search for Atlantis...in the Atlantis resort, no less. That was as likely to peg him for a lunatic as it was to explain their actions. He also didn't want to let on that he knew what organization the shooters were from, that he knew who the lead gunman was. That would tie them up in an interrogation room for hours, and they might even be prevented from leaving the country. Meanwhile, Daedalus would still be on the loose, stopping at nothing to reach the treasures of Atlantis.

At least they had Maddy back, though. Hunt embraced her and looked into her eyes. "I'm sorry you had to go through that."

"Thanks for saving me," was all she said.

Then the questions started. A man wearing a suit walked up to Hunt and introduced himself as the Director of the aquarium. Hunt gave him a short explanation that he and his friends were standing in the grotto pool when gunfire erupted, so they jumped the fence and jumped down into the aquarium. Jayden and Maddy backed up his story with occasional interjections or well-placed nods.

"We just did what we had to stay alive," Hunt finished up. "We're all certified divers, we saw the scuba rig and just went for it!"

The aquarium director frowned at this but then shrugged. "We're certainly glad all of you are unharmed. We'll be happy to comp your entire stay as a small token of our empathy at having to go through such a traumatic experience. I hope it won't reflect poorly on us."

"Oh no," Hunt assured him. "We love this place, right guys? Now that it's free of active shooters, I mean. Speaking of which, were they apprehended—the shooters?"

"Unfortunately, no. But they were seen fleeing the resort premises. Police are looking for them now. You'll be safe here, we've got police presence 24/7 until further notice. Is it just the three of you?" the director asked, a quizzical expression growing on his face.

Hunt saw him looking at Maddy standing between he and Jayden and realized the social implications. Almost blushing, he said, "Oh no, my wife's down on the beach somewhere. She didn't want to see the aquarium so I came up with these two. They're the lovebirds."

"I see. Well, I'll see to it that all *four* of you are comped, all the same." His gaze lingered on Maddy before he bid them good day and left the platform to exit back into the main building.

Hunt and Jayden talked to the divers a little more, making sure to thank profusely the one who had helped them underwater, and then they were free to go. After being given towels and dry outfits courtesy of the aquarium gift shop, the three of them left the aquarium and walked to the hotel room Hunt and Jayden had booked. They walked through a grand lobby, ornately furnished with a nautical theme, including a wall mural depicting the fabled city of Atlantis in its heyday. Maddy paused in front of it, pointing to the center.

"This is historically accurate. You see the concentric ring structure? That's how Plato described Atlantis, as being a city designed around a system of canals that led to the inner island, where the seat of government was."

"What were the walls that make up the rings supposed to be made of?" Hunt asked.

Maddy smiled as she gave her answer. "Precious metals. Gold, silver, orichalcum. No one can say for sure, of course."

"Could be cubic zirconium," Jayden said with a shrug.

"Not likely," Maddy said. "Those are lab-made. 11,000 years ago that technology didn't exist."

Hunt held up a finger. "Ah, but the Atlanteans were supposedly quite advanced for their time, were they not? Reason I bring it up is because this orichalcum—it's an alloy, right? Doesn't exist in nature, so they were creating their own precious or at least semi-precious metals, so why not gemstones?"

Maddy threw her hands up with a smile. "Hey, it's Atlantis. Who knows, right? How did the head of a statue that was in the Azores, the rumored birthplace of Atlantis, end up in an Egyptian pyramid?"

"And how did a statuette of Anubis, an Egyptian figure, end up in the Azores?" Jayden posited while considering the mural, the busy harbor with wooden vessels plying its waters, actively engaged in thriving trade, loading and unloading goods at the port of Atlantis.

"Speaking of Anubis," Hunt said, pointing up through the ceiling, "we should get to our room."

They walked to the elevator and enjoyed the ride up, made spectacular by the fact that the elevator was made of glass and faced out toward the beach and the sparkling blue Atlantic beyond.

"You really think Atlantis was out there somewhere?" Jayden wondered.

Maddy shrugged. "Could be. We are in the Bermuda Triangle, after all. This is one of the possible places rumored to be a resting place for it." She turned to Hunt. "Is that why you chose this place as a meeting location with Daedalus?"

Hunt gave her a smile that came with a twinkle in his eye, but before he could answer, a chime sounded and the doors opened. A family of three waited to get in while they exited onto their floor. They walked down a nicely appointed hallway, with custom maritime art on the walls and clean, blue carpet with golden, stylized tridents. Hunt stopped at a door and inserted a key card.

"Whoa, nice place!" Maddy said upon entering. The lavish suite faced the ocean, and below them sprawled a labyrinthine series of swimming pools connected by rope bridges and dotted with palm trees. But Hunt's eyes were not on the view. His gaze roved around the room carefully, checking for any signs of forced entry. He knew an organization like Treasure, Inc. would have the resources to find out their room number, once they knew he was here. It wouldn't have surprised him to find the room ransacked, but everything appeared as they had left it, with the exception of the beds being made and the bathroom being stocked with fresh towels, twisted into the shape of an octopus, no less.

"Looks like Daedalus and his goons had to skip town fast—they didn't get to our room," Hunt said.

"Maybe we should change rooms, just to be safe," Jayden said. "And speaking of safe, maybe we should—"

There was no need to complete the sentence. Hunt strode to the hotel safe and unlocked it, breathing a sigh of relief when he saw the Anubis artifact—the original they'd dug up in the Azores—still there.

"That's good," Maddy said. "But, uh…guys? I can think of another reason to change rooms."

"What's that?" Hunt asked.

"Well, unless you two plan to share a bed…" She eyed the two beds. "We could get adjoining rooms."

"Preferably on a different floor, to throw them off, if they do plan to come back," Jayden added.

"All right, let's get our stuff and check out." They cleared out their minimal belongings, including two small bags and the Anubis artifact, which Hunt placed in his bag. Then they made the trip down to the front desk, where the concierge was able to assist them with the desired room change, still compliments of the hotel. When that was taken care of, the three of them checked into their new rooms, Maddy in her own next to Hunt and Jayden's.

While Jayden raided the mini-bar, Hunt set the Anubis artifact up on a table and turned on the hanging light above it. Freshly showered, Maddy entered their room wearing a new sun dress and sandals, closing and locking the door behind her.

"Thanks, I feel a tiny bit safer now," she said, looking out the window, which, while not quite as impressive as the last suite, still offered a fantastic view of the ocean beyond the sprawling, manicured grounds of the resort. "I tried to see if I could get a local news channel on my TV to see if they'd caught Daedalus yet, but they didn't have anything about the story at all."

"I'm sure they know it's not in their best interest, for the island's tourism economy, to have that kind of thing in the news. I'm sure it'll break eventually, but they'll keep it under wraps as long as they can. Daedalus himself may even be playing some part in that. I chose this location partly because he has no connections here that I know about, but that doesn't mean he doesn't."

"Great." Maddy's eyes were downcast until she looked up at the statuette and snapped out of it. "Hey, so let me check this guy out!" She moved to the table and took a seat in front of the artifact. From the small backpack she had with her, she removed a pair of latex gloves and put them on. "Should really have been wearing these all along, you know," she said with a frown.

"Sorry," Hunt offered. "We really weren't expecting to find much."

"Yeah, when he handed me the metal detector, I was really looking for old coins, I mean, seriously, that's all I thought I would find. Maybe some cool souvenir type stuff, like those flattened pennies you buy in the machines, if I'm lucky."

Maddy turned back to Anubis. "Don't worry about it. Fortunately, this material, whatever it is—some kind of metal alloy inlaid with onyx—doesn't seem prone to oxidation or other chemical reactions when exposed to the air."

"Is there a way we can date the material to see how old it is?" Hunt asked. "That would give us a lot of clues as to its origins."

Maddy held up her smartphone. "I can set it up, but we'd have to send in the whole thing or a sizable sample."

"We already took a chunk out of his foot," Jayden reminded.

Maddy picked up the artifact and took a look at the sole of the foot, where a small piece was missing. "That really is a weird-looking metal. At first, when Daedalus showed me the picture, I thought you were trying to pull the wool over his eyes, with Photoshop or whatever digital trickery."

Jayden held his hands up. "We don't have the skills for anything like that."

"Maybe it really is orichalcum," Hunt joked.

"Or some unknown alloy, at any rate," Maddy added, picking up the artifact. "I'd really like to get a look inside."

Jayden's eyes bugged out. "Inside? Isn't it solid?"

She nodded. "Probably. I just mean, so we could see the composition throughout the entire artifact. Judging the entire piece by that tiny chip you gouged out of the foot is hardly conclusive. It fooled Daedalus for just long enough, though."

"Is there a way to get a look inside without breaking it open?" Hunt asked.

Maddy shrugged noncommittally. "X-ray machine might offer some information, but even that might miss some things. Besides, I don't have access to one here. I miss my field lab already."

"Maybe we should just break it open," Hunt said.

The archaeologist looked horrified at the thought. "You don't want to wait until we can x-ray it and see if it's worth breaking open?"

Hunt and Jayden shook their heads in unison. "It could hold a clue to the whereabouts of Atlantis. Why was Daedalus so interested in it?"

Maddy exhaled sharply at the mention of his name. "He's an artifact hound, sniffing around anything that might be of value. He might have had no idea of any significance it might hold."

"Still," Hunt went on, gesturing animatedly now, "it can't be a coincidence that we dug it up in the Azores, of all places, near where the horse and rider statue was reportedly found by the Portuguese explorers."

"Right, right," Maddy said in an exasperated tone. "Go west. Well, here we are. In another supposed Atlantis hot-spot, the Bahamas. So I don't see how you can be so sure that—"

A jarring cracking noise caused Hunt and Maddy to break off their conversation and look sharply to their left, in time to see Jayden holding half of the Anubis figurine in his right hand, while the other half—from the waist up to the dog's head—lay on the table next to a few fragments that had separated from it. Jayden looked over at them with a sheepish grin.

"I took care of it."

Maddy looked mortified. "Took *care* of it? You took care of it all right, it's in pieces now!"

Hunt stood and moved to the table, holding up a hand. "Maddy, it's okay. What's done is done. You said yourself this piece may well have no archaeological value whatsoever, and meanwhile it could hold a clue to one of the greatest treasure troves mankind has ever known, so we may as well have a look inside and be done with the speculating. Because—"

"Whoa!" Jayden sounded excited. "Look at this!" He reached out onto the table and picked up the other half of the statuette.

"Something's in there," Hunt said.

"Wait, don't touch it yet, let me document it." Maddy activated the camera on her smartphone and snapped off a picture of the cracked-open find. Inside the statuette, a small, oblong object, golden in color, lay nestled inside the otherwise solid construction of the figurine. "A nested object!"

"Can I pull it out?" Hunt asked.

"That's what she—"

"Jayden!" Hunt cut him off.

"Let me do it," Maddy said, eliciting a smirk from Jayden. Maddy ignored the snickering men while she held the broken, top half of the Anubis figurine upside down a few inches over the table with her palm outstretched beneath it. Nothing happened, the golden object remained ensconced inside the figurine.

Maddy looked to Hunt. "Do me a favor and tap it—*gently*—from the top."

Hunt shot Jayden a withering stare as he positioned his hand above the artifact. Balling his hand into a fist, he rapped on Anubis' head three times. After the third knock, the piece of golden metal slid from the figurine into Maddy's hand.

"Got it!" She stood and gently placed the piece of metal on a folded towel on the table's surface. The specimen was roughly rectangular, but with rounded edges and a notch out of it in place, maybe a couple of millimeters thick.

"Looks like solid gold to me," Hunt said.

Maddy picked it up, hefting its weight. She nodded while putting on a pair of reading glasses and leaning forward. "I'm looking for an inscription..." With her latex gloved hands, she turned the gold piece over. "Got something here!" She reached into her bag and pulled out a magnifying glass.

"Wait a minute," Jayden asked, "How'd you get that field kit stuff?"

"I was wearing my backpack when Daedalus kidnapped me. He had his goons rifle through my stuff to check for weapons or communications devices, but other than that he didn't care and gave it back to me. Plus, he wanted me to work for him, leading his illicit dig sites."

"His recruitment policies leave something to be desired," Hunt said.

Maddy nearly snorted. "You could say that, yeah. I told him where to stick it."

"So what's it say?" Jayden asked, leaning in, his impatience getting the better of him

Maddy leaned over the gold piece with her magnifying glass. "It's just three characters...letters...they look like known Egyptian hieroglyphic symbols that I happen to know translate to letters, hold on..." She picked up her smartphone and used it to access the Internet. "My university pages have the standard hieroglyphics key, here it is...let's look for a match..."

Maddy enlarged the pictorial key on her phone, then handed it to Jayden while she picked up the magnifying glass again. "This symbol here..." She aimed the point of a pen at the first symbol..."Corresponds to our letter 'M'. And this one..."Letter 'i'. And the last...letter 'N.'"

"Min?" Hunt spelled out for all of them.

Jayden had a blank look on his face, but Maddy appeared thoughtful. "Interesting..." She faded off, lost in thought.

"What's interesting?" Hunt prodded.

"The Egyptians had a God named Min."

"Figures," Jayden said. "They were really into gods."

"What was he—or she—the god of?" Hunt asked.

"*He* was the guardian of explorers. And Bimini was a far-off territory for them, so it makes sense that he would be worshipped."

"Wait a minute," Hunt said. "Who said anything about Bimini? We're on Nassau. Bimini's in the Bahamas, but it's a whole 'nother island."

Maddy gave a knowing nod. "Notice how the word 'Min' is contained within 'Bimini'?"

"You're hurting my brain," Jayden said, staring at the gold metal.

"Stay with me. It's not that complicated. Then we have, 'ba' which means *soul* and 'ini' which means *reverence*. So, all together now…"

Hunt and Jayden looked confused. "Ba?" Hunt faltered.

"The original word was 'Baminini'," Maddy explained.

"Another Egyptian connection," Jayden said.

Hunt pointed to the gold piece. "So this little piece of gold, hidden in the statue of Anubis, was put there to remind…whoever found it…that Bimini is important somehow?"

It was Maddy's turn to shrug. "That's the way I see it. As for who or what…I have no idea. But there's one more thing. The very shape of the gold piece—it's a well known shape, do you recognize it?"

Jayden furrowed his eyebrows. "I just thought it was because that was the shape that let it fit all snug-like into the figurine."

Maddy shook her head. "No. Have you heard of the Bimini Road?"

Jayden shook his head but Hunt nodded. "A trail of stones in shallow water off of the island of Bimini. It's long been associated with both the Atlantis myth as well as the Bermuda Triangle."

"Right," Maddy said. "And the stones—although many times larger—are shaped just like this golden representation here." She picked up the oblong gold piece and held it up to the light, turning it over in her fingers.

"Well then that settles it," Hunt said, reaching for his smartphone.

"Settles what?" Jayden asked.

"It's time for a trip to Bimini."

CHAPTER 17

Island of Bimini, Bahamas

"Can you believe this guy knows how to fly?" Jayden called from the backseat of the de Havilland Twin Otter floatplane. "I'm glad Carter's up front with you, though, Maddy. Seriously, I'd rather sit next to this pile of scuba gear than listen to his crap at this point."

"I heard that." Carter turned around in the pilot's seat.

"Now, now, you two," Maddy chided from behind mirrored sunglass and a baseball cap. As was customary, she wore her long hair tied back in a ponytail, through the back of the cap. "Aren't you excited for the dive? I mean, what's a trip to the Bahamas without scuba diving, am I right? So if we can check out the Bimini Road while we're at it, so much the better. I love how it all fit together."

"I love how chipper you are about waking up at five in the morning on vacation!" Jayden said. Once they'd decided to explore the water surrounding Bimini, Hunt had suggested a seaplane rental. The flight itself was a short hop from Nassau, but in order to have a full day of diving and also return the rental plane by that afternoon to the Nassau airport, it meant a bright and early start. "Try not to spill my Starbucks with your wacky flying, Carter."

Hunt raised a hand to give Jayden a universal hand signal. "You didn't complain that time over the Persian Gulf."

"True that." Jayden had no desire to relive the classified mission that had helped to form a bond between them, but all kidding aside, he had the utmost of faith in Hunt's flying abilities. Likewise, he knew Hunt could count on him to back him up in the most dicey of situations. This was merely an adventurous vacation outing. Certainly it was made more exciting with the Atlantis connection, but deep down, that was all just an excuse to have a little adventure, wasn't it? None of them, including the processional archaeologist among them, expected it to pan out into anything real. Even though Treasure, Inc. seemed to think it was real enough. Jayden's hand slipped off one of the scuba gear bags as Hunt rode them through a pocket of turbulence and he focused his attention back on the dive that was coming up.

Outside the plane's windows, the day was sunny, the sea calm as they flew at low altitude—a hundred feet or so—above the water. Perfect conditions for diving the Bimini Road. The dive site itself was well visited enough. A shallow water site, only fifteen or twenty feet deep, depending on the tide, it was made somewhat inaccessible only by virtue of the fact that there was no commercial airliner service to Bimini itself, making either a private flight or boat ride from either Nassau or Miami the most convenient modes of access. Even so, Hunt had to wonder how they would find anything that had been overlooked at a site that had been dived so often, including by professional treasure hunters with state-of-the-art equipment such as magnetometers, underwater metal detectors and bottom profiling scanners. And yet the scant finds they had made so far, which had led them here, had come from equally well-trafficked sites.

The coordinates to the site had been entered into the plane's GPS at the rental airport, and soon Hunt informed them that they were closing in on the location. He coaxed the floatplane down lower until they skimmed only a few feet above the ocean's surface, reducing speed at the same time. Jayden and Maddy eyed the water for bottom characteristics while Hunt flew.

"White sand bottom," Jayden said. Then, "Okay, I'm seeing some patch reefs now." Darker, mottled areas became interspersed with the lighter-colored sand. Then they passed over a sun-dappled, dazzlingly bright white sandy area until Maddy pointed out her window.

"There it is!"

Jayden looked out his window and spotted a dark line that meandered away from them.

"Straight lines, definitely looks manmade, like a wreck, but it's too big to be a wreck."

"Must be a lost city!" Maddy suggested.

"Let's check it out," Hunt veered the aircraft to the right and then leveled out in preparation for a water landing. First he flew low over the formation, following a course of what appeared to be dark colored stones—large ones—laid out in a line.

"That's the Bimini Road, all right," Maddy declared, craning her neck to look out the window.

"And the stones look like giant versions of the gold one from Anubis," Jayden said.

"Let's see what the overall pattern is," Hunt said, veering the plane slightly to the left as he followed the underwater path of stones.

"I see the end up ahead," Maddy said. "The whole thing is sort of a "J" pattern. Mostly a straight line, but then curving at one end of it."

They flew on for another minute, until they reached the hook-shaped formation and Hunt began banking the craft into a lazy 180-degree turn.

"Wait a minute, if this is the Bimini Road, then what's that over there?" Jayden pointed out of his left side window. Hunt took a look in that direction.

"Looks like a parallel track of stones, but much shorter. It's probably a mile away from the main road."

"Maybe we should dive that instead?" Jayden suggested.

"Maybe we should fly over it, see what it looks like closer up," Hunt said. They all agreed and he took the sea plane out of the banking turn and onto a straight course toward the outlying section of the Bimini Road.

"An altitude of fifty feet should let us get a good, close look at the structure," Hunt said, hands manipulating the plane's controls. "I'll slow us down some, too. Here we go…"

All three of them looked down out the windows as Hunt flew just to the right of a linear path of oblong stones, a mile from the main underwater track. Looking down at the stones, it was easy to see their individual shapes and how they fit neatly together, interlocking to form a paved road beneath the waves.

Maddy took photographs as they passed over the structure. They had almost reached the end, with Hunt preparing to bank the plane into a turn, when Jayden called out.

"Wait a minute, can you go back? I see something."

"What is it?" Hunt asked.

"One of the stones we just passed over. Hold on…where's the gold piece we got from Anubis? Can I see it?"

Maddy reached into her backpack and then passed him the oblong piece of shiny, gold metal.

"Go back around over the same spot at the same altitude, would you?" Jayden asked Hunt.

"Will do." Past the end of the structure, out over a featureless plain of white sand, Hunt put the plane into a tight arc and headed back to the end of the parallel, second road. This time, as they passed over, Jayden held the Anubis gold piece up to the window as he looked down on the mysterious stones. "Should be right about on it," Hunt said, also looking down.

"There it is! Maddy, get a picture!" She clicked off snapshots as Jayden alternated his gaze between the gold piece in his hand and one of the Bimini Road stones below.

"It's a match! One of the stones down there is the *exact* same shape as the piece of gold we got from Anubis! What are the odds? I mean, it has that same little hook shape in it and everything!"

Maddy brought up one of the photographs she had just taken of the stone in question and enlarged it on her digital camera's screen. She reached her hand back over the seat. "Let me see the piece, please?" Jayden handed it to her and then went back to looking down from the window, checking to see if any other stones had the same shape.

"I don't see any other ones with that same exact shape," he declared.

"And it is the same shape," Maddy concluded, looking up from the camera while holding up the gold artifact. "I'd say they're perfect replicas of each other, except for the scale, of course. Hard to say which came first, though, without some carbon dating on each piece."

Hunt banked into a turn yet again. "You two up for a dive to check it out more closely?"

They both agreed and Hunt coaxed the plane into a landing pattern, giving himself a wide enough approach that they would end up near the site at the end of their water taxiing. He slowed the plane as he decreased altitude, the tops of the turquoise waves looking closer beneath them with each passing second. Then the plane's floats bounced off the water's surface, skipping like stones a few times until they stayed on the water, coasting like a boat. Hunt decreased speed until the plane coasted to a stop under its own momentum. He stuck his head out the rolled-down window, craning his neck to see where they were in relation to the target stone. He saw some blurry stones, fifteen or twenty feet below them, some distance out in front of the seaplane. He pushed on the throttle a little, taxiing the aircraft on the water like a sluggish, ungainly boat until they were right over the stones.

"A little more that way." Maddy pointed toward the end of the subsea roadway, and Hunt directed the plane accordingly.

"That's it, we're right over it," Jayden called out after a few minutes of sloshing over the waves.

"Should have brought some seasickness pills," Maddy said. "I'm starting to feel a little queasy already."

Hunt shut off the plane's engines and a quiet calm settled over them. "You'll feel better once you hit the water. Let's dive!"

They opened the doors to let fresh air inside and began gearing up. Jayden handed Maddy her set of gear first, while Hunt helped her put it on. Then he passed Hunt's to him, and he and Hunt donned their equipment.

Each of them would enter the water from their respective open doors, then they would drop down to the seafloor as a group.

When they were ready, Hunt initiated a countdown. "On three, two, one...splashdown!"

The three divers rolled backwards into the waters of the Bermuda Triangle, the Bimini Road beckoning below.

CHAPTER 18

Off Bimini, Bahamas

The phrase "gin clear water" was an expression that was almost cliché among scuba divers, but Hunt couldn't deny how apt it was here. Looking down after splashing out of the plane, he recoiled, it looked like the bottom was so close he could reach out and touch it. But in actuality it was twenty feet deep.

After a quick check of their equipment, the three divers vented the air from their buoyancy compensator vests and began their short descent to the bottom. To the Bimini Road, or at least the strange parallel track they had found next to the main road. Hunt had heard of it before—knew it existed and had been photographed and dived before, but it got nowhere near the traffic that the main road did.

When they reached the bottom, they landed on one of the smooth, flat stones, to avoid stirring the sand up on the bottom, which would cloud the water and reduce their visibility. The stone of interest, the one matching the shape of the Anubis gold piece, lay only five or six stones to their left. After checking their depth gauges (twenty-one feet), and their air pressure (nearly full tanks) to confirm all was working properly, the three of them were ready to begin work.

First, Hunt traced his fingers along the stone they had landed on, figuring that they may as well get a feel for what the normal ones were like before examining the target stone. To Hunt, it felt like smooth limestone, weathered over the centuries by wave action. He was aware that many geologists and oceanographers dismissed the Atlantis related stories about the stones as fiction, claiming that wave action and coastal erosion patterns were sufficient to explain the shape of the stones. Also, their mineral composition, they maintained, was consistent with that of the nearby shoreline. Others were not so convinced. But to Hunt, he would take neither side's word for it. That's why they were here today, to find out for themselves.

He got to a standing position and then kicked off of the rock, launching himself toward the target stone. Maddy and Jayden followed, swimming a few feet above the smooth stones. Hunt found it a bit strange that there was no sea life of any kind near the road. No schools of fish, not even crabs scuttling along the bottom. He supposed there could be myriad creatures buried in the sand, but for such a sunny, shallow spot, with rocks, he would have thought there would be more life. Only a thin patina of green algae grew on the stones; their natural pale color was still plainly visible.

Jayden pointed excitedly as he spotted the distinctive hook shape of the target stone. He didn't bring the gold piece with him, for fear of losing it, but he was confident they'd be able to identify the stone in question without it.

And here it was.

Hunt, Jayden and Maddy settled onto the stones surrounding the target stone. The road was either two or three stones wide in most places, and three wide here, with the target stone in the middle position. Visually, it appeared the same material, color and texture as the rest of them, with only the slight irregularity of its shape to differentiate it.

Hunt removed a dive knife from a sheath on his calf and dug the point into the rock on which he knelt, to test its consistency. Normal limestone, it chipped with sufficient force, but he found nothing unusual about it. Jayden tapped him on the shoulder and pointed to the target rock, indicating he wanted to move onto it. Hunt nodded, and all three of them hopped over to the stone in question. Approximately eight feet long by four wide, it accommodated the three divers, who knelt on its surface, Maddy and Hunt at one end, with Jayden in the middle.

Together, they carefully eyeballed its surface, looking for any telltale sign that it concealed an artifact, or was in some way unusual. But they saw nothing. It looked exactly like all of the other Bimini Road stones. Hunt held up a gloved hand and made a show of running it down along the side of the stone where it disappeared into the sand. He pushed his fingers into the sand as far as they would go and ran them along the side of the stone. The others started doing the same. After a few minutes they had gone all the way around the perimeter of the strange stone and still had detected nothing out of the ordinary.

Hunt checked his air pressure, urging the others to do the same. They all still had plenty left, but it served to give them a little breather and to remind them that time was limited. They needed to try something else. Maddy photographed the stone with her camera in a plastic housing, taking some closeups of its top face. But inwardly, Hunt was disappointed. Nothing seemed significant about this stone, compared to all the others. They had come a long way for nothing. Maybe the shape of the gold piece from the Anubis statuette was simply a coincidence?

Jayden and Maddy grew bored and swam off over the neighboring stones, leaving Hunt to stare at the mystery stone by himself. He again turned to his dive knife, this time using it as a tool to stick as far down as he could along the edges of the stone. He wanted to figure out how thick the stone was. Were they thin, paving-stone like entities, or several feet deep? He soon had his answer when the knife plowed through the resistance of the sand into…into what? Hunt used the hand not holding the knife to fan away the sand particles in his way. Into…open water?

Digging some more with the knife, he found that he could scrape along the underside of the stone. It wasn't more than a few inches thick. Was it just one thin section, or the same thickness all the way around? He tried the same thing with the knife on a couple of different points along the stone's edge. It was the same thing each place he tried. He could picture the stone as a thin cap, lying on the bottom.

But then he got to thinking, if they're so thin, why hadn't some of them been taken? Thousands of people had dived the main Bimini Road, and all of those stones were still there. Even this outlying section of road had probably seen hundreds of underwater visitors over the decades. He found it hard to believe that none of them had been chipped away at or taken altogether if they were so thin…and therefore so movable.

He looked up from his work to glance over at Jayden and Maddy, who swam lazily over a section of road some distance away. Hunt moved one stone over. He took his knife and set to work in the same manner, attempting to determine the thickness of the stone. This time, however, the tip of his blade was met only with more stone as he thrust it as deep as he could into the sand along the limestone's edge.

He smiled inside his dive mask. The target stone was different! Thinner than the rest. He thought about it while breathing slowly through his regulator and watching his bubbles float lazily toward the sunlit surface. *One stone different than the rest….we were led to it by a miniature model found in a statuette of Anubis—also a miniature—which was in turn found in the Azores…*Hunt ruminated on the facts, but after a couple of minutes he was still no closer than before to figuring out what the thin stone could mean. He decided to get hands on again.

Moving back to an edge of the stone, he inserted his knife blade against the flat rock until he felt it pass beneath the bottom edge. Then he pried upward with the knife. Nothing happened, so he ran the blade sideways along the length of the stone, loosening the sand and sediment that was holding it in place with the suction created by it laying there for untold decades or centuries.

Then Hunt had an idea. He rapped the butt of his dive knife on his metal scuba tank, creating a piercing ring that immediately caught the attention of Jayden and Maddy. He waved them over. When they reached him, Hunt held up his knife and pointed to the one Jayden carried on his leg. Jayden looked confused, so Hunt demonstrated what he had been doing with the stone, trying to pry it up. After watching that, Jayden gave him the okay sign and set to work alongside Hunt. Hunt wasn't sure if Maddy carried a knife, but he was glad to see her hold one up and join them on the side of the limestone.

Together, the three of them wedged their metal implements beneath the stone slab and pried with all their strength. Just as Hunt thought he was going to snap the blade, he felt the limestone move. He signaled his friends to reposition and try again. Once more they repeated the process, and once again the slab moved, this time a little higher off the seabed.

He heard a muffled grunt and looked over to his right to see Jayden with his arm wedged beneath the slab up to his elbow, eyes bulging with physical effort. Immediately, Jayden curled the fingers of his left hand beneath the slab and began to lift. As it separated from the bottom, his knife blade snapped with an audible *crack*. He dropped the ruined knife and replaced it with his right hand. Redoubling his efforts, he planted his fin-clad feet against the sand bottom next to the stone slab and put his leg muscles into the lift. Looking to his right to gauge the progress, wondering if he should drop the slab and rush to Jayden's aid, he saw the Asian-American ex-Navy man still bearing down on the lifting and smiled.

We can do this.

Maddy was also not giving up. She dropped her own knife and also gripped the stone with both hands, putting all her strength into it. A thick curtain of air bubbles floated up above them with their heavy exertions. In the back of his mind, Hunt made a mental note to check their air remaining when the lifting was done, since they were breathing very heavily with the hard labor. But right now, there was no stopping. The curiosity factor was too strong. What lay beneath this stone slab? The fact that the stone was even movable at all was exciting enough.

So they kept at it, coordinating their bursts of lifting power, pushing with their legs while their gloved hands raised the lip of the slab. After five grueling minutes, they had the slab three feet off the sea bottom. Hunt began to push forward instead of up, looking to his right while yelling, "Hey, look!" into his regulator. The words themselves were not really distinguishable, but the noise itself got his friends' attention. They saw what he was doing and followed suit.

With the three divers straining, shoving and pushing, they were able to pivot the stone slab off of its resting place until it was clearly in a different position. They dropped it halfway on top of its neighboring stone and then sat in place, waiting for the swirling sand particles to dissipate so that they could see.

During this waiting period, Hunt checked his air gauge: he was down to about one-third of his supply remaining. Not yet critical, but definitely something to keep an eye on; it was easy to become distracted by exciting finds underwater and forget about things like how much air you had left. Knowing this, he tapped Maddy on the shoulder and pointed to her air gauge. *How much left?* She glanced at the gauge before handing it to him. Also one-third left. Hunt smiled behind his mask. They say that women have better air consumption than men, and it must be true in Maddy's case, since she was much less an experienced diver than Hunt. But it was good news right now, and he was glad for it. He knew Jayden was experienced enough to keep track of his air supply, and that he would be about the same as him, so he didn't bother asking him. The visibility was clearing now, and it was time to see what they had uncovered.

Hunt peered down at the space the block had uncovered, which was equal to about half of its length and width. Enough to see what it had been concealing, if anything. Hunt wished now that he had brought an underwater metal detector with him, to pass it over the sand the stone had been covering. But as he peered down at the uncovered area, his breath caught in surprise.

There was only water there.

How is that possible? His mind screamed, and yet, he was looking down into *deep* water. Particles of sand and detritus swirled around ten, twenty, thirty feet below him, removing all doubt. Hunt leaned down, sticking his head into the hole that had been revealed by uncapping the stone slab. As he suspected, the opening was the exact dimensions of the thin stone. He could see the undersides of the other road stones jutting down below around the opening.

Hunt could not see the bottom of the uncapped zone. He imagined it to be like a *cenote*, a natural geological formation that was essentially a deep hole in the Earth, on land, filled with fresh water. In the ocean, a hole in the seafloor was known as a "blue hole." Hunt himself had dove one before, in the coral reefs of Belize in Central America. They were well known features of the Caribbean, and even in the Bahamas. But he had never heard of one in connection with the Bimini Road.

Jayden and Maddy swam over beside him and also peered down into the newly revealed passage. Hunt knew that he and Jayden, at least—probably Maddy, too, out of professional curiosity—were dying to go in there. But he didn't want to literally die by going in there. Glancing at his air gauge, he knew it was time to return to the surface. They had an extra set of fresh scuba tanks in the plane. They could switch them out for the dry ones and return to explore the new area.

That would have been the prudent thing to do, he knew. But staring down into the that unknown void, it beckoned, pulled at him with a siren song all its own. It was a lure he had heard before from shipwreck divers exploring passages of famous wrecks like the Andrea Doria or a newly discovered German U-Boat from World War II. The allure was so hard to resist that it became dangerous.

Hunt just wanted one look at what it was like down there right now. Just a little taste, to see what they were getting into. Maybe see how deep it was. A couple of minutes' look-see, at the most. Then he'd swim right back up out of there and they'd get back to the plane, swap the tanks and come back properly equipped. Proper dive lights would be good too, since it looked dark down there, but he had a small back up light clipped to his vest. It would have to do for now.

He signaled for Jayden to wait at the opening with Maddy while he checked it out, tapping his dive watch and holding up two fingers. *Two minutes—be right back.*

Then Hunt positioned his body and swam head first into the hole.

He swam down into the inky void, making sure he dove below the protruding road stones before moving laterally. There he floated, dangling in the open void, allowing his eyes to adjust to the dim light after the dazzling, sunlit shallow bottom of white sand.

Geez, it's *deep*, he thought. He could not see the bottom. He knew that some blue holes were several hundred, even a thousand feet deep. He really had no idea what to expect here, but he was only a little ways below the opening, so he swam down some more. When his depth gauge read one hundred feet, he stopped and floated in the water column. One hundred feet meant that he was eighty feet down into the hole, since the seabed where the stones lay was already at twenty feet deep.

He glanced at his air pressure gauge, now in the red. It was reckless to remain any longer. He was about to press the button to add air into his buoyancy vest to aid his ascent, when he caught something in his vision, far below.

The bottom! But wait, he realized, it wasn't the bottom, because it only occupied a narrow part of the hole, in the center. More like a pinnacle. Some kind of rock formation, stalagmites, perhaps. He unclipped is tiny backup flashlight from his vest and turned it on.

Just a little further. Hunt dropped down deeper into the hole, feet first now, since he didn't want to hit his head on anything now that he knew something was down there. Down he went, ten, twenty, thirty more feet. That's it, absolutely no more, he told himself, knowing that nitrogen narcosis, a narcotic effect from nitrogen caused by breathing compressed air at depth, would be setting in any second now if it hadn't already. It affected a diver's judgment, much like having too many alcoholic drinks.

*Let's see what it looks like now…*He aimed his puny flashlight beam down toward the pinnacle he'd seen…

And felt a numbing chill envelope his entire body.

CHAPTER 19

Atlantic Ocean, near Bimini, Bahamas

The sleek mega-yacht plowed along at a sedate pace across the azure waters. With state-of-the-art automation permitting a crew that would have been considered skeletal only a decade earlier, the few passengers who were aboard enjoyed extreme privacy and plenty of luxurious space while at sea.

Daedalus lounged by a swimming pool—one of two aboard—that overlooked the diving platform off the ship's stern. A thirty-six foot speedboat hung from davits over the stern rail, and above, forward of the pool, a small passenger helicopter sat waiting on a pad. Having just emerged from the pool, Daedalus reclined in a chaise lounge wearing a plush robe with the stylized letter 'H', short for the yacht's name, the *Historica*.

In his hands he held a tablet computer that allowed him to see the ship's navigation information—its current position on a chart—as well as to communicate with the crew and captain, and even to control the ship directly if need be. Presently another man, also of Greek descent, walked over to Daedalus but remained standing. Phillipo, carrying a tablet identical to the one his older brother used, removed his Costa del Mar sunglasses in order to make eye contact with Daedalus.

"The thieves' exact location is unknown at this time, but we have strong reason to believe they are somewhere on or near the Bimini Road formation. Do you want me to take up the helicopter?"

Daedalus looked up from his tablet and frowned. "No, it will be too obvious. We don't want to spook them into running. Let us do some work, and perhaps, as with in the Azores, we can be on hand to reap the spoils."

"I will instruct the Captain to continue course for Bimini Road then."

Daedalus nodded. "Yes, but tell him to maintain distance. We want to be nearby, not on the site or again, they will become suspicious. Have him take us within striking distance."

"Agreed." Phillipo paused, obviously struggling with some thoughts, before speaking again. "Daedalus, I have to ask: our company is spending a lot of money in pursuit of these people, all for the Atlantis myth. Do you think it to be worthwhile? There are other less fantastic, but much more concrete, treasures—the kind that have allowed us to build our fortune in the first place. There is a war going on in Syria right now, for example. We could—"

Daedalus' face flushed red. "Enough, Phillipo! These people, especially this Carter Hunt-have somehow stumbled across a trail of finds that could lead to one of the most exciting archaeological discoveries of the millennium. Atlantis!" He leaned up in his lounger and spread his arms wide. "Can you *imagine* it? The precious metals—the gold? The unknown artifacts awaiting discovery? It would be the find of a *lifetime*, brother. A lifetime."

Phillipo's mouth turned down at the corners. "If it is even real, Daedalus. Meanwhile, there are plenty of other treasures whose existence is not debatable. While we float around out here, literally burning money by the minute to keep this ship running, other artifact seekers are making moves on solid pieces that, until now, have always been our bread and butter."

Daedalus scowled and rose from his lounger. "If the accomplishments of our company are insufficient for you, dear brother, then please, feel free to go your own way. You should be more than comfortable from this point on. Unless, that is, your penchant for gambling has gotten the better of you.

Down on your luck in Monte Carlo on your last visit, were you?"

An awkward silence passed while the two brothers stared one another down, then Daedalus continued.

"At any rate, I myself am driven by a genuine interest in humanity's past, not avarice." He waved his arm about the opulent yacht. "I feel I have done well enough for myself to this point to be able to indulge in a little hobby. But again, Phillipo, if you disagree, you are free to resign your position with Treasure, Inc., and we will go our own separate ways. Professionally, of course. I do still hope I'd be invited to your next family gathering."

At length, Philppo replied. "For now I am happy in my role with the company. And who knows, maybe our treasure hunting friends will find us something of value, even if it turns out not to be from Atlantis. A profit is a profit is a profit, am I right?"

Daedalus gave a slow nod. "Of course."

"I will visit the bridge personally to convey the orders to the Captain."

"Do that. And Phillipo?"

"Yes?"

"Do not make suggestions about our company's direction again. Until, that is, we are dining in the Hall of Poseidia, walking the golden streets of Atlantis. Then, I will hear you out. Until such time, the strategic course for Treasure, Inc. has been set and is no longer a matter of discussion. *Is that clear?*"

Phillipo stood there holding the tablet, staring at his brother with a slack jawed look.

"Is it *clear?*"

Phillipo let the hand holding the tablet drop down to his side. "Yes, it is clear." Then he turned and strode away toward the staircase that led to the bridge.

CHAPTER 20

Bimini Road

Hunt steadied the pathetically anemic beam of his mini-light in his shaking hand. He simply could not believe what he was looking at. *I must have nitrogen narcosis*, he thought to himself. It certainly wouldn't be the first time a diver had succumbed to the so-called rapture of the deep and imagined fantastic visions deep underwater. Divers had even been known to offer their breathing mouthpieces to passing fish because they thought they needed air.

But Hunt knew this was no illusion. It was too solid, and he was far too experienced a scuba diver to have that vivid of a hallucination.

He was looking at the top of a pyramid.

The feeble light from his beam glinted off what appeared to be a crystal surface. Astounding, Hunt thought. Absolutely amazing! The structure was massive, descending into the dark depths beyond the reach of his meager light.

It took his next breath to tear his mind from the exotic sight. It was hard to pull. Air! He clawed at his pressure gauge and read the dial: deep in the red. He would be out of air, his tank completely dry, with any breath now. Time to go!

Hunt mentally kicked himself for being so complacent, so lax about his situation, as he physically kicked for the surface far above. He remembered to check his depth gauge so that he could report to the others on how deep the pyramid was: 150 feet. Very deep, at the edge of what was safe for the recreational diving gear they had with them. Still, it was doable. Kicking hard for the surface while keeping his mouth open to avoid an air embolism—the expansion of the lungs due to decreasing water pressure while going from deep to shallow water—Hunt allowed his mind to wander. He had so many questions. How big was the pyramid? From what he could see of it, plenty big, maybe the size of a three-story building if it was intact all the way down, but who knew? What was a pyramid doing here at the Bimini Road, concealed beneath a capstone identical in shape, though not in scale, to a gold piece found in a statuette of Anubis in the Azores? What, if anything was inside the pyramid?

He only knew one thing for sure as he continued to kick toward the small oval of bright light that represented the capstone opening to the shallow seabed above. They had to get fresh tanks and come back down here for a full dive.

#

On the seaplane, Hunt explained to Maddy the dangers of the dive. The deep depth, the unknown factor of the pyramid itself, having to exit through the narrow capstone opening. But despite acknowledging these hazards, Maddy insisted on making the dive with Hunt and Jayden.

The three of them set up their gear with fresh air tanks, and then prepared to hit the water again. Hunt rummaged around the plane's safety equipment and found a full-size waterproof flashlight that would suffice as a real dive light, and added it to his gear. Sitting backwards with the door open, Hunt glanced all around the plane, checking for any boat traffic. He saw a large vessel on the other side of the main Bimini Road, perhaps a mile away. High above them, a small airplane passed by. Double-checking the seaplane's anchor, he gave the go-ahead for his team to enter the water.

Once at the open capstone, the three divers conducted a quick check of their equipment as before. Satisfied all was in order, Hunt led the way down through the narrow opening into the hidden blue hole below. Once they were clear of the stones that jutted down, Hunt straightened his body out and began dropping down feet first. Jayden and Maddy followed suit. Hunt shined his powerful dive light beam all around, but so far it was as if they had entered a liquid void. The only direction in which he could see anything was up, to the Bimini Road's underside.

The trio of explorers dropped down through the inky void. Hunt's light beam was flanked by the weaker backup light rays of Jayden and Maddy. Hunt kept his own small backup light he'd used on the first dive in reserve in case his primary light stopped working. Around 100 feet down, Maddy had to pause the descent in order to equalize the pressure in her ears to avoid pain in the ears from increasing water pressure. Hunt and Jayden were able to do this while on the move, but Maddy, having less experience, needed to remain in one place while she pinched her nose and breathed into it until she felt her ears pop, relieving the pain. Once that was done, the three of them continued their descent.

Hunt again marveled at the total lack of sea life down here. He saw no fish, no floating jellyfish, nothing. He stabbed his beam into the darkness below, searching for the tip of the pyramid. Still nothing. He glanced at his depth gauge: 125 feet. The tip was at about 150. Or was he at 150 when he first saw it and it was deeper than that? He felt confused, and a little panicky that he'd imagined the whole thing due to nitrogen narcosis and would be embarrassed that he'd brought Jayden and Maddy down here for nothing. Or maybe they'd drifted too far to the right or the left? He swept his light in both directions, angled downward, but still saw nothing. He forced himself to calm down. They continued their descent, and a minute later, he spotted a gleam down in the gloom.

Hoping it wasn't the sides of a silvery fish, which would be the first one he'd seen down here, he continued dropping down while steadying his light on the object. *Yes!*

The pyramid.

But this time he wasn't looking at the tip of it. They'd come in to the left side, and Hunt had to aim his beam up to see the pointy tip.

He consulted his depth gauge, cautioning himself to stay on top of his diving metrics. *What's your depth? What's your air?* 160 feet, and about three-quarters breathing gas remaining. *Okay.*

Jayden and Maddy floated next to him, facing the unknown structure, gawking at it with unabashed wonder. *What is it?* He could practically hear them thinking the question. But there was only one way to find out. Hunt tapped each of them on the shoulder and pointed to the pyramid. Then he began to swim toward it.

As they neared it and more detail became visible, Hunt speculated on it construction. He would have thought that it would be made of limestone blocks, the same as those of the stones that comprised the Bimini Road above. The lack of growth was to be expected because the structure had existed in total darkness, with the capstone in place for who knows how long, there was no plant life marring the stone. But what he hadn't counted on was the building material.

Gold.

The metallic luster was unmistakable. It didn't gleam like a polished jewelry piece, but had the dull glow of something that had existed underwater for centuries. Although no plant life marred the surface, there was a patina of other growth, coral perhaps, sponges, encrusting worms. But overall, the structure appeared to be in remarkably good shape.

Hunt reached the structure and ran a hand over it. Gold! He removed his glove so he could really feel the material. Solid, it certainly felt like the real thing. He went so far as to take his dive knife to one of the bricks in order to feel how hard it was. He knew that real gold was actually a fairly soft metal, malleable and relatively easy to gouge and chip. He drove the butt end of the knife into a section of gold brick and grinned when he saw it leave a mark, brighter gold gleaming beneath the dented surface metal.

Jayden and Maddy also inspected the surface of the pyramid. Hunt checked his gauges again. Unfortunately the depth was great enough that they really didn't have much time to spend down here. He aimed his beam up until it glinted off the pyramid top. Way above that he could see the rectangle of light representing the open capstone. Then he shone the beam in the opposite direction, down along the widening base of the pyramid. It was all smooth tiles as far as he could see; there were no openings or protruding features that he could make out.

Now he aimed the beam horizontally along the pyramid's face, attempting to see how wide it was. He couldn't distinguish the end. He decided they had enough air to check out at least one more side of it, so he signaled Jayden and Maddy to move along the strange monument's face.

Hunt used the lines of the blocks or tiles, whatever they were, which were tightly sealed together by some unknown construction technique, to keep him oriented on a straight line course as he swam along. He kept his light sweeping from top to bottom, searching for any extraneous feature as they swam, but so far he saw only the smooth gold bricks of the pyramid's alluring exterior. Then it occurred to him that he'd been thinking of this pyramidal structure like it was the Great Pyramid of Giza—hollow inside, or at least parts of it—with sculpted passages, chambers and cutouts. But maybe it was solid all the way through? Hunt chuckled at the staggering amount of gold that would represent. Probably enough to drop the international market price, he mused. He supposed it could have an inner solid core of limestone, like the road stones above, with only the outer surface layer being comprised of gold blocks, or even tiles. Who could say without taking some penetrating radar and other gear down here, which would be tricky due to the single, narrow entrance and exit.

At least that was the only entrance or exit he knew of so far. Maybe there were others, deep down somewhere in this blue hole? Something else to investigate another time, he told himself. Right now, the prudent thing to do was to head back to the surface with plenty of time to do so safely. Then they'd discuss what to do next—who, if anyone, to tell about this remarkable discovery, what gear to bring back—and act accordingly.

They reached the end of the pyramid's side and turned right along the next face. Hunt tapped Jayden and Maddy on the leg to get their attention. He pointed to his watch and then up to the surface, which beckoned through the small capstone opening. *Time to go.* Both of them nodded and gave him the "okay" sign. Maddy snapped off a few pictures of this side of the pyramid while Hunt and Jayden scrutinized it visually, checking for any external features. They saw none.

Hunt gave them a thumbs up sign, indicating it was time to begin their ascent. They did so slowly and as a group, only a few feet away from each other. Rising vertically, Hunt watched the pyramid as they lifted away from it. He burned with the desire to know what secrets it held, but diving safety dictated that they leave now. *We'll be back,* he thought.

They swam up toward the distant rectangle of light, each thinking about the pyramid and what it meant. When they reached a depth of forty feet—twenty feet below the capstone opening—Hunt signaled for them to level out at this depth for a decompression stop, which entailed remaining at a shallow depth while breathing in order to avoid ascending too rapidly, which could result in nitrogen bubbles forming in the blood, otherwise known as "the bends."

Hunt looked down while he waited and breathed, straining to pick out the pyramidal form that he now knew waited in the gloomy depths, but he could not see it this far up. He lost himself in thoughts of what might lie inside the enigmatic structure until his dive watched beeped, indicating the preset decompression time had elapsed. Hunt gave the others the thumbs up sign to ascend.

Then, just as they began to swim up toward the opening, they heard a heavy grating sound. Hunt looked up in time to see the piece of limestone they had removed sliding back over the opening. He caught his breath and stopped kicking for a moment, so stunning was the revelation.

Someone was sliding the capstone back into place!

Hunt kicked hard for the rapidly eclipsing aperture. Jayden and Maddy followed right behind him. Even as he swam, his mind rejected the less ominous theories: a local scuba outfit wanting to correct the out of place Bimini Road stone to keep their tourist attraction in place, or a strong current moving the stone by chance. With the empty sea plane floating at anchor on the dive site, scuba dive flag up on the plane as Hunt had left it, no one in their right mind would cover the opening without waiting for the divers to emerge. And since visibility was stellar on the sandy flats where road was, it would be plain to see that no divers were nearby, which meant they had ventured down through the rabbit hole…

A chill overtook Hunt as he strained for the diminishing portal to the world of air. There was only one explanation.

Treasure, Inc.

And then, while Hunt was five feet from the last sliver of opening, the capstone slid fully into place, sealing Hunt and his friends in total darkness, except for their artificial lights.

Like Arctic seals trapped beneath the ice when their breathing hole freezes over, Hunt, Jayden and Maddy had a limited amount of time before their air ran out and they would drown if they couldn't find another way out.

CHAPTER 21

Daedalus stood on the expansive bow deck of the *Historica* and looked down into the water, where a row of stones lay across the bone white sand. The expression on his face wasn't what one would call happiness, yet might be called smug satisfaction. He checked his Rolex and then turned to his brother, Phillipo, who stood next him at the yacht's rail.

"An hour from now and they will have succumbed. It is great to have finally gotten rid of that thorn in my side, Carter Hunt."

Phillipo nodded. "Later today I will send down a dive team to locate their bodies, so that we know for sure."

Daedalus nodded. "Leave them down there, though. We don't need any bodies recovered. Weight their corpses so that they sink to the bottom of the hole."

Phillipo said he would. With tensions running high between him and his brother regarding the running of the company, whenever he did find a simple task he had no issues with, he made sure to comply with enthusiasm and without delay.

"In the meantime," Daedalus went on, "we can speculate on what's down there. How do you think they found it—how did they know where to look?"

Phillipo shook his head. "No idea. This site, while not as common as the

146

main Bimini road, has nonetheless been dived on by hundreds of people. It was as if…" He trailed off as though suddenly lost in thought.

"As if what, brother?"

"As if they were somehow led right to it."

"We've been following them, surveilling them. They don't seem to have been in close contact with anyone."

Phillipo nodded. "They won't be in close contact with anyone ever again after another few minutes." He looked at his own watch and then excused himself to go supervise the dive team getting ready on the aft deck.

#

Hunt pounded his fists on the underside of the limestone slab. Seconds later, Maddy and Jayden joined him. Hunt switched to using the butt of his dive knife to bang on the rock, because it would be louder. Jayden followed suit. He was pretty sure that if people were on the other side of the stone— which they had to have been in order to move it back into position—that they could hear the noise. But alas, the stone did not move.

All three of them tried to push up against it in various ways—Jayden even removed his fins and planted both feet against the underside, pushing with all of his leg strength—but the limestone cap would not budge.

Trapped.

The word echoed about in Hunt's head like a menacing ghost. He descended a few feet down and switched off his light to see if he could see sunlight leaking through anywhere. He saw only complete darkness. The capstone was the only way in or out.

He felt Maddy's hand grip his arm tightly. She showed him her pressure gauge. It was low, about how it should be at the end of a normal dive. He had a little bit more, and he knew Jayden would, too, but if there were no other exits…

He blocked out the panic from his mind and tried to visualize their situation as if he were someone watching it on TV, to reduce the fear and think more rationally. *Three divers in a capped off limestone blue hole. Low on air.*

*It's completely dark, meaning no light is coming in from topside, so there must not be any other places to get in or out...*He pictured an illustration of a blue hole, the kind geologists would make, that depicted the ocean surface and then the blue hole formation and the various rock deposit layers that made it up, as well as the surrounding seabed. In his mind, the diagram, typical of those he'd seen both in geology lectures and by scuba divemaster briefings when he'd dove blue holes and Mexican *cenotes*, featured tunnels and passageways formed by water flowing eons ago when the entire reef was above sea level. One or two of these passages opening out into a cave on the bottom of the reef or sand shelf some distance away, connected beneath the seafloor.

That's our only chance, Hunt told himself. *The only way out is down!*

He waved his dive light back and forth to gain his friends' attention. Then he pointed down. He could see Jayden nod grimly. He understood what the goal was, but no doubt also the low odds of success. But Maddy had no idea why they would go down. Hunt took a precious couple of seconds to write on his slate: MAYBE TUNNELS UP TO REEF DOWN BELOW.

Maddy nodded slowly, her face ashen.

Then, after one last unsuccessful attempt to move the stone cap, the trio began their descent. Hunt did his best to block out the white hot anger he felt toward Daedalus and Treasure, Inc. as they fell through the blackness that most likely would be their eternal tomb. *How could I have been so stupid, so naïve?* he lamented. Of course Daedalus had been shadowing them in country after being duped about the Anubis figurine.

Hunt's flashlight blinked off just as the top of the pyramid came into view, leaving them with only two tiny specks of light held by Maddy and Jayden. He hit it against the palm of his hand and it came back on, but he knew what it likely meant. The seal was no longer water tight, and seawater was affecting the electrical connections inside. Hunt twisted the head of the light until it was screwed as tight as he could get it. The last thing they needed to do was to make a near impossible task any more difficult by not being able to see.

Hunt put the beam back on the top of the pyramid because it was nice to have a reference point while descending instead of only a black void. As they sank past the pyramidal structure, Hunt lamented that they would likely never be able to unlock its secrets. All three of them were doomed to perish down here in this blue hole, this black hole, really. Feelings of rage and helplessness again welled up within Hunt, and this time he had trouble beating them back. He and his friends were going to drown! They would never find a blue hole tunnel that led to the reef. Even if they found an opening in the side of the hole, it would likely just be a dead end. Literally.

Hunt watched the golden pyramid slip by until they reached its base, which also meant that they had reached the bottom of the blue hole. He checked his depth gauge: 200 feet. His minutes, his very breaths were numbered at this great depth. Maddy especially, being the least experienced of the three, she was more prone to panic and would consume air more rapidly in this situation. To have any chance of finding a tunnel, they needed to swim out to the side of the hole now and start poking around.

The three of them touched down on the bottom, which, as Hunt expected, was limestone with a thin covering of sand that trickled down from above. Hunt didn't bother asking everyone what their air situation was; he knew it wasn't good and that there wasn't anything they could do about it, anyway. It would only be a time-waster at this point, so he simply pointed along the base of the pyramid toward the side of the blue hole and began to swim.

Jayden and Maddy followed him as they finned along next to the pyramidal edifice. It occurred to Hunt that this was one of the sides they hadn't seen yet, and so he played his beam along it as they moved past it. Same gold tiles. Same smooth, uninterrupted surface, just like the—*Wait, what's that?* Hunt stopped swimming. Was he seeing things? But Jayden and Maddy were tapping on his arm and pointing at it, too.

It appeared to be an entrance of some sort. A doorway leading inside the structure. The vertically oriented rectangular opening was set perhaps ten feet up from the base. From down on the bottom it appeared only as a dark hole. Hunt kicked off the bottom and rose to the level of the doorway, unable to contain his overwhelming curiosity even in the face of death. He stared into the opening. A narrow passageway that was also constructed of gold tiles. It extended some distance inside, perhaps fifty feet back, where his light beam landed on a wall of some sort.

Then the light blinked out again, plunging the internal pyramid into blackness. Hunt banged on the light a couple of times but it wouldn't come back on. On the fifth try, as Jayden and Maddy reached him, it illuminated once again.

Hunt shrugged while looking at Maddy and Jayden, pointing into the pyramid. Both of them nodded. *Let's check it out.*

The three divers, perilously low on air, swam into the golden pyramid.

CHAPTER 22

It reminded Hunt of swimming through one of the dry pyramids in Egypt. Narrow, constricting walls with a ceiling that would barely be head-high for most people if they were walking. First Hunt, then Maddy, and then Jayden swam through the claustrophobic passageway, constructed of the same gold tiles as the pyramid's exterior. When Hunt neared the end of the passage, about the same time he could see that it opened up into a wider space, his air became harder to pull through the regulator.

He kicked faster, if for no other reason than to see one more thing—what lie beyond this tunnel—before he died. He knew now that he never would have made the edge of the blue hole, how futile it would have been to try to find a limestone tunnel that connected to the reef. But at least he would see the inside of an underwater pyramid. He thought about what pyramids were for—basically they were fancy tombs—but to have one underwater made little sense since it meant it would be wet inside, unless there was a section totally sealed off. But then again if it was totally sealed off, they would not be able to gain entrance.

These thoughts accompanied Hunt as he emerged from the hallway into a flooded chamber as his air became harder to pull, the air pressure needle now firmly in the red. He knew any second now Maddy and Jayden would have the same problem if they didn't already. He felt so terrible that he let them both down, and even now, they still followed him.

He was surprised to find the room unadorned, except for the same gold tiles he'd seen everywhere else. It was more gold than he'd ever seen in his life. The room widened into a roughly square shape, and extended both above and below the level of the passageway from which they had just emerged.

Looking up, Hunt saw nothing interesting, only a vaulted ceiling with no openings or accessories. Turning his attention in the opposite direction, he eyed something that looked like it could be a door or portal of some sort, but he couldn't be certain. With no time to waste, he swam down into the underwater room. Although there were no inscriptions or anything that could be interpreted as signage of any kind, Hunt felt a surge of adrenaline upon looking at the structure set into the floor.

It had to be a door!

A door to what, he had no idea, but it was something. But then he thought about it—once opened, even if it was dry beyond, the ocean water would rush inside, flooding whatever lay beyond. It would not be possible to close the door again against the raging flood, therefore whatever lay beyond would be submerged before long. With them inside.

He turned and looked back to see if Jayden and Maddy had followed him inside the room. And that's when he saw it, something that made perfect sense to him in a flash of inspiration. Jayden and Maddy had already entered the flooded chamber and now hovered in the middle of the space, surveying it in all directions as Hunt had done.

But Hunt was focused on what lie just inside the entrance.

Up above the doorway was a massive stone slab. Actual limestone, not gold, supported on four cylindrical posts that jutted from the wall above the doorway exiting the passage. Hunt eyed the stone slab, then turned his gaze back to the construct on the floor that looked like a portal of some sort. Instantly it clicked into place for him: they were inside an airlock.

Hunt knew from his navy days that the way an airlock worked was to have a room with two airtight doors. You entered through one, flooding the room if it wasn't already, such as with the wet room of a submarine. Then that door was sealed, preventing new water from entering when the second door was opened. *Where are you right now?* He asked himself. *In a flooded room! What's on either side of you? Two doors.*

But as he gazed at first one, then the other, the problem became apparent. How to open the one in the floor and close the one at the entrance? Hunt opted to concentrate on the outer door first, since it would do no good to open the inner one first with the outer still open. He had to seal the airlock, and then open the inner door so that only the water trapped inside would flow through to the new area.

He saw Jayden looking at him and pointed to the stone slab above the entrance. Then he pointed sharply down, hoping that would get the message across. He saw his friend's eyes brighten as he nodded and began to swim toward him. Hunt then turned and focused on the mechanism that was holding up the stone slab.

He could see that if the four circular rods were pushed in so that they were flush with the wall, the slab would fall into place, blocking the doorway and effectively sealing them in. But how to push in the rods? Hunt swam to them and shoved on one, not surprised at all when it wouldn't budge. *Of course it's not that easy. Think, if you want to live!* He glanced back down at the floor, dropping down through the water towards it as he did so.

The people who built this place, if they had wanted to use it as an airlock, wouldn't have had dive masks, Hunt reasoned. So to be able to trigger the stone gate mechanism from inside meant that the trigger must be operational to someone who couldn't see well. Hunt noticed the tiles on the floor, where the door would fall into place should the rods be withdrawn into the wall. Gold, like the rest of them, and unmarked. No *press here to release gate*, Hunt thought. *What a surprise.* But as he looked up at the rods, and back down at the tiles, he saw that each rod did in fact line up exactly with one of the gold floor tiles.

Hunt swam down to the tiles, moving to the leftmost one. After getting a glimpse up of the rod supporting the door to make sure it lined up, he then slammed his fist into the tile.

Nothing happened.

He wasn't sure what he expected—if it would click or move somehow, but he tried a couple of more times, with varying degrees of pressure, and still nothing happened.

Then his flashlight winked out. He banged it on the tile, hoping it would flicker back to life, but no such luck. He dropped his main light and activated his mini backup light that he'd had to rely on earlier. The three of them now worked in near darkness, three pinpoints of light their only illumination.

Jayden swam up and put his face close to Hunt's, a *what now* expression plain to see. Hunt showed him the tiles that lined up with the rods above. Jayden swam to the next one over, and Hunt tried pressing on the same one again. Both of them pushed on the tiles at once, and still nothing happened.

But it gave Hunt an idea. What if all four tiles had to be pressed simultaneously? He turned and saw Maddy swimming very fast over to him, giving him the OUT OF AIR signal as she swam, moving her finger in a slashing motion across her throat. Her tank had run dry. In anticipation of her reaching him, Hunt found his octopus and handed her the emergency mouthpiece. His air was already hard to pull, and he knew that now with two persons breathing off of it that they would have only a few breaths each. Hopefully Jayden had a little more, but he knew they had very little time left, regardless.

Hunt got Jayden's attention and pointed to Maddy, then pointed to one of the tiles. They were spaced just close enough together that he could press on one while Maddy reached over and pressed the adjacent one. But that still left two more, meaning Jayden would have to somehow be able to push on two of them at once. Hunt was glad to see his old navy buddy comprehend the problem immediately, and swim into position between the two tiles. He stripped off one of his fins and placed that foot on the last tile in the row, while the fingers of his left hand barely reached the other tile. It would have to do.

Hunt and Maddy got into position on their respective two tiles. He knew they wouldn't be able to hold the position for long, not to mention they were almost out of air anyway, so there was no time for any kind of coordinated countdown. It would either work or it wouldn't. He looked over at Jayden and nodded.

All three of them pressed down on the tiles at once, with Jayden stepping on one with his foot. This time Hunt could tell something was happening. The tile beneath his hand depressed into the floor about an inch, and he felt the grinding of stone on stone somewhere from deep within the walls. Then he remembered what was poised above them.

Move!

Hunt yanked Maddy back by the arm, while grunting loudly to alert Jayden. He felt the pressure wave of water as the stone block above their heads began to fall as its support rods were withdrawn. Jayden's legs were already in the clear, but his chest and head was still in the impact zone. Fortunately, he had been on his back to be able to reach both tiles, so he saw what was happening without Hunt's warning. He pushed off the floor with his left hand, the one deepest in the impact zone, and did a slow-motion roll out onto the chamber floor.

The stone block slid straight down into place as it had been designed, not more than a single millimeter away from the pinky finger of Jayden's left hand. A small cloud of silt billowed up, displaced by the falling block, which made a dull thud that all of the divers could feel in their bones.

But it was done, it had worked! The room was now sealed off. What's more, Hunt thought, now allowing himself to feel the faintest tinge of optimism for the first time since they began their descent from the blocked opening far above, he now knew that there was something to this. Someone had engineered this room! It could really be an airlock, and an airlock meant the one thing that was now more important to any of them than they could eve have imagined: *air.*

He whirled around to look at what he thought of as the other piece of the puzzle, the inner door that was set into the floor. Immediately he felt resistance; he forgot that Maddy was tethered to him by way of his second regulator. She was out of air! They had to hurry. His own air was about to run out at any second.

He tugged on Maddy's arm and moved toward the other door. Jayden was already moving toward it. The three of them aimed their dim keychain-sized flashlights at the mechanical contraption that now represented their only hope of continuing existence.

This one was a circular limestone lid of some sort sticking up out of the gold tiled floor. Hunt could only pray that it opened up into a space that was now dry and large enough to accommodate the water from this single chamber, which would flow down into it. But that point was moot if they couldn't figure out how to open it in the first place. Already, Jayden was trying in vain to brute force turn the stone wheel with both hands, feet planted firmly on the floor. But that had zero effect on the mute stone. Hunt took a closer look at the mechanism.

A circular wheel with smooth sides, made of limestone, with no apparent handles or levers, of any kind. Hunt leaned in over the top of the device and shined his feeble light on it. He took a hand and brushed off a fine layer of sediment, which temporarily clouded the water, but cleared a few seconds later. When he looked again at the top of the wheel, he was able to discern something he hadn't seen before: a hexagonal shape comprised of six very thin grooves cut into the limestone.

He felt a surge of elation followed by a jolt of sheer panic as he went to pull his next breath and found nothing there. His tank had run completely dry! Sure enough, he felt Maddy's fist pound into his shoulder in a silent, primal cry for help. She, of course, was now out of air, too. Hunt pulled on Jayden's calf. When his friend turned around he gave him the out of air signal, feeling a deep pang of sadness as he registered the look of shock, surprise and understanding in Jayden's eyes. They weren't going to make it. It was amazing they'd gotten this far, really.

Jayden swam over and gave his emergency second regulator to Maddy first, who took one breath and then passed it to Hunt, who gulped a quick one and passed it back to her. He could see her crying behind her mask. With all three of them breathing off of one very low tank, and Jayden exerting himself, they were probably down to mere seconds of air supply remaining. They would perish down here in this strange monument beneath the sea.

But Hunt wasn't about to give up. He turned back to the hexagon carved into the circular stone top. *Think, think, think!* On the plane ride to the Bahamas, he had read in his research that six was a sacred number of Atlantis. That bolstered his thought that this place had been designed carefully, and might possibly be connected with the fabled lost city. But it sure didn't help his real situation right now. What could it mean that there was a hexagonal pattern in the stone, from a mechanical standpoint?

He was out of breath now and turned to Jayden for another. But his friend shook his head and gave the out of air signal.

They were done.

He heard Maddy start to scream into her regulator. Any second now she would spit it out and breathe in water and it would all be over. With nothing left to try, Hunt turned back to what he hoped was in fact a door mechanism. Jayden had tried to turn it. He now took both hands and pressed down firmly in the middle of the hexagonal section in the middle of the cylinder.

To his great surprise, he felt the now familiar grinding of stone on stone as the entire hexagonal piece slid down within the circular stone. Jayden heard it and swam over. Hunt pushed again and the hexagonal stone moved again. Jayden saw what was happening and added his hands and arm strength to Hunt's, using his last remaining ounce of strength to hopefully accomplish something useful. The hex piece moved faster now, receding deep into the circular stone until they had to reach in almost up to their shoulders to push it. Then Jayden, already not wearing one fin, shoved Hunt out of the way and stood on top of the recessed section. He hopped up and down on it, and Hunt heard the grinding of stone inch by inch with each jump.

His lungs were afire, and he knew he had a few more seconds left before his body would involuntarily betray him and cause him to spit out his mouthpiece and breathe in water. Meanwhile Jayden kept stepping down on the hexagonal block, grunting with exertion on each kick.

Maddy came over and clutched at Hunt, getting in his face, staring at him with wide-panic eyes to let him know she was about to succumb, when Jayden let out an *ooomhp*, and Hunt heard a last grating of limestone before he began to feel an enormous suction.

Jayden had pushed the hexagonal piece all the way through the circular door stone, and now all of the water in the room was pouring out through the new opening...which could mean only one thing.

There was an air space on the other side, below! If there wasn't, then the water couldn't rush in.

As Hunt watched, mystified, surprised and relieved all at the same time, Jayden slipped through the hexagonal opening like a kid down one of the water slides at the Atlantis resort, dropping rapidly out of sight. Hunt grabbed Maddy and positioned her feet first over the hole, but the force of the water grew stronger as it began to drain faster, and she ended up with one leg in and one leg out. He unhooked her right leg, bent at the knee, from the rim of the opening, and then she went sliding down the chute.

Even though they had now opened a portal that led to somewhere with air, Hunt still couldn't breath yet, he was still underwater. He could feel his lungs start to convulse, and knew that he had arrived at the outer limit of biological tolerance for his body without oxygen.

With his last ounce of controllable energy, Hunt dove headfirst into the hexagonal hole after Maddy and Jayden.

CHAPTER 23

A raging torrent of water rushed Hunt straight down for what seemed like forever, but was in fact only a few seconds. He impacted hard on a limestone surface but his fall was cushioned by the water that poured in from above. He heard his empty scuba tank clanging against the rock. Aware that his hands felt air before being plunged back into the riotous current, he spat out his mouthpiece and gulped. He took in one glorious breath before being plunged again beneath the deluge. He was then washed horizontally for an appreciable distance until the water thinned out some and his body began to tumble more slowly across the rock floor of the subsea corridor.

When he came to rest with is legs up against a wall and his head and shoulders on the ground, he stared up at a rocky ceiling for a few moments while a thin layer of remaining water sluiced around his inert form. He wiggled his fingers and toes, then slowly rotated his body. So far it seemed like nothing was obviously broken, although he could tell already he had bruises that would be around for weeks. Hunt groggily lowered his legs and pushed himself up from the ground, or floor or....where was he, anyway?

And where were his friends? He called out Maddy and Jayden's names, his voice reverberating in the damp, tunnel-like space.

"Over here." Jayden's voice came from somewhere up ahead, apparently having been washed further forward since he was first down the chute.

"You okay?" Hunt called out as he shrugged out of his scuba tank and vest, letting them drop to the tunnel floor. If not for his feeble mini-light, still clipped to his dive vest, it would be pitch black in here. He unclipped it from his gear and carried it in his right hand. As it was, he had just enough light to see in order to move forward without worrying about smashing into something. One of his swim fins had already been ripped off his foot, but now he stripped off the other. He tucked it into the waistband of his shorts and then lowered his mask and snorkel around his neck. He might need the snorkel gear again, who knew, and it was best to be prepared.

"I'm not sure a doctor would agree with that assessment, but I can still walk." Jayden's voice sounded shaky, but carried well enough in the confines of the dank passageway.

"Same here." Hunt's ears perked up at the sound of Maddy's voice.

"I'll be right there." Hunt started walking toward them, his first tentative steps becoming steadier and more confident as he progressed. He examined the passageway with the aid of his tiny light as he moved. All of it was limestone, the remnants of coral reefs from eons ago. He could pick out seashells here and there locked in the substrate. The ceiling was barely above his head, and in fact he found himself stooping here and there to make sure he wouldn't be hit. The walls, though irregularly shaped, were perhaps three feet apart. He shined his light up ahead but still couldn't actually see Jayden and Maddy, though he could hear them talking now in quiet tones.

Hunt saw an object lying on the passageway floor and shined his light on it: the hexagonal keystone that Jayden had kicked through the door mechanism. It had been washed and rolled to this point. He bent down and picked it up. It was heavy, but not to the point of impeding his mobility, so he decided to keep it for later examination. What if it really was connected with Atlantis? The six sides, the mysterious Bimini Road location…that would make invaluable in and of itself.

But first things first, Hunt reminded himself. They still had to get out of here somehow. They had entered the pyramid at its base level, and then gone down through the door with the hexagonal piece, which meant that right now they were not only below sea level, but below the seabed itself! Hunt tried to block that thought from his mind as he continued down the passageway. He found Jayden and Maddy a few yards further on, still in the process of removing their now unnecessary dive gear.

Hunt pointed to his mask and urged them both to keep their snorkel gear in case they had to get wet again. Receiving no arguments, Hunt set off down the passageway in single file formation with Maddy in the middle and Jayden bringing up the rear. The corridor remained much the same for what seemed like a long distance—Hunt guessed it was at least a mile the soggy trio marched—with a level floor. After a while he noticed they were trudging along at an incline, gradual at first, but becoming noticeably steeper as they went on.

"Wonderful weather for a hike, isn't it?" Jayden quipped. They were too tired to laugh. What's more, Hunt found he had to concentrate more and more to keep his footing. More than once he almost lost his balance and slipped backwards onto Jayden, who offered some choice curse words for advice on how to maintain his footing. Just when Hunt was about to call out that it was too steep to continue, his feeble beam picked out a large hole in the limestone wall a couple of feet above his head.

"Got some kind of opening right up here," he called down to them.

"Is it wet?" This from Maddy.

"Don't see any water dripping out of it," Hunt said with a grunt as he clawed his fingers into the rough rocky wall. "Can you two sit tight where you are for a minute? No reason for all three of us to try and scramble up there. Let me go up first and I'll see if this leads anywhere."

"It better lead somewhere," Jayden said, "or we're beyond screwed, unless your idea of a good time is living out the end of our days in that pyramid in the dark with no food or water."

Hunt sighed. "I can always count on you to brighten things up. Here I go, hang tight for a minute. If I fall on you, I don't mean to, believe me."

Hunt knew he would need both hands in order to make the climb, so he unzipped his wetsuit and crammed the hexagon cap into the front of it, and then zipped it most of the way back up, holding it in place against his body. It was awkward, but it would work if this chute was climbable, Hunt thought. He dug the toes of his rubber dive boots into the porous rock wall and tested his footholds before attempting to spring upward. After a couple of test movements, he jumped up and dug the fingers of his gloved hands into the more level rock surface above. He scrabbled to gain purchase with his hands and feet. A few loose bits of rock crumbled away, raining down on Jayden and Maddy, but Hunt held on and pulled himself up.

He found himself in a very enclosed space, a vestibule of sorts, with the only way to go being up. His heart sank on seeing only darkness in that direction—it must only lead into another enclosed space like the pyramid, he thought, or maybe not even that—it could be a dead-end chimney. He aimed his light up there—was it a little dimmer now?—and saw a series of crude steps hewn into the stone.

Hunt dug his right foot into the bottom-most rung and began to climb. Ten, twenty, thirty feet vertical he went, holding his mini-flashlight clenched between his teeth. He still saw no light emanating from above, yet forced the negative implications from his mind and kept climbing. He climbed on until he almost hit his head as the angle of the chute changed, slanting up at about forty-five degrees rather than vertical.

What's this all about? At first he thought it was due to his flashlight aiming up into his eyes, but then, as he saw that it was dangling down, illuminating the front of his chest, he felt a surge of elation.

Light! Natural sunlight filtering down from above! *But how is that possible? If this tunnel leads up onto the reef why doesn't the water fill this passageway?* But right now the answers to those questions would have to wait. Jayden was calling up to him.

"Can't see your fat ass anymore, Carter, what's going on?"

Hunt swiveled his neck and shouted down: "Come on up. The tunnel angles here, and I see light!"

"Say no more!" came Maddy's exuberant voice. She and Jayden started climbing the vertical chute while Hunt assessed the new section of tunnel. Aiming his light up into it against the walls, he saw more of the same limestone rock, only this section didn't have the rungs cut into the sides. Due to the shallower angle, they weren't needed. Hunt cautiously loped up the incline, on all fours, wary of hitting a loose or soggy section that could fall through, but the passageway floor remained solid beneath him as he progressed.

By the time he was near to the opening, he could hear Jayden and Maddy entering the inclined section below.

"Nice ladder!" Jayden called up. "What's this next part like, Carter?"

Hunt turned around and bellowed down to them. "No more ladder, but you don't really need it. Just walk like a dog on all fours, I'm sure you're used to it, you knuckle-dragger."

He could hear Maddy's laughter bubbling up from below, followed by Jayden's voice.

"Normally I'd say something to that, but right now I'm still in shock that I'm alive at all."

"Hopefully it'll stay that way," Maddy said.

"I'd say our prospects have improved dramatically," Hunt said, looking up to the natural light filtering into the chute from above. "I see trees!"

"Are you sure the oxygen deprivation didn't have an affect on your already questionable brain, Carter?" Jayden asked.

"No, I can see it, too!" Maddy called out. "Light!"

Meanwhile, Hunt crawled the rest of the way to the end of the passageway, the hexagonal stone chafing uncomfortably against his skin beneath the wetsuit. The exit flared out in a stone lip that was overgrown with green vegetation. Hunt listened, wondering if perhaps Treasure, Inc. might be waiting right outside the exit, somehow knowing where the passage would lead, but he didn't hear anything except the twittering of birds and the rustle of leaves in a light breeze.

Hunt took the final steps and emerged from the dark tunnel into the world of light.

CHAPTER 24

Daedalus stood on the bow deck of his yacht overlooking the stern dive platform, which was currently a hub of purposeful activity. Below, crew members set up scuba tanks and prepared dive equipment, including double-tank rigs with exotic gas mixtures that would allow increased bottom times. He glanced at his jeweled watch and then spoke into a handheld radio to his brother, Phillipo, who supervised the dive operations down on the platform.

"Carter and his team have certainly expired by now. Split your divers into two groups: one to see what lies in the blue hole that might be connected to Atlantis, and another to locate the bodies of Hunt and his team. I want confirmation that they are dead."

Phillipo did not bother replying over the radio but merely looked up to his brother from the dive deck and held his fingers in the "okay" sign before turning to address one of his men concerning specifics of the dive operation. While the operation was prepped, Daedalus stared out over the water above the Bimini Road, occasionally raising a pair of marine binoculars to his eyes, looking for heads bobbing in the water that might indicate Hunt and his friends somehow made it to the surface, alive or dead. But he saw only the sparkling blue sea surface. One question burned into his mind while he stared into the uncaring sea.

What did you find down there, Carter Hunt?

As he heard a splash near the boat and looked over in time to see the first diver entering the water, his lips spread into a thin smile.

He would have his answer soon enough.

#

Hunt shook his head in wonder as he, Jayden and Maddy stared at their new surroundings. Sunlight, blue sky, trees, sand, dry coral, birds…

An island.

They stood immediately outside the passageway entrance, in a copse of scrubby trees rooted in sandy soil, on a small hillock shrouded in foliage at the highest elevation point of what was little more than a sandspit of an islet. Hunt summed up what they were all thinking.

"So the passageway we were washed down into from the pyramid--it travelled beneath the seafloor a mile or so until it angled up beneath this island, right through its base. Coming out in the middle of it."

Maddy nodded. "I'm pretty sure this is that same island we saw on the way in from the plane."

"Let's check it out." Jayden pushed through the foliage until he was outside the heavily shrouded tunnel exit. "I think it's safe to say we've got this place all to ourselves."

Hunt and Maddy also fought their way through the brush until they, too, could see the rest of the island. Scrubby green plants dominated the center while brown coral rubble defined the perimeter, with a ring of white sand encircling that. The blue Atlantic sprawled in every direction beyond the island, with no other land masses within sight.

"Which way do you think our plane is?" Jayden asked. All of them turned slowly in circles, visually inspecting the horizon in every direction, but none of them had an answer. Hunt offered the closest thing to a solution.

"Wherever it *was*, I think 'was' is the key word, since Daedalus obviously found our secret underwater blue hole and tried to make us a permanent part of it. I doubt he'd leave our plane floating around so people can find it and say, 'Hey I wonder what happened to whoever was on it?'"

"You can bet that the rental company will start looking for it when we don't bring it back later today. You're right, he'll probably sink it rather than risk a lot of questions that he thinks could lead to not only some dead bodies being found, but the entire underwater area beneath the Bimini Road."

"And he doesn't even know about the pyramid yet," Maddy added.

"I can think of one advantage this has given us," Hunt said, staring out across the ocean.

"What's that?" Maddy asked. "Because from where I'm standing, all we did was show Daedalus where a monumental treasure is and meanwhile, after almost drowning, we're stranded on a deserted island with no food or water and no way to call for help."

Hunt turned to look at Maddy, her disheveled, waterlogged form in a posture of defeat, even through the elation of still being alive. He felt bad for what she had been through, and so was glad to think of something positive to buoy her spirits. "Daedalus and Treasure, Inc. think we're dead."

He let that sink in for a moment as the three of them stood there and gazed about the uninhabited island. At length, Jayden said, "Interesting. But I'm hungry."

"I don't think they deliver here," Hunt said.

Jayden pointed to a tall palm tree some distance away. "Coconuts will have to do for now. Going to go get us some."

Hunt pointed to the nearest edge of the island. "Maddy and I will see if we can flag down a passing boat or aircraft. Meet us on the beach when you're ready."

They agreed to the plan and set off through the scrub brush until they reached the palm tree. It was a good three stories high, but brimming with ripe coconuts at the top. Jayden assured them that he would be all right and then Hunt and Maddy continued on across the island until they reached the beach, which didn't take long. Once there, Hunt was glad to set down the heavy hexagonal door piece while he and Maddy surveyed the scene.

They scrutinized the sea and horizon, and while they saw a couple of large boats far in the distance, there were no craft in the immediate vicinity. "Waving our arms for help and being picked up anytime soon isn't looking so good," Hunt admitted.

Maddy shrugged. "This area's not all that remote. The Bimini Road is a popular dive destination. Bimini itself is a major tourist destination with lots of charter fishing and diving activity. Someone'll come along. Meanwhile, let's have a look at this thing you lugged all the way up here." She moved to the hexagonal door piece and picked it up. She stared at it closely for a couple of minutes, and then began turning it over in her hands, pausing to study each of the six facets, basically a six-sided cylinder, longer than it is wide. Exotic hieroglyphic style drawings were etched into each of the six longitudinal facets.

Finally, she studied the end pieces, noting that neither of them featured any markings. The rock itself they were composed of was different than the limestone of the area, nor was it a metallic substance—gold or otherwise—as with the submerged Bimini pyramid itself. Gray slate was what it looked like to her, although she was no geologist, but as an archaeologist she had dug many holes into the Earth, and had on more than one occasion collaborated with earth scientists.

But the sides of the hexagonal object were composed of a different rock, a conglomerate of sorts, she guessed. She set the piece down on the ground on one end. Then she rapped a knuckle on the slate cap.

"It's sort of hollow—hear that?" She put her ear up to the hexagonal piece while she rapped on it again. Hunt drew closer, taking a keen interest.

"Maybe we should open it?"

Maddy looked up at him with a frown. "We can't break it! This thing is an artifact in itself."

"Who said anything about breaking it?" Hunt knelt next to Maddy and rapped his fist on the opposite end cap of the artifact. It, too, resulted in a hollow echo. "Do me a favor, will you?" He gripped the hexagonal chamber by its base.

"Depends what it is!" She gave him a coy smile. Hunt pointed to the opposite end of the artifact. "Just hold it by that end, okay?"

"What for?"

"I'm going to try something. Watch…" Hunt proceeded to twist the base of the hexagonal tube counterclockwise while Maddy held the other end firmly in place.

"Nothing's happening," she said, eyes on the artifact.

"Let me try the other way." Hunt steadied his grip on the end-piece once again, but this time turned it clockwise. At first, the result was the same as the last time, but then he felt something start to slip. He looked closer at the surface of the hexagonal cylinder. He now saw a tiny puff of dust dislodged from turning the object. He tried again, turning the base clockwise, and this time part of the structure rotated.

"It moved!" Maddy exclaimed.

Hunt released his grip on the artifact and eyeballed the faces. Sure enough, the pictographs decorating each facet were now out of alignment. Looking at the device now, he realized that's exactly what is was—a machine that was designed to exact specifications. He looked at Maddy.

"It appears to be a machine with two functions: one, to act as the door stopper for the underwater pyramid airlock system, and two: as a safe, it looks like."

"Safe?" Maddy arched an eyebrow as she stared at the hexagonal machine.

"It's hollow inside, and it has six six-sided sections that turn, each with a different drawing on them. What if when the drawings are lined up a certain way, the device is unlocked?"

"Kind of like a Rubik's Cube or something?" Maddy suggested.

"Yeah sort of, but cylindrical instead of a cube. It just has to be lined up a certain way and then it unlocks. So let's take a look at these pictures, there are…wow, six vertical sections, each with six sides, for a total of thirty-six pictures."

Maddy squinted hard at the artifact. "You're calling them 'pictures', but it looks to me like they're actually *parts* of pictures.

Hunt eyed the strange drawings. "Right, I see a lot of random shapes, lines, maybe runes."

"Let me hold it for a minute." Maddy picked up the artifact and turned it over in her hands. "I'm looking at the bottom section, the one you just turned."

"They look like two outward facing 'L's."

"You call them 'Ls", I call them feet."

"Feet?"

"Bear with me, I could be wrong, but hear me out. The middle pieces are harder to visualize, but I think I can make sense of the topmost pieces…here." She pointed to a triangular shape next to the end she had held when Hunt turned the first piece, and then then a more rectangular polygon on the section below that.

"What are they? Seriously, they look like Greek to me."

"Not Greek, but Egyptian. If I'm right, that is. Not sure yet. But let's try it. This time you hold the other end, and I'll turn the section." They worked together to turn the device until the next section of pictographs lined up the way Maddy thought they should.

"An animal head?" Hunt guessed.

Maddy nodded. But not just any animal head. Watch this—next section down. Hunt held one end of the device while Maddy rotated the next section.

"Now that does look like some kind of animal head," Hunt admitted. "Kind of a pointy nose or muzzle, like maybe a fox?"

Maddy gazed down at the aligned pictograph. "Or a dog. But let's keep going and see if there's a body in the middle."

Hunt eyed the series of lines on the middle sections as Maddy turned the hexagonal segments. "I think there might be a big rectangle or square formed by a double-section."

Maddy turned the segments until, sure enough, a polygonal shape close to a vertically oriented rectangle manifested. "Looks like part of a body to me," Maddy said.

Together they examined the remaining two segments of the puzzle, seeking to identify a recognizable shape that might come together with proper alignment of the hexagonal wheels.

"I can see an inverted triangular form being constructed by turning this wheel three facets to the right, and the other one two to the left."

"Let's give it a go," Hunt said.

Together they held the artifact and made the requisite turns. "Yes!" Maddy squealed when it was done and she leaned back to view the results of their image manipulation. "Does that look familiar to you?"

Hunt held his breath as he took in the astonishing sight. He was nearly speechless. "How…"

"How did we get here? I mean what led us here?"

"Anubis, the statuette of the dog."

"I think there's your answer. Because it's a good likeness, wouldn't you say?" Both of them stared at the image a moment longer. Taken as a whole, on one half of the artifact, the image depicted a figure with a canine-like head, a blocky body tapering to a pair of outward facing feet. On the reverse of the device, there were only a series crisscrossing lines that made up a background of sorts, perhaps as though the figure stood in a field of vegetation or reeds.

"Could be Anubis," Hunt had to admit. "But right now, I have another question: did we unlock this thing?"

"Let's see. Each of us should hold onto one end, and then pull straight back." Gently, Maddy and Hunt performed the action. "Mine's not budging." No sooner had Maddy said the words than Hunt's end piece came free from the device.

CHAPTER 25

"There's something inside." Hunt set the lid of the hexagonal chamber aside on the sandy ground. Together, he and Maddy gently tipped the device up on the closed end so that they could both peer inside from above. Inside the device was a tube-like chamber that contained one object.

"Looks like a scroll of parchment or papyrus!" Maddy said, reaching into the tube. "Oh, we really should get this to a lab immediately. I can't stand that we've exposed it to this salty, humid air."

"It's already been exposed, now," Hunt pointed out. "Might as well read it quickly, if we can, see if it means anything to us, and then we can put it back in there and cap it up. When we get back to the States, you can take it to your lab and give it the full treatment."

Maddy agreed and then carefully reached inside the tube and extricated the roll of parchment. It was not held together by any kind of fastener, but simply rolled tightly.

"There's no writing on the outer side," Maddy said. "I'll have to unroll it, which is unfortunate because the risk of damage is higher, but, we do need information, don't we?"

Hunt looked around nervously. "Yeah. In fact, do you still have your camera?" Maddy nodded, indicating her underwater camera still clipped to a wrist strap, and Hunt continued. "We should take a picture of it once it's unrolled, just in case our friends from Treasure, Inc. decide to check this island out. Because if they find us here, it'd be lucky if they only took our new treasure and left us here alive."

"First of all, let's see if I can get it unrolled in one piece. Parchment, or vellum—various material that typically supports old manuscripts—is notorious for falling apart after coming in contact with air after long periods of storage. That's why museums keep this kind of thing in carefully climate-controlled conditions."

Maddy began to carefully peel back the leading edge of the heavy, paper-like material. At first she used one hand to hold it and the other to peel it back, but then decided against it and turned to Hunt. "I think it would be better if you hold it so I can use two hands to unravel it from each end. I don't want to put too much pressure on one end and tear it."

Hunt complied and Maddy bent to her task again, this time having success as the paper made a rasping sound while it was unrolled. "I see writing…it's a long manuscript with a lot of text." She continued to gingerly handle the scroll as she unfurled it. Hunt was able to focus some on the content since he was only holding the scroll in place while Maddy handled the more delicate task of unrolling it.

She took a long look at the lettering itself, hoping to recognize a language, and said, "This is all Greek to me, Carter."

Carter's face revealed his disappointment. "Looks like we'll have to get it in front of more eyes, then, maybe—"

"No, Carter, I mean it's literally in Greek. As in the Greek language-- Attic Greek to be precise, meaning it's a Greek dialect from the city of Attica."

Hunt's laughter rolled across the island until he heard footsteps approaching and whirled around, hand reflexively reaching for the dive knife still strapped to his calf. But he relaxed as soon as he saw Jayden's lanky form running across the sandy soil. His gait looked off for the normally spry ex-Navy man, though, and Hunt focused in on the load he carried—an armful of coconuts.

"You two lovebirds hungry or thirsty? Because these things have food and water. Love 'em!"

He reached his friends and dumped the fruits of his tree-climbing labor on the ground.

Sounds good to me," Maddy said. "How do we open them?"

Jayden unsheathed his own dive knife and demonstrated on one green coconut. He jammed the point of his blade into the soft spot near one end, then held it upside down to let the flow of clear, sweet liquid pour into his mouth.

"Nothing like fresh coconut milk," he said, turning the coconut back upright and wiping his chin. "You can eat the meat inside them, too, but I thought refreshments would be in order first." He proceeded to open two more coconuts, handing one each to Maddy and Hunt.

"Whoa, you guys got that thing open? What *is* that?" Jayden pointed excitedly to the roll of parchment Maddy set back inside the hex chamber when she picked up her coconut for a drink.

"Not sure yet," Maddy replied. "It's written in Greek, though, which I am reasonably capable at deciphering. But it's a long document, and like I told Carter, the proper environment in which to make sense of it is not here on a glorified sandbar drinking coconut juice, but in a controlled laboratory setting."

"We can try, though, right?" Jayden said with a wet coconut juice smile. He looked down at the scroll. "I mean, first of all, what is it? Is it a letter that says, 'Dear Mom, I'm not sure I'll be able to leave the island to come home this summer...' kind of thing, or is it more like some official political document from ancient Greece?" He shrugged off his own questions by opening another coconut.

She shot him a look of grudging respect. "I suppose I could take another look," she said, "if I can wipe off my coconut juice hands on your shirt. Can't have that stuff getting on the parchment."

"I knew my services would come in handy sooner or later," Jayden said. Maddy wiped her hands on his shirt and then picked up the scroll again. She and Hunt repeated the careful process to unroll it and hold it steady while Maddy read it. Jayden quickly grew bored and came up with a suggestion.

"How about if while you guys are reading that Greek novel there, I'll walk around the beach and see if I can flag down a ride to get us off of this rock."

"Sounds good," Hunt said without taking his eyes off the scroll. Jayden polished off the last of his coconut before dropping it on the ground and heading off onto the beach.

Maddy gazed intently at the words on the old paper. "It seems to me like whatever it is, it's continued from something else. It literally seems to begin in the middle of a sentence," she concluded, wiping sweat from her forehead with the back of her hand.

"Can you translate any of the actual words?" Hunt asked.

"Let me give it a shot. With access to a computer it would be easy for me, but let's see what I can do from memory. I always knew that classical training all those years ago would come in handy." She gave Hunt a smile before looking back down at the parchment.

"It looks like dialogue...Someone is addressing a crowd...."

#

Daedalus paced the stern deck of the *Historica* restlessly as he looked down on the dive platform. He glanced at his watch yet again. None of his divers had returned yet. He brought the handheld radio to his mouth and was about to call his brother when he spotted thick bubbles, the kind produced by scuba divers, not far off the port rail. His divers—or at least some of them—were returning!

He ran down the steps to the dive platform, eager to hear from his underwater team first-hand. He knew that the underwater operations had been given two broad missions by his brother, one to search and recover the bodies of the thorn in his side that was Carter Hunt and his friends, the other to determine, what, if any, kind of artifacts—related to Atlantis or otherwise—lay beneath the Bimini Road capstone. He saw two heads break the water's surface. The two divers—he didn't recognize them through their masks and probably wouldn't have known their names anyway—began swimming toward the dive platform to make their exit from the water, but Daedalus waved them over to his position along the port rail. He called down to them, already disappointed that he did not see dead bodies in tow.

"Did you find their bodies?" Maybe they spotted them but they were too deep to recover, he hoped. But both men shook their heads while one answered.

"Negative, sir. We searched both the water column and the bottom of the blue hole and we saw no sign of them or their gear."

"But," the other diver interjected, pulling off his mask and grinning, "they may have gone inside the pyramid."

Daedalus' expression changed to a rare mixture of confusion, delight and concern. "Pyramid?"

The same diver—a bearded Middle-eastern man in his late twenties—continued. "Yes sir, there is a large pyramid, similar in size to some of the smaller Egyptian ones, at the bottom of this blue hole, in about 200 feet of water. It has an entrance corridor that looks like it might lead to an interior."

"You went inside?"

"We couldn't because there is a stone door that is shut, but the rest of the dive team is trying to open it right now. We came back to let you know the status."

"Something else, sir," the first diver added. "The pyramid appears to be made of gold tiles or bricks. Solid gold!"

Daedalus nodded slowly, connecting the precious metal to the lost city in his mind. "Interesting. You will go back down to help with the pyramid investigation, no?"

"Yes sir. We're going to change for fresh tanks now and dive again."

"Excellent. I suspect you will find the bodies of our friends inside that pyramid. Fitting that Carter Hunt meets his end inside a tomb. Now hurry, do not keep me waiting!"

#

Down at the base of the pyramid, the team of six Treasure, Inc. divers examined the stone slab that seemed to block what should be the entrance to inside of the pyramid. All of these men had been to the Egyptian pyramids and knew that they usually had rooms, tunnels and chambers inside. The exotic gas mixtures ands double-tanks they carried gave them much longer bottom times than Carter, Jayden and Maddy had, so they took their time to investigate the structure with bright, halogen headlamps and handheld dive lights.

The stone block was immovable, but an astute diver found a grouping of tiles to the left of the entrance that were not gold like the rest, but composed of ordinary limestone, like the Bimini Road stones above and indeed the entire blue hole itself. He called over a couple of his divers and three of them tapped on the incongruous tiles with the butts of their dive knives. Upon hearing a hollow knocking sound, they nodded to each other and proceeded to fracture the tiles with their knives, breaking them away until their was a small passage to the interior of the pyramid.

One of the divers peered inside with his flashlight, then backed out of the opening. He nodded to his fellow dive team members and pointed inside. *It's the way in!* The only problem was that whoever had built this pyramid had not envisioned scuba gear, since it was just wide enough to allow a human adult male to pass through without any sort of encumbering equipment. But the men had a solution for that.

The first diver removed his scuba tanks and handed them to one of his dive buddies, who held the gear for him while maintaining position next to the opening. Then, holding his breath after taking a deep pull from his rig, the diver swam headfirst through the smashed tile opening into the pyramid. He then turned around and pulled his scuba rig through after himself, taking a breath from it before putting it back on his person. The process was repeated for four of the other divers, with one man remaining outside.

Inside the pyramid, the group of five divers were stunned to discover what was a large air pocket. Or at least, they noted, it would be until it filled with water from the incoming stream now pouring through the group of smashed tiles. They quickly found the opposite side of the stone door and noted the same mechanism that Hunt had used to activate the airlock. They walked, not swam, for a time around the main chamber, but kept their masks on out of fear that the atmosphere inside the pyramid was somehow contaminated. Initially disenchanted to find neither artifacts or dead bodies, that feeling dissipated when they came across the open chute down into a dry tunnel.

Curiosity piqued, the team leader instructed one man to inform the diver left outside the pyramid that they would be penetrating deeper inside the structure. Then he aimed his powerful dive lights down into the chamber, saw that it was dry, and dropped down into it.

CHAPTER 26

Jayden had made it about halfway around the island when he spotted the boat. An old fishing trawler, it plowed through the waves looking like it had all the time in the world. And in fact, it would take some time to reach their little isle yet, but that was a good thing, since he still had to gain its attention. Jayden thought about Hunt's larger dive light—even though it no longer worked, it had a larger reflecting mirror behind its bulb. Maybe that could be used as a signal mirror to reflect sunlight to the passing boat?

But first he had to reach Hunt. He decided to walk directly across the little island rather than continue all the way around by the beach. He'd already found what they needed, why risk losing it by taking the long way back? With a last look back at the approaching vessel, he stepped off of the sand onto the scrubby vegetation that covered most of the island's interior. The plant life grew denser the more toward the middle of the islet he went, culminating in the profusion of vegetation and small trees that shrouded the small hillock that concealed the chute entrance by which they had entered the island.

Jayden took a path to the right of the hillock, not wanting to scale it and pass through the thicket of foliage. As he passed by he thought he heard voices, then figured it must be Hunt's voice carrying over the wind from the beach. But then he heard the rustling of branches coming from the hillock. His first thoughts were that maybe a search party had come looking for them, and he was about to call out to them, when he saw a man wearing scuba gear, including a snub-nosed spear-gun strapped to a thigh, step out of the trees. That could mean only one thing.

Treasure, Inc. found the pyramid tunnel and followed it to the island. He had no idea how they got inside the pyramid, since they had closed the stone door over the opening, but somehow they found a way. Now it was a matter of minutes before they came across Hunt and Maddy with their noses in yet another priceless treasure probably related to Atlantis. Jayden flattened himself to the tall scrub-grass before the newcomers could look in his direction. He had little doubt as to his fate should he be discovered.

As he, Hunt and Maddy had done, Daedalus' divers stood atop the highest point on the islet and surveyed the small spit of land. Could they see Hunt and Maddy from here? Jayden wasn't sure, but he was about to find out. He watched from his concealed position among a cluster of scrubby foliage as the interlopers glanced about in all directions. Apparently not, for they made no decisive moves.

As he watched, they stepped down from the hillock, six men in all, Jayden counted, registering the fact that they were badly outnumbered should this come to a fight, which looked likely given the close confines of the islet. The black market treasure hunters headed off in three different directions in pairs of two. One of the groups headed away from Jayden and Hunt, toward the beach where Jayden had sighted the fishing boat. Another pair headed almost directly toward Hunt and Maddy's location, while the third moved off on a course that would put them to within twenty feet or so of Jayden.

All of the men were relatively young and in extremely good shape, Jayden noticed, as well as being of either middle eastern, Greek or Spanish descent. Each of them carried the same model of spear gun, as well as having a dive knife strapped to a calf. Jayden passed a hand over his own knife to make sure it was still there, but didn't see how a single knife would be of any help against two foes with spear guns. The element of surprise would be his strongest weapon. That, or simply staying hidden, but with

Hunt and Maddy unaware as to this new development, he didn't see how that could last long.

For now he remained frozen against the ground, holding his breath so as not to disturb the grass around him and give away his presence. The Treasure, Inc. hunters talked in low tones, and Jayden thought he caught a few words of Greek, but couldn't be sure. He was glad the men were in conversation, though, since it meant they weren't fully focused on their surroundings, compromising their situational awareness.

The pair of treasure seekers walked past Jayden, not fifteen feet away, continuing on toward the water. Jayden dared to glance left, looking for the other pairs. He spotted one, the two men moving steadily toward the beach where they would find Hunt and Maddy with their noses in an ancient scroll. Craning his neck awkwardly to look back in the other direction, Jayden could not find the other team. He waited silently in his prone, hidden position for another two minutes, racking his brain to come up with the best course of action.

If possible, he decided, it would be best to reach Hunt and Maddy before any of his adversaries, and without being detected. But how to do that? The most direct route would take him past the pair of foes already heading that way, so that was out. To his right was where the other pair had gone, so he opted to move to the hillock and then straight across the islet to the coast, where he could then follow the beach around to Hunt's position.

He low-crawled through the scrub until he reached an area where there was simply not enough vegetative cover to conceal him. He would have to do a mad dash to the thick cover of the hillock. Rising to a kneeling position, he pushed off the ground and sprinted to the copse of scraggly little trees. He scrambled up to the vertical chute exit, slowing as he neared the apex. What if they left a lookout posted? He heard no signs of human presence, though, and so he broke through the last layer of foliage into the chute area.

Here there was dive gear on the ground, where the Treasure, Inc. hunters had shed some of their equipment—masks, weight belts...no tanks, though, he laughed to himself, since those were not able to carried up that last vertical section. He couldn't resist peering down into the chute, where he saw a couple of dive tanks at the bottom, but that was it.

Jayden crept to the opposite edge of the hillock and stealthily moved through the foliage there until he could see out across the other side of the islet. The other team was in the distance now, moving fast toward the beach Hunt occupied!

Got to go!

Jayden's military training allowed him not to let the sense of urgency compromise his need for stealth. He proceeded slowly yet deliberately to glance behind him, checking the position of the other team. He found them, moving toward the beach on that end of the island, where the boat....the boat!

It was moving toward Hunt's beach now, and would be there soon. A plan coalesced in Jayden's mind as he slipped through the foliage toward the quarter of the island that was unoccupied. He didn't have time to entertain the details of it, only that he had some inkling of what he would do when he got there. He ran faster and louder than he knew he should, but figured he had that luxury given that the Treasure, Inc. goons had gone in completely different directions than him. His feet pounded across the low-lying island and soon he could see the shore, the blue, sun-dappled ocean beyond. He swiveled his head left and right as he ran, but saw no one, so he kept on running, kept on striking his feet against the earth until it turned soft with the sand spraying up around his wetsuit boots.

He dropped to his knees and breathed deeply, taking in great lungful's of air until he wasn't about to pass out. The he rose and, after looking left and seeing no one, he ran to the right. Running on the sand was hard, but quiet as well as being below the line of sight for most of the island. He flashed back on his naval training, of being made to jog through the sand until some of his fellow cadets were vomiting, and smiled at the memories. *You can do it,* he told himself, *this isn't even as bad as that...*

Then he was rounding the island's curvature as the beach continued around toward the side Hunt and Maddy occupied. Would he reach them before Daedalus' thugs? The thought tortured his oxygen-starved mind as he sprinted down the sandy strip. He leapt over a heap of driftwood and sidestepped a pile of dried seaweed before continuing on his frenetic way.

Up ahead he recognized a palm tree that leaned way out over the beach he saw earlier. Hunt and Maddy were only a few yards inland from that point on the beach. But as he came closer to the tree, his heart sank as two dark-dressed figures came into view on the opposite side of the tree. The pair of armed scouts walked at a normal pace, not hurrying but not leisurely, either. And their heads were on a swivel, Jayden could see. It was a matter of minutes until they sighted Hunt and Maddy.

Jayden acted decisively, ducking off of the beach into a stand of high nettle grass that offered minimal concealment, but which was better than nothing. He elbow-crawled through that until he was far enough away from the beach that he could stand without being seen. Then he ran toward Hunt and Maddy's position.

He found them in the same spot in which he'd last seen them, still hunched over the ancient scroll, in deep discussion about its finer particulars. Jayden scuffed a foot on the ground to alert them to his presence, which he thought would be not as loud a way to do it compared to using his voice, which might carry on the wind to the beach.

Jayden was pleased to see Hunt reach for his knife before looking up to see the source of the noise. When he did see Jayden, he started to relax but Jayden knelt beside him and whispered, "Keep your knife ready. Two tangos coming up the beach right over there. Four more in two pairs on different parts of the island." He pointed in two different directions to indicate the last known positions of the other two sub-teams.

Maddy looked like a deer caught on the road in headlights. Jayden pointed to the scroll. "Put it away, hurry! If they see it, they'll take it."

She rolled it back up while muttering something about improper handling procedures, and then stuffed it back into the hexagonal door chamber. Jayden spotted one of his coconuts on the ground and picked it up, testing its weight in his hand.

And then they heard the crunch of foliage under booted feet as Daedalus' deadly explorers walked up from the beach. Jayden didn't know if they had somehow given their presence away or if it was simply bad luck, but either way, there was no time to think about it. One of the men went rigid as he made eye contact with the three people a few yards away. His associate was quicker to act, raising his snub-nosed spear gun and pointing it right at Hunt.

Jayden hurled the coconut at the man wielding the spear gun. He raised the shaft of the spear to deflect the organic projectile, but missed. The green nut smashed into his Adam's apple, causing him to stagger back. Meanwhile, the other gunman drew his weapon while Hunt raced for the staggering man.

Jayden bent down to scoop up another coconut but this gunman was able to get off a shot. The spear tip glanced off the very coconut Jayden had his hand on, the tip ricocheting up into his face, drawing blood from his cheek. He grabbed the spear with two hands and yanked on it, knowing it was connected to the gun with monofilament line that spooled from a mounted reel. The shooter holding the gun was too slow to let go and was pulled forward, stumbling, until he tripped and fell onto Jayden in a grappling heap.

While that man and Jayden rolled on the ground fighting, Hunt caught up with the other assailant, landing a right hook to his jaw. The man reeled back, stumbling but somehow keeping his balance. Hunt took the opportunity to launch a high kick with his right leg at his opponent's chest, and down the foe went, landing hard on his back on the ground. If it weren't for the sandy soil, it would have been much worse of an impact. As it was, the man was not getting up anytime soon.

Jayden rolled off of the fighter he had been grappling with on the ground. Both combatants were preparing for Round Two when suddenly Maddy stepped forward holding the hexagonal stone. She held it above her head as if she was about to smash the man's skull in with it, but she took no action. She didn't need to. The treasure hunter put his hands in front of his face to ward off the blow, and that was enough for Jayden to make his move. The Asian-American pinned his foe's arms behind his head. When the opponent swung his legs up, he grabbed one of the ankles and twisted it until he heard it snap.

Out of his peripheral vision he saw Hunt pointing. He was saying something, too, but the downed fighter's screams of anguish drowned out Hunt's words. But Maddy saw something happening and came over to tug on Jayden's sleeve. "Got to move, come on!"

"What's up?" Jayden shot to his feet. Maddy pointed to Hunt, who in turn pointed across the beach and out to sea, where the old fishing boat was plowing into view.

"We've got to get their attention!" Hunt shouted, before moving out onto the sand. Jayden and Maddy, who still carried the hexagon, followed suit, but not before Jayden collected the spear guns and dive knives of both defeated foes. He gave Maddy one of the knives, kept one for himself to strap to his other leg, and then caught up with Hunt on the beach.

"Present for ya." He handed him one of the spear guns.

"No time to catch dinner," Hunt joked, eyes on the fishing boat coming their way.

"It's not for dinner, it's to fight off those guys." He pointed to their right, where two more Treasure, Inc. soldiers came running toward them down the beach.

"Great." Hunt checked the spear gun to make sure it was cocked and loaded, then stood facing the oncoming attackers. Jayden looked out to sea, jumping up and down and waving his arms at the boat while Maddy did the same. "They're slowing down!"

Hunt planted his feet in the sand and fired off the spear gun at the onrushing assailants, who dove out of the way, flattening themselves on the beach to avoid the metal-tipped projectile.

"Maddy, I'll carry the stone. We have to swim, let's go!"

"Swim?" She stood there looking confused until Hunt grabbed the hexagonal scroll chamber from her and spun her around until she faced the water. "See that boat? That's our ticket out of here. Come on."

She hesitated a moment longer, but when she looked over to see the two newcomers pushing up to their feet, she mobilized along with Hunt and Jayden. The three of them ran into the water with long, splashy strides, stealth no longer a factor at play. The sea was calm and so waves were not a factor to contend with as they waded out into deeper water, Jayden in the lead because Hunt was burdened with the hex chamber that was keeping the scroll dry.

The fishing boat slowed as its operator clearly saw the three people rushing out toward it in the water. Hunt, Jayden and Maddy launched themselves horizontally into the sea and began to swim toward the boat. Hunt held the hexagon which meant he was only able to swim one-handed, but he kicked furiously to make up for it and made progress toward what he hoped would be their ride away from here.

Some kind of small shark splashed out a few feet in front of Hunt, no doubt as startled as he was by the sudden activity, but he paid it no mind and kept on, and the fish disappeared from sight. Jayden was out in front, unencumbered by the artifact, while Maddy was a little behind Jayden.

Hunt couldn't resist looking back toward the beach, where he saw the two thugs stopping on the beach where their quarry had entered the water. He managed a smile as he continued to kick toward the boat, for the men were out of spear gun range. They started running into the water, though, and that's when Hunt knew this was serious. These mercenaries would stop at nothing. They were diving into the water now, swimming fast, no doubt hoping to get into range with their spears.

The fishing vessel, its metal hull streaked with rust, idled just beyond a reef line, where the bottom dropped off to deeper water. Hunt hoped it would stick around; commercial fishermen were sort of like truck drivers of the sea—they were known to help fellow boaters in need—but this was an odd situation indeed, and if whoever was on board saw the violent divers threatening with spear guns, they might change their mind about sticking around to help.

Hunt called on every ounce of his strength to propel himself toward the old boat while lugging the cumbersome artifact. Jayden and Maddy plowed on ahead of him, while behind, the Treasure, Inc. predators pursued their prey.

Jayden reached the boat first. A black man of Caribbean descent leaned over the rail and called out: "Need help? Stranded here?" He pointed to the sandy islet.

"Yes!" Jayden reached the boat and the fisherman lowered a rope ladder over the side. Jayden climbed the side and shook the man's hand, thanking him. Then he helped Maddy aboard. When Hunt got to the boat he grabbed the hexagon from him and then handed it to Maddy for safekeeping.

"Crab trap?" the fisherman asked, pointing to the artifact.

"No, we're not sure what it is, just looks interesting."

"All kind of things wash up here!" the captain said with a laugh.

"If you could just take us over there..." Hunt pointed toward the main Bimini Road where he had anchored their seaplane, we would appreciate it very much."

The boat captain pointed to the two Treasure, Inc. swimmers, now about halfway to the boat. "As soon as your friends get here, yes? Wouldn't want to forget them, or is one of them your ex-husband?" He grinned at Maddy.

"Actually, they're not our friends," Hunt explained. "They're bad people, trying to hurt us with their spear guns."

The fisherman scowled and looked over at the men to see a glint of sunlight off of one of the spear shafts. "Why?"

Hunt took a deep breath. "Look, there's no time to explain it right now. But I don't want to cause any trouble for you, and I'm afraid if we stay here, those men will attack you."

The fisherman shrugged, not looking too concerned. "You want to leave them here and go that way?"

"Yes sir, right away, before they get here" Hunt said.

The fisherman made eye contact with Hunt. "You pay me?"

Hunt nodded. "Absolutely." Then he patted his wetsuit-clad legs. "I don't have any cash on me, though, but..."

"You will send it? I have PayPal."

Hunt smiled and nodded.

Without a word, the fisherman moved to the helm and put his boat into gear.

CHAPTER 27

"It's still there!" Jayden pointed to their seaplane, floating at anchor where they'd left it. Daedalus' massive yacht lay sedately at anchor about a hundred yards away.

"Not for long, by the looks of things," Hunt said. He pointed to a small boat tied up to the plane. One man was affixing an object to the side of it.

"Looks like they're preparing to blow it!" Jayden said.

"We need to scare them off." Hunt looked to the boat captain. "Do you have any guns aboard?"

The captain gave Hunt a serious stare, but nodded slowly. "If you want, I'll fire a warning shot for an additional hundred dollars. But if they shoot back, we're leaving."

"How about you drive the boat, and I shoot?" Hunt asked.

But the captain shook his head. "The only one using my gun is me. Sorry, but you've got a whole lot of trouble around you, buddy. My gun, my rules."

"Fair enough," Hunt said. "We just want to hop in our plane and get out of here. You get us a little closer to the plane, provide us with a little distraction, and we'll do the rest."

"Including the money transfer? I am trusting you."

"Deal." Hunt shook the fisherman's hand on it, and the captain then retreated into the boat's small wheelhouse, emerging a few seconds later with a rifle, which he cocked. "You get one pass on this," he reminded them. "I drive by once, you do what you do, and that's it, I'm out."

"Understood." Hunt heard the men shout something by the plane and for a second he thought they had been outed and were about to be under attack. But whatever it was had to do with their own activities, for neither of Daedalus' operatives on the small boat looked away from the seaplane.

The captain got behind the wheel. Hunt stepped over and offered a hand. "What's your name, anyway? I'm Carter Hunt—those are my friends Jayden Takada and Madison Chambers."

The captain leaned his rifle against the control panel. "Call me Darcy. Here we go. Remember, she's not all that fast but she can go for a long time." He grinned broadly and throttled up the old boat's diesel engine. "Almost forgot." He reached out and opened a side window in the cockpit, and then picked up the rifle and stuck the barrel through it. "All better now!"

Hunt nodded with a mischievous twinkle in his eye. "Be safe, Darcy. And thanks again!" Then he turned and stepped out on deck, where Jayden and Maddy hunkered down while peering over the rail. He ducked down also, thinking they might be about to be fired upon, but Jayden filled him in.

"We saw them about to turn around so we hid. I'm sure they see the boat, but they haven't seen us yet, I'm pretty sure."

"Pretty sure?" Hunt clarified.

The *ping* of a bullet ricocheted off Darcy's wheelhouse. "Actually I'm not very sure," Jayden added.

Suddenly the fishing boat accelerated, not as fast as a speedboat would, but fast enough to cause all three of them to put their hands on the deck to keep their balance.

"Be ready to jump!" Hunt yelled.

"What about this? I can't jump with it!" Maddy clutched the hexagon.

Hunt glanced at it quickly. "Take the scroll out and leave the hexagon. It served its purpose. Just try not to get it wet. Wait hold on…" Hunt crawled into the cabin. He was gone for a minute during which the boat picked up additional speed. Then he returned with a gallon-size Ziploc bag. "Stick it in here."

"Maddy gave him a wide smile, removed the scroll from the hexagon and sealed it inside the plastic bag.

And then they heard the shot. Hunt looked left and saw the wisp of smoke escape the rifle barrel protruding from Darcy's window. He didn't know exactly what he was expecting, but to his mind it came too early. Now the Treasure, Inc. saboteurs on the small boat by the seaplane trained their full attention on the old fishing scow. Hunt saw one of them raise a handheld radio to his mouth and gesture excitedly toward Darcy's vessel.

Then the outboard motor of the small inflatable boat Daedalus' operatives used whined to life and the tender vessel sped away from the plane toward the fishing boat. Hunt didn't see them raise any weapons yet, but they had surely heard Darcy's shot and they didn't seem worried. Darcy angled his boat toward the seaplane, straight at it.

"Get ready!" Hunt warned. He gripped Maddy's shoulder. "You have the scroll?"

"It's good!" She patted her chest, where she had stuffed the plastic bag down her wetsuit top.

"Let's go. Jump!" Hunt stood up as he felt the big vessel began to turn. He saw the rental plane bobbing in the water. It looked operational, but he could only hope, since he didn't know what they had done to it. He was glad he'd taken the keys with him and put them in the little wetsuit pocket up by his neck, an old surfing habit from when he'd park his car on the Pacific Coast Highway in Southern California and then catch waves for hours out in the ocean.

Jayden went overboard first. Maddy hesitated on the rail, staring down at the fast-moving water below the boat. Hunt grabbed her and took her over the side with him. They were sitting ducks on the rail, easy targets for a shooter. In the water they would be slower, but also harder to see.

Now unencumbered by the heavy hexagon, Hunt was able to swim fast. He left Maddy behind since he knew she could swim, and that Jayden could look after her if need be. But he needed to reach the cockpit and start up the plane. It had a certain warmup period and was not like a car where it could be immediately driven off. He swam a fast, efficient, fast crawl stroke that had once been the envy of his high school swim team. He even passed Jayden on the way to the plane, all the while listening to the sounds of outboard motors carrying underwater—the low rumble of the fishing boat versus the high-pitched, waspy drone of the Treasure, Inc. inflatable boat.

He had to give Darcy credit—his erratic boat driving was leading the Treasure, Inc. boatmen away from the plane—as well as Hunt, Jayden and Maddy. There was now nothing but a few feet of open water between them and the aircraft. Hunt reached the plane and crawled up onto a pontoon. He flung the pilot-side door open and climbed into the cockpit dripping wet. He fumbled for the key in his wetsuit, pulled it out and dropped it, but it landed on the pontoon.

Hunt muttered a silent prayer that the key hadn't fallen into the water, and quickly but carefully climbed back out of the plane and snatched up the key. Jayden was almost to the plane now, not even looking to see what Hunt was doing, just kicking like mad. Hunt pulled himself back into the plane and jammed the key into the ignition. He turned it and the motor cranked to life. He then went through the hastiest pre-flight check of his life, confirming the bare minimum he knew was needed to get the plane aloft. Then he began to rev the engine, giving it the RPMs it would need to take off.

Jayden reached the plane next. Hunt looked out his window to see where Maddy was and pleased to see her not far behind Jayden at all. Then beyond her, he saw Darcy's fishing boat heading away from the scene. His job was done. He had done all anyone could ask for, Hunt thought.

But now the Treasure, Inc. criminals were speeding back toward the plane in their inflatable boat, waves of spray pushing out from under the sides as it bounced over the waves. But the real adrenaline struck when Hunt looked behind them, for there, a helicopter was lifting off from the deck of Daedalus' mega-yacht. Hunt leaned out leaned out the window.

"Gotta go, come on. Hang onto the pontoon, they've got a chopper coming for us."

Jayden hauled himself up onto the pontoon as Hunt had done, and while Hunt put the plane into slow forward motion. Jayden encouraged Maddy to swim the remaining distance faster, and then assisted her up onto the pontoon.

The first bullet ricocheted off of one of the seaplane's metal struts as soon as Jayden opened the rear door. "You go first, go ahead." He pulled Maddy toward the door and shoved her inside to the plane's backseat. Jayden wished he had another coconut; the only weapon he had at his disposal was the dive knife on his calf.

"Hunt, we need weapons, what do you got besides a knife?"

The plane was moving fast now, bounding along the waves, and Jayden almost fell off after they went over the inflatable boat's wake. The little boat zipped in front of them and swept into an arcing turn that was no doubt designed to give its occupants the best possible shooting angle. Hunt tried veering slightly to the right—he couldn't turn too sharply without losing all of the plane's momentum needed for takeoff—but the nimble boat tracked them easily.

Hunt saw a muzzle flash and then a crack appeared in the plane's windshield, fortunately on the passenger-side. The bullet glanced off, but Hunt knew their luck wouldn't hold out for long. He reached into a storage compartment and pulled out a package.

"Jayden—here, take this!" He held the object out the window and felt Jayden's hand grab it from his.

"Flare gun, nice! Let's light this candle!"

"Hurry up about it, we're taking hits!"

While Hunt steered the plane and Maddy laid low in the back, Jayden balanced on the pontoon while trying to load the flare gun. The first flare bounced out of his hand and into the water as he tried to force it into the gun when the plane launched off of a swell and smacked back down into the water. He looked at the bag—there were four of them. He got the second one loaded and then took aim with the gun at the pesky inflatable boat as it zoomed past them, no doubt intending to circle back around for another strafing pass. Then a line of bullets stitched across the water, kicking up little fountains of spray until Jayden heard the ping of lead on aluminum and holes appeared in the pontoon that was supporting him.

He aimed the flare at the small boat and pulled the trigger. He heard the familiar whooshing sound as the incendiary device lit and was then launched out of the device. A red streak cut the air until it landed in the ocean a couple of feet behind the boat's motor.

Missed!

He steadied himself again on one of the pontoon-struts and repeated the loading process with another flare. But this time Hunt changed the plane's course erratically, nearly throwing Jayden from the pontoon and dumping the new flare into the water in the process.

One flare left!

Jayden felt the tingle of fear grip his body and pushed it away by concentrating on the task at hand. He eyed the boat, which was now circling around behind them as he had expected. He glanced to the right, saw no large waves that might bounce him around, and went ahead with loading his last remaining flare. He slid the flare into the chamber and locked it.

He couldn't take aim yet because the boat was now on the other side of the plane. He could see it if he crouched down low and put his head sideways to look beneath the plane, while seawater splashed his face. But he had no clear shot.

Inside the plane, Hunt knew Jayden hadn't scored a hit yet with the flares, and that he was now on the wrong side of the aircraft to take a shot. He looked back and to his right to check the boat's position, but he couldn't help but notice Maddy hunched down on the floor of the backseat. She had the scroll out, unrolled, staring at it while moving her lips as though reading aloud.

"Maddy, what are you doing?"

She looked up as if in a daze. "Reading the scroll. I had an idea and wanted to see if it makes sense..." She looked back down at her work, and Hunt decided to let her be. Everyone had different ways of coping with stress, he knew from experience after serving in the Navy in the middle east.

He turned his attention back to driving a plane. Seaplanes were not as maneuverable as boats when on the water; they were made mostly to go in a straight like to land and take-off, not to turn on a dime or have rapid acceleration. But he wanted to put Jayden on the same side as the boat to give him a shot. He banked the aircraft—watercraft at the moment—to the left as sharply s he dared, creating a wall of spray that washed over the plane.

That should give Jayden something to work with. But no sooner had he completed the thought than a new sound registered. Deeper, more powerful-sounding. And then Hunt flashed on the helicopter he'd seen taking off from Daedalus' mega-yacht. It was getting closer. He wondered what its purpose was—he doubted it could be an actual gunship, but he supposed people could shoot out of it with regular guns. Or simply drop men onto the small boat and plane to fight, he thought grimly.

He heard the whoosh of one of Jayden's flares, and then caught sight of a flaming inflatable boat fish-tailing across the plane's nose, totally out of control.

Hit!

Hunt didn't allow the flare-up of hope in his chest to distract him from minding the new and more formidable incoming threat, the helicopter. Where was it now? He twisted around in the pilot's seat to see its blue undercarriage swooping in low over the water, on Jayden's side.

Damn! They were going to catch them. Hunt nudged the throttle up, more to change their speed than to think he could outrun the helo. But then the seaplane skipped over a swell and went airborne, and Hunt remembered that besides trying not to be shot, he was also flying a plane.

The airplane returned to the water like a skipped stone, but this was to be expected. Hunt knew he just needed to control the "bounce" and make sure he didn't dig a wingtip into the water, which would send them cartwheeling. The erratic motion also served to give the helicopter pilot pause, since the chopper dropped back a little bit out of fear of colliding, but it was enough to let Hunt concentrate.

Until Jayden climbed back into the plane, that is. "Outta flares! Any more?"

Hunt shook his head without turning around. "Negative. Shut the door, we're going airborne."

Jayden pulled the door shut. "The 'copter has a gunner standing on the skids. I flipped him the bird but that didn't seem to convince them to leave us alone."

"If they only knew you," Hunt called back.

Jayden looked over at Maddy, who was still on the floor. "Is she okay?" he asked Hunt.

"Yeah, she's reading the scroll. Hold on!" The plane ramped off a wave and took to the sky for the first time, actually flying. It dipped back toward the water but this time stayed above the ocean. Hunt grinned broadly. They were flying.

As Hunt wrestled with the controls, Jayden gazed down from the window. "The helicopter is not stopping to pick up their guys who jumped off the burning boat."

"What a surprise," Hunt called back. "Daedalus probably told them they're fired if they stop chasing us."

"Planes are faster than helicopters, and we have longer range, too. Not worried about them, unless they start shoot—"

They heard the ping off a bullet bouncing somewhere off the plane's metal. "If this thing's got more speed to give, Carter, now's the time," Jayden said.

"Speed is increasing. Hang tight for a little evasive maneuvering." Hunt suddenly banked left, and then right again before resuming an upward altitude-gaining trajectory.

Jayden looked back at the helo, nodding. "Threw them off a bit. Keep it up."

Hunt repeated his actions on the controls, and the 'copter dropped back a little further. "We're pulling away from them now. Only one question..." He interrupted himself to pull back on the stick and tweak the rudder.

"What's that?" Jayden asked.

"Where to?"

Jayden thought about it for a few seconds. "Daedalus probably looked up where we rented it from by now, so going back there is out."

"Agreed. So where do we go? Florida?"

"No!" They were surprised to hear Maddy's voice. Jayden looked over at her. She was staring at the unrolled manuscript.

"Why not?"

Maddy looked up from the old writing. "I know where we should go! Head due south."

CHAPTER 28

"You sure this is the right way?" Jayden shot a nervous glance at the fuel gauge from his seat in the back. Hunt's reply was swift.

"Pretty sure."

"Pretty sure? Are—" Jayden looked like he was about to jump up out of the aircraft before it dropped from the sky.

"Kidding, relax. We're on track. We may have to do a water landing, but it should be within sight of land."

"Should be, great," Jayden intoned sarcastically. Looking down, he saw only the deep blue of open ocean, topped with whitecaps. He looked over to Maddy, who had been looking out the window but quickly buried her nose once again in the mysterious manuscript.

"And how do you know, again, that Cuba is the right place to go?" Jayden inquired.

Maddy answered without looking up from the musty old paper. "*My God...*"

Jayden stared at her but she did not elaborate. "My God, what?"

"I...I do believe I hold in my hands the lost pages of Plato's *Critias*."

"I've heard of Plato," Jayden said with a shrug. Maddy looked up at him, eyes wide with wonder.

"The two documents that contain everything we know about Plato's

197

Atlantis story—the *Timaeus* and the *Critias*!"

"Of course, how could I have forgotten," Jayden replied.

Maddy frowned at him and yelled to Hunt in the front seat. "Do you know what we've got here, Carter?"

"Yeah, about an eighth of a tank of fuel left."

"That's not what I meant. I mean that we are now in possession of what will surely be one of the most sought-after documents in the world once it's authenticated."

"Great," Jayden droned from the co-pilot's seat, "another reason for Treasure, Inc. to come after us."

She stared at him open-mouthed. "You don't understand." She shook her hands ever so slightly, emphasizing the paper. "This paper is about 2,000 years old—containing words written by *Plato*—that I believe lead to an actual location of Atlantis."

"Now would be a good time for that actual location," Hunt called from the pilot's seat. "Because I see land."

Jayden and Maddy both looked out their respective windows. A dark mountainous mass loomed in the distance, part of it obscured by clouds.

"Is that Cuba?" Maddy asked, voice tinged with tension.

Jayden made like he was sniffing the air. "I can smell the cigars from here."

"Cuba's a huge island—need to know which part of it we should focus on," Hunt said.

Maddy squinted down at the ancient manuscript again, burying her nose in it for almost a minute before replying. "Northwest corner. Sorry, that's as specific as I can be right now."

"It'll have to be a boots-on-the-ground thing from there, is that it?" Jayden asked.

Hunt answered. "That's literally it, because our boots are going to be on the ground all right, when this bird runs out of gas." Hunt consulted his gauges, GPS and compass before making a course correction, then eased back a little in the seat. "I set us on a course that should take us to *Bahia Honda*, a circular natural cove that's about fifty miles west of Havana."

Maddy looked up from the document again. "Did you say circular?"

Hunt called back from the cockpit. "It's roughly circular, yes. Small inlet leading to a big circular bay surrounded by mangrove forest, probably, but we'll see. Hopefully, anyway," he finished, tapping the fuel gauge with his pointer finger.

"Oh, my…" Maddy went back to the manuscript while Jayden rolled his eyes.

"This is turning out to be one heckuva working vacation, I gotta say."

"It's all coming together now. In the *Critias*, a speaker is addressing a crowd, in an amphitheater, which is of course, a circular arrangement. But then again, the entire city layout of Atlantis was supposedly circular, with canals connecting the concentric rings…"

"But there must be thousands of circular bays around the Caribbean, or south of the Bahamas, anyway. What's so special about Bahia Honda?"

"According to the lost pages of the *Critias*—" Maddy began, but she broke off at the sound of an alarm emanating from the plane's dashboard.

"I hope that means the beverage cart service is ready," Jayden said, "because I'm thirsty."

Hunt turned around to answer. "Unfortunately, the plane's thirsty, too. For fuel. That's the low fuel alarm signifying that we're on our last reserves."

Jayden looked out the window ahead of them, where Cuba still looked like an indistinct land mass far away. "Reminds me of that time over the Persian Gulf, with that radio operator guy—remember him?"

"Rather forget him," Hunt called back. "But it worked out okay."

"Yeah, well let's hope this works out okay, too. How close do you think we'll get before we need to make a water landing?"

"The closer the better, that's all I know. Get ready to bail out. Have all the important stuff ready to take with you." Hunt turned back around and dedicated himself fully to flying the plane.

Jayden turned around to look at Maddy. "That means you, too, and that magic scroll of yours."

She looked up from the missing *Critias* pages and started to roll them back up. "Right. I think reading it was taking my mind off the stress of being shot at and now possibly running out of gas."

Suddenly the plane's motor's began to cough and sputter. "Not possibly," Hunt shouted. "Definitely. We're out of gas."

Jayden looked out his window. "Hey Carter, I see a little barrier island we might be able to make."

Hunt stared out of his window from the cockpit, eyeing the flat strip of sandy land dotted with a green band. Then he gauged the distance from the island to the Cuban mainland, and shook his head.

"That'll have to do. I'm going to set her down." Hunt put the plane into a controlled dive in preparation for a water landing. Just as the plane levelled out over the water's surface, the engine sputtered once more and then died, casting a pall of silence over the group as they hurtled through the salty air in a non-functional aircraft. The air was not still, and frequent gusts required Hunt to react swiftly with the plane's rudder to keep it level, lest they turn over and land upside-down in the ocean.

"I'll try to land us as near the island as I can, but no guarantees," Hunt shouted. As Jayden gazed out the window, with no other craft in sight, no populated land of any sort in sight, it dawned on him that they had gone out of the frying pan and into the fire, from one dangerous situation to another—stranded on a Cuban barrier island—and that's if they managed to stick the landing.

Jayden sat back in his seat and put the seatbelt on, encouraging Maddy to do the same. He knew from experience that even a good seaplane landing could be quite bumpy, and given their lack of engine power, this was not going to be a good one. Maddy stowed the scroll and braced for a hard landing.

In the pilot's seat, Hunt's eyes scanned the gauges, his brow furrowed in concentration, sweat beading on his forehead. He white-knuckled the steering wheel, pulling back on the stick to bring the nose up a little as the beleaguered aircraft approached the sea surface.

"Brace, brace!" he shouted as the small seaplane bashed nose-first into the ocean. Water washed over the windshield and Hunt was shocked to see a school of fish dart away from the plane in surprise, before it floated back to the surface and rays of sunlight greeted his wide-open eyes. The aircraft rocked back and forth, nose to tail, before settling down into a sloshy floating pattern.

"Everybody okay?" Hunt shouted.

He was glad to hear Maddy's voice first. "I'm fine."

"The expression is, 'Any landing you can *walk* away from, Carter, not swim away from. But we all seem to be in one piece, so I'll give you the benefit of the doubt on this one."

"Thanks." Hunt cranked the plane's controls, turning it to the left toward the barrier island, wishing to coax every ounce of remaining momentum from the plane's landing to their advantage. After a couple of minutes it was clear that, while it wasn't sinking, the plane was no longer drifting toward the island. In fact, it was being carried slowly away from it, back out to the open waters of the Florida Straits which they had just crossed over.

Hunt let go of the controls. "We're going to have to get wet, people. Grab the essentials and let's go." He opened his cockpit door and lamented the fact that he no longer had the anchor he'd used in Bimini, thanks to Daedalus' vandals and their hasty departure. The plane would drift away once they left it. But as he glanced over at the island—a swimmable distance away—he was grateful that at least they would be alive.

Hunt ducked back inside the plane and loaded his backpack with the plane's remaining useful safety equipment—a small tool kit, a first aid kit. "Time to go." He glanced back at Jayden, who had moved into the back with Maddy to prepare their bags. Jayden opened the rear door.

Hunt stepped outside onto the plane's pontoon, staring down into the sea and trying to gauge the water depth. He guessed it was about seven or eight feet, mostly sandy bottom. Too deep to stand, but he knew it would get shallower as they approached the island, which he judged to be maybe an eighth of a mile away. He could tell by the drift of the airplane that a current was running through the area, though, taking them away from the island, so they'd have to work against that.

Hunt opted to slip quietly into the water from the pontoon rather than make a big splash that might attract sharks. He encouraged Jayden and Maddy to do the same. He treaded water while Jayden and then Maddy slipped into the sea alongside him. They began to swim toward the low-lying land, kicking hard against a current that felt like a freight train coming in the opposite direction. They kept at it, though, with some choice curses from Jayden and some encouraging words from Hunt, and some time later Hunt stopped swimming and put his feet straight down.

He was rewarded with the feel of soft sand beneath his wetsuit boots, the water about shoulder high on his six-foot frame. A large shadow materialized from the sand below and Hunt raised his arms in a defensive posture, but he quickly saw that it was only a large stingray, wings flapping furiously as it moved to escape the intruder who had disturbed it as it lay beneath the sand. He watched it disappear into the distance and then turned around, waving to Jayden and Maddy.

"I can stand. We're almost there." He waited for Maddy to get close and then reached out and pulled her to him, holding her while she got her footing on the sandy bottom. Jayden caught up with them next, appearing not the least bit winded from the strenuous swim. He nodded to the low-lying isle that was now not so far away.

"Looks a lot like the one we came up on in the Bahamas."

Hunt nodded as he took in the scrubby vegetation atop a low-lying sand hillock. "Let's check it out. Shuffle your feet so you don't step on a stingray."

"I call it the 'stingray shuffle', kind of like a moonwalk." Jayden broke out into song as he slid his feet across the sand bottom. "Do the stingray shuffle, every day, the stingray shuffle, look out for those rays!"

"I think I'd rather be stung by a ray than be subjected to your singing," Hunt mocked.

The waterlogged trio shuffled across the sandy bottom that sloped gradually up toward the flat island. The tropical sun warmed them, but also burned their faces as it reflected off the water's surface. Hunt was grateful for the aviator sunglasses he still wore. As they neared the island's fringing beach, the water became shallower; they were waist-high, able to walk faster, and then trudging through only calf deep water until they reached the beach and flopped down on the dry sand, exhausted.

"So this is Cuba," Jayden said at length, after they had rested.

"Where's your cigars?" Maddy wondered.

"We need to figure out how to get to the Cuban mainland," Hunt said, rising to his feet. He turned around 360 degrees and stopped when facing the Cuban mainland. "It's got to be two, maybe three miles away," he estimated, the dejection evident in his voice.

"I can't swim that far," Maddy said bluntly.

"We'll figure something out," Hunt said. But what? As he continued to look around, he saw no signs of human activity whatsoever—no boats, planes, no noise from the mainland—nothing. Jayden got to his feet and went to explore what little there was to see of the rest of the islet, while Maddy took out the *Critias* scroll.

"I hate to expose it to the elements here," she said, unrolling the ancient parchment, "but something's been nagging at me."

Hunt watched her while she buried her nose in the lost manuscript once again. "Tell me more about what led you to think Cuba is a possible location for Atlantis? I've heard unfounded reports of an underwater city somewhere along Cuba's coast, but it wasn't connected to Atlantis as far as I know."

"Don't be too sure," Maddy said cryptically, still staring at the pages. She reached into her pack and took from it her digital camera. "I snapped a couple of pics right before we began our descent, while we were still high up." She turned the device on. She nodded on seeing the screen fill with an aerial image. "Yeah, you can see the Cuban mainland coast as well as the barrier islands...including this one." She held up the camera so that Hunt could see the photo.

He stared at it for a minute before nodding slowly. "Okay, it shows the surrounding area, the islands. The bird's eye view could help us plan our way out of here, is that the point?"

Maddy shook her head. "No. Try to imagine the scene without any water, as if it was one of those topographic maps showing valleys and mountains."

Hunt eyeballed the photo while mentally picturing it as she suggested. The Cuban mainland formed one side of a ring, while the barrier islands, including the one they were currently stranded on, formed the opposite side of the ring. In between were smaller, isolated islands and islets. Hunt had seen imagery with the oceans' water removed to show the bottom contours and seamounts, and knew that many islands were really just the tips of huge undersea mountains.

"Okay, I can picture it. But I still don't get your point. How does it help us?"

"What if, tens of thousands of years ago—say eleven thousand-- the sea level wasn't as high as it was now?"

Hunt shrugged. "I suppose there would have been more land back then, which today is submerged under the ocean."

Maddy beamed. "Right. But look at the shape that land—this land," she said, waving an arm at the sea beyond their little sand islet—"would have taken." She pointed back to the image on the camera's display, tracing the contours of the islands with a finger. "Imagine just a little more land on each of these islands—picture these islets in the middle here as the tips of large mountains, with some water still at the bottom....what shapes would it take on?"

Hunt felt the realization wash over him like the waves lapping at the beach a few feet away. He gazed at the tiny screen in amazement, staring at it until it made sense to his eyes like one of those blurry posters that slowly materialized into a recognizable shape after squinting at it long enough.

"I see it now," he said, his voice low and even. "It would form a series of concentric rings, wouldn't it?"

CHAPTER 29

Aboard the Historica

Daedalus shot his brother a hard stare. "You mean to tell me that you've found no trace of them whatsoever—they've vanished?"

Phillipo shifted his weight from leg to leg while he answered. "Unfortunately, that is correct." His eyes were downcast as he said the part he looked forward least to delivering. "We found a tunnel that leads from inside the underwater pyramid."

"Did you follow it?"

"Yes, it came out on that island there…" He handed his brother a pair of binoculars and waited while he put them to his eyes and focused on the distant spot of land among the Bimini Road area of ocean.

"It came out on that island?" Daedalus lowered the binoculars to look at his brother.

"Yes, and on the island, three of our divers engaged the targets in combat, but they escaped by boarding a passing fishing boat."

Daedalus clenched his jaw tightly in barely-controlled anger. "Which men were responsible for this failure?"

Phillipo pointed to two employees down on the dive platform taking apart their scuba gear, and then to one more man on the opposite side of the platform who was smoking a cigarette.

Daedalus glanced at them for a split second before saying, "They will be punished. But we must stay on site for now in order to work on the golden pyramid. That alone is worth astounding benefits. I will alert my specialty team as to Carter Hunt's activities."

Phillipo's expression grew fearful for a moment before he resumed the hard façade. Treasure, Inc.'s "specialty team" was a euphemism for Daedalus' hit-man, an Israeli ex-special forces sniper who defected some years ago, and who was reportedly wanted by the Mossad. The fact that he was still alive, Daedalus claimed, was testament to the fact that he was a very talented agent, indeed.

And now this individual would be set loose on Carter Hunt and his unsuspecting friends.

On the dive platform, a technician gave a countdown. Phillipo pointed to the Bimini Road over the missing capstone that led to the pyramid. "Watch this…"

And then a low rumble was heard as the underwater explosives were detonated.

"We're blowing away more of the road stones to hopefully make an opening big enough to get a mini-sub down to the pyramid. Then we can remove the gold tiles with the grapple arm, get more heavy equipment down there."

Daedalus watched the slow wave that formed from the blast as it reached the ship, rocking it gently.

"At least something's going right. You are to inform me immediately with any word on Carter Hunt or his associates."

Daedalus' brother nodded. "In the meantime, I put out the word to our operatives in the Bahamas to be alert at all ports of call."

"The seaplane—I thought I told you to scuttle it?" Anger rose again in Daedalus' face, his skin reddening.

"There was a shootout, Daedalus. We tried but failed to stop them from taking off."

He glared at his brother. "Did you note how much fuel was in the gas tank of the plane?"

Slowly, Phillipo shook his head.

Daedalus let loose a sigh of exasperation. "We will need to address these systemic failures once this situation is resolved. For now, find out the range of the plane assuming it had a nearly full tank of gas, and draw a circle on a map around the Bimini Road with the plane's range as its radius. Can you do that much?"

Phillipo squinted ever so narrowly at his brother. "Of course."

CHAPTER 30

Bahia Honda Bay, Cuba

Maddy shook the lost pages of the *Critias* in her hands while she talked to Hunt. "Why couldn't Atlantis have been in Cuba? It's the Atlantic, it's not far from Bimini, which has been proposed as an Atlantis location. The concentric ring pattern is here."

Hunt shrugged as he looked around at the islet and sea. "If it is, though…then where is it? The buildings, the roads…the treasure?"

Maddy stared back down at the ancient manuscript, brow furrowed in deep concentration. "There's something special about these pages."

Hunt's eyes widened. "Well, yeah—they're about 2,400 years old! That makes them pretty special."

"No, something more than that." She paused for a few moments in deep thought, then continued. "Consider for a minute what the story of Atlantis as told by Plato was really about?"

Hunt took a deep breath as he looked out across the sea to the verdant Cuban mainland. "it's an allegory for what happens to a civilization that becomes greedy and corrupt."

Maddy nodded slowly as a smile spread across her face. "Precisely. Because what supposedly happened in the *Critias* and *Timaeus* documents that already existed before we knew about this?" She shook the scroll in her hand.

"The gods punished the people of Atlantis by unleashing a deluge of floods and massive tidal waves that destroyed the city and submerged it permanently beneath the ocean."

"Also correct. But what if the Atlanteans had a plan to escape and rebuild after that catastrophe? To relocate to another area and start a new life?"

Hunt held her gaze for several moments during which he reflected ever so briefly on their past times together, before replying. "Sounds like that would be called a second chance."

"A *second chance*—exactly!"

"But how would the logistics of that work—moving all the building materials, which were supposedly exotic, rare Earth metals, and the treasure, the cultural items like books that made them a people to be admired in the first place—how would they preserve and move all of that?"

"Good question." Maddy held the pages up to the sun and looked up at them. "See how some of the words are fainter than others? When you look at it straight down against a surface it's not really noticeable, but when I shine light through it like this, it's much more apparent."

Hunt leaned in and looked up at the unfurled scroll of parchment Maddy held up to the sunlight. "Oh yeah, I do see that. It's like they had a bold font all those years ago!"

Maddy's laughter carried on the sea breeze along with the squawks of gulls. "They did it the old fashioned way, with a quill using extra ink — probably some kind of plant extract mixed with animal blood-- on select words. But why these particular words, Carter?"

He took a closer look at some of the words. "Sorry, but the words themselves are all Greek to me."

She smiled at him. "I see you haven't lost that sense of humor I remember."

"Some things are worth holding on to." He looked away from the manuscript and into Maddy's eyes. They sparkled for a moment and then she pointed to one of the words on the parchment that was emboldened by the sun. "I really do need to be in my office for this, but I can make some sense of it. This word here, I don't know what it means, for example. It is literally Greek to me!" She gave Hunt a playful shove. "But take this one here..." She moved her finger across the parchment to another boldened word.

"Vacated..." She moved her finger to another part of the scroll. "Southern..." Again, she moved to a different bolded word. "Province."

Hunt made prolonged eye contact with her. "And Cuba is the 'southern province'?"

Maddy nodded emphatically. "I'm sure of that, based on what I read earlier before we left the Bahamas. And look at these other words: They're ancient Greek and have no direct translation today, but as best I can tell, if I look at only that series of bold words, it says, *In this new place they learned the evil of their ways and were able to live for generations of fruitful activity.*"

Hunt appeared perplexed. "So this...Cuba...is the old place...but where is the 'new place'?"

Maddy bit her lip while continuing to stare at the manuscript she held up to the sunlight. "Well that's the funny thing...it doesn't say. The story— the *Critias*, which is the end of Plato's Atlantis tale, the first part being the *Timaeus*, ends here by saying..." She squinted at the scroll while interpreting the ancient Greek. "...*from the sea it rises again.* I'm pretty sure that's what it says, anyway."

"You're probably right, Maddy. But okay, so Atlantis was destroyed, the people relocated in anticipation of those God-induced floods and tidal waves, rebuilt the city somewhere else, meaning it rose again from the sea...right?"

Maddy shrugged. "That's how I see it."

"But where?"

Maddy looked up at the scroll again, shaking her head. "It doesn't actually say where that I can see—either in the bold words or the regular text. I guess I'll have to have a more thorough translation done back at home, and then—"

"Guys, hey—over here—I found something!" In addition to his voice, they heard the sound of Jayden's footsteps pounding across the island to the beach. He stopped at the edge of the beach and beckoned them. "Come with me, check this out!"

"Everything okay?" Hunt asked.

"Yeah, no emergency, just found something cool. Not sure what it is, though. This way!"

Maddy carefully rolled the scroll back up and tucked it away. Hunt took a last look at the water, checking for boats or planes, but saw none. Then he and Maddy jogged across the sand and caught up with Jayden, who led them across the island's thin cover of scrubby vegetation. They trekked across the middle of the island, which was roughly crescent-shaped, while a flock of gulls wheeled around overhead. Before long, Jayden reached the edge of the beach and stood in place for a second, hands on his knees, out of breath.

"Found a campsite!"

"What? There are people on this island?" Maddy's eyes widened, but Jayden stood up straight and shook his head. "Come on, I'll show you."

Hunt and Maddy left the beach and followed Jayden at a trot toward the middle of the barrier island, finding the going easy over the flat, hard ground. After a few minutes, Jayden stopped walking and looked around. He pointed into the distance, along the curving crescent of the island's natural shape. Colored swatches of fabric contrasted sharply with the brownish-green of the island's terrain.

"Those are tents," Jayden said. "Come on."

They trekked the rest of the distance to the campsite. Maddy stopped a few yards short of the camp, balking at the obvious remnants of recent human activity. "Jayden, are there...did you see...are there dead people here?"

But Jayden shook his head immediately. "No. Saw no people, living or otherwise. Not that I checked every single area, but I'm pretty sure it was left in haste. Come on, I'll show you."

They walked over to the nearest tent, a green fabric two- or three-person affair, the stakes of which had been bent and twisted beyond repair, collapsing the fabric so that it no longer had its intended dome shape.

"Whose camp was this?" Hunt asked, getting right to the point.

"Not sure yet, but whoever it was, they had some technology." Jayden picked up an ethernet cable off the ground from inside the tent and held it up.

"Any actual computers or drives left behind?" Hunt wanted to know.

"Not that I could find so far, but let's have a look around." Jayden ducked farther inside the collapsed tent while Maddy combed the ground nearby and Hunt ventured to the next tent over. This one was also ruined, mangled into unusable scaffolding supporting a shredded, orange fabric. Inside, he saw a mix of soda pop and *Cristal* beer cans on the ground, along with a sleeping bag and a battery powered lantern. He moved to the sleeping bag and lifted it off the ground. Beneath it he saw a pile of books. He dropped the bag and picked up the volumes, which were relatively recent hard covers with titles like, ATLANTIS: THE EIGHTH CONTINENT, MEET ME IN ATLANTIS, THE TRUE MYTH OF ATLANTIS, and the like. He opened the pages of a few, looking for handwritten notes or any sign of the owner's identity. He found nothing inside the first couple of books, but third caused him to suck in his breath when he opened its cover.

The pages had been cut away and inside the book was a 9mm pistol. Hunt carefully extracted it from the book and checked that the safety was on and that the magazine was full. Looking for the serial number, he saw that it had been filed off. He started to put the gun back in the book but then thought better of it and tucked it into the waistband of his shorts, pulling is shirttail over it.

He looked around the tent some more but found nothing further of interest. Outside the tent, Maddy was stooped down on the ground, combing through the vegetation with her fingers. She picked up something and held it up to Hunt as she heard him emerge from the tent. It was small and brass-colored. "Look at this, I'm finding some bullet casings."

Hunt nodded and lifted up his shirt. "And I found a gun. Let me see one of them."

Maddy's eyes widened at the sight of Hunt's new acquisition and he took the brass shell from her, inspecting it briefly before dropping it to the ground. "Yep, 9mm, it could be from this gun. But let me see that one..." She handed him one of the other spent shells in her hand.

"This one is a different caliber. So there are either more firearms still on this site, or there was some sort of shootout here, with all the players long gone."

Jayden emerged from another tent and walked over. "Look what I found?" He held up another pistol, of a different model than the one Hunt found.

"Found a 9mm myself," Hunt said, showing Jayden the gun in his waistband. "I figure we may as well keep them until we get out of here, since we never know what kind of jam we may find ourselves in." He looked all around at the sea surrounding the island and thee sky above.

"But what do you think happened here to make someone want to leave their guns behind?" Jayden asked.

"Is the serial number filed off that one, like it is on the one I found?" Hunt asked. Jayden inspected the gun before answering. "Sure is. Just like the VIN number was gone from that sweet El Camaro I used to have."

"Your taste in cars it what concerns me the most about that statement."

"Hey, you two—over here!" At the sound of Maddy's voice they broke off their conversation and looked farther into the camp, where Maddy stood in an open, grassy area in the middle of a circle of ruined tents. They trotted over to her, where she stood next to a wide pit that had been dug into the Earth. A couple of shovels, one of their handles broken, lay alongside a rock-hammer lay in the open hole.

"They tried to excavate something, it looks like. At the very least, they wanted to see what lay beneath the top layer of soil."

Hunt peered into the hole, where a flat layer of exposed dead coral, limestone, lay exposed.

"Not only that," Maddy said, "but this isn't the only pit they dug." She pointed farther away in the campsite. "There are at least two more that way."

"Let's check them out," Hunt said, moving off toward the other freshly dug pits. Maddy snapped off a photo of the current pit and then she and Jayden joined Hunt at the next nearest one. It looked much like the other one, with one important exception.

"Oh my goodness!" Maddy exclaimed, looking down inside it. "Is that....could it be?"

Both Jayden and Hunt stayed on the rim of the pit while she climbed down into it. The object of interest was white and tapered, protruding from the dusty limestone.

"If I didn't know any better, I'd say it looks like an elephant tusk," Hunt said.

Maddy's voice echoed off the bottom of the pit since she couldn't bear to turn away from the amazing find. "Not elephant," she shouted, "but wooly mammoth! Oh, I really shouldn't be doing this, but look!"

Jayden gawked at the white tusk as Maddy began to tug at it where it disappeared into the coral. "Wooly mammoth? You mean, like those big hairy elephants that went extinct....how long ago?" He and Hunt slid down into the pit to give her a hand.

"It's been documented that mammoths still existed 10,00 years ago."

"And Atlantis flourished about 11,000 years ago," Hunt pointed out as he put an arm on Maddy's leg to steady her while she worked at extracting the gargantuan tusk.

"Did you know," Jayden said, his voice brimming with childlike enthusiasm,. "that wooly mammoths were alive when the great pyramids of Egypt were being built?"

Maddy looked up from the pit. "But not in the same place."

"If this was Atlantis," Hunt said, waving an arm around the Cuban island, "then there were mammoths roaming around Atlantis?"

"I like to picture Atlantean hunters riding them," Jayden said, staring at the partially unearthed tusk. "That's what I would have done."

"No doubt," Hunt said. "But even with this impressive find, it seems like we're getting farther away from Atlantis, not closer. In the Bahamas we actually found a gold pyramid. Here we've got an animal tusk. Not to mention, whoever was camped here—Treasure, Inc. or someone else—didn't think it was worth coming back to after they left in a hurry."

Maddy again looked up from the tusk to answer. "This looks like a pretty standard camp to me—either archaeology or maybe paleontology. Except for the guns," she said with a frown.

"Could be that a regular archaeology or paleontology team was working here, and just like with what happened to your team in Giza, they got run off by Treasure, Inc," Jayden offered. "They seem to monitor important dig sites around the world."

"The number of spent shell casings around here seems to bear that out," Hunt agreed.

Maddy suddenly took off her pack and removed from it the rolled up scroll. Once again she unfurled it.

"It's like that thing is a Harlequin Romance novel or something—you just can't get enough of it!" Jayden quipped.

"Seeing the mammoth made me remember something I read in here earlier that made no sense, but now it might..." Her eyes scanned the document's Greek words.

"How about if Jayden and I see if we can get this thing out of the ground while you work with the manuscript," Hunt suggested. Maddy nodded absentmindedly without taking her eyes from the scroll while Hunt and Jayden maneuvered into place around the mammoth tusk. The two men worked at chiseling more coral away from the tusk while Maddy pored over the manuscript, lips moving silently as she worked through the cryptic words.

Jayden chipped away at the coral with one of the rock-hammers left behind while Hunt pulled on the tusk. Jayden would break chunks of coral loose and Hunt would pull out another section of tusk, until they could see the base of the massive tooth.

"Hold up," Hunt said, stooping to examine what they had uncovered. "Wow, it looks like it's still attached to the skull!"

"Geez, what if the entire skeleton is in there?" Jayden exclaimed.

Maddy glanced up from the manuscript. "Oh my God. It is! I mean, it will be, you'll see. This place *was* Atlantis. But they moved it and reestablished it in another location. And now I know where."

CHAPTER 31

Bimini Road, Bahamas

Daedalus paced the foredeck of the *Historica* impatiently as his brother climbed the steps leading from the lower deck. He was eager for news of the search efforts to find out where Carter Hunt had escaped to in the seaplane. Phillipo paused for a bit at the top of the stairs, catching his breath while smoothing out his pants and tucking in his shirt.

"What are the results of the search?" Daedalus asked, not waiting for his brother to begin when he was ready.

"We have not yet actually located the subjects or their plane," Phillipo said, smoothing out his shirt and walking the rest of the way to Daedalus, but I am confident that I know where they are."

"Continue," Daedalus ordered.

"Our operatives tell me that they have still not attempted any conventional landing at a Bahamas airport, including the one they rented the aircraft from, which would have been the fastest and easiest thing for them to do."

"Except that they knew we would locate them if they did that," Daedalus said smugly. "So it's really not the fastest or easiest. Go on."

Phillipo took a deep breath before continuing. "They've also not checked in at Miami, Fort Lauderdale or other major Florida airports within range. It's possible that they landed the plane near a remote part of the shoreline, a mangrove area, perhaps, and then abandoned the plane to come ashore on foot."

"Do you have people looking into that?" Daedalus asked.

"We do. But I think the most likely scenario is that they went south."

"South? To where, the Florida Keys?"

"Even farther south, although they would have been very low on fuel."

There was a beat as the two brothers locked eyes. At length, Daedalus answered. "Cuba."

His brother nodded.

"Site 6?"

"That's right."

Daedalus looked stern, but gradually his expression lightened until he laughed out loud. "Good! Let those buffoons waste their time in the abandoned camp. There is nothing for them to find there. And if we're lucky, they'll end up in a Cuban prison for a few years while Castro figures out if they might be spies."

Phillipo had to chuckle at this. "Yes, and speaking of that, brother, for that reason it is not wise for us to pursue them there, do you agree?"

"We are an antiquities trading company, Phillipo, not a military outfit. I quite agree. Unless we know for a fact that the lost city lies within Cuban territorial waters, we have no reason to go there."

"If we are really lucky," Daedalus went on, seeming to ignore his brother, "they'll be blasted with one of those sonic weapons that was used in Havana on American diplomats! Wouldn't that be perfect?" He erupted into cackles of laughter.

"I have a feeling that the means used by Cuban authorities for intercepting persons arriving in an unannounced aircraft with no visas would be far less subtle."

"Of course you are right," Daedalus said, his laughter fading out. "I'm just trying to have a little fun in the midst of all this chaos, brother, perhaps you should try it some time."

Phillipo stared at his brother without saying anything for a moment before continuing. "They will almost certainly find the wooly mammoth remains."

Daedalus shrugged dismissively. "Let them have those old bones if they want them. We have more important work to do."

"Such as?"

"Such as figuring out where Atlantis is and getting there first."

CHAPTER 32

Bahia Honda Bay, Cuba

Hunt threw his hands up and looked around the little island. "If this was Atlantis, then we already succeeded. We found Atlantis!" He grinned at Maddy and Jayden, hoping to cheer them up. Jayden especially appeared less than convinced.

"Yeah but the treasure's not here. Nothing is here, except for some old animal bones. Which are cool—don't get me wrong. I love old animal bones. But they're not really part of Atlantis."

Maddy pointed emphatically to the lost *Critias* pages. "Actually, it says in here that 'strange beasts from another time were kept inside the city's gold walls'. That could mean mammoths, I don't know. But what it does say that's important is that the beasts, whatever they are exactly, were moved to the 'mirror island.'"

"Is that like an island covered with mirrors, like a funhouse or something?" Jayden asked, only half joking.

Maddy frowned at him. "No. It means it's a lookalike island, but a mirror image, like left and right hands."

"So an island that looks like Cuba. But it's not Cuba?" Jayden clarified.

"Now you're getting it. If you were to look at it on a map, it would have the same basic shape, but somehow inverted so that similar features like coves and peninsulas would match up if swapped back to the original position. For example, the Greek island of Crete would fit the bill. Crete is a lot smaller than Cuba, though, but if they were fleeing they might have lost a lot of people and things and had to scale down."

"When we get back to civilization, we'll have a look at some maps and try to figure it out. But right now, the way I see it, our best ticket out of here is floating away as we speak." Hunt pointed to their seaplane, still floating nearby, but definitely farther away from where they had left it.

"You didn't anchor it this time?" Maddy asked.

Hunt shrugged. "My first priority was getting us safely to land, not the plane. Also, since it's out of gas, it doesn't do us much good. But it's still basically a boat at this point, and with the current heading toward the Cuban main island, it means we can sit in it to get there."

"Cuban cigars, here we come!" Jayden ran across the beach toward the water. Hunt helped Maddy to secure her things in her backpack, then donned his own small pack and met Jayden down at the waterline.

"At least it's warm," Jayden said, wading out into deeper water.

"We're going with the current this time," Hunt pointed out.

"But so is the plane," Jayden said. As if to emphasize this point, a gust of wind picked up and sped the drifting boat-plane along even faster.

"Jayden, if you can get to it first, see if you can fashion a sea-anchor out of something to slow it down," Hunt said, recognizing that Jayden, already out front and the only one of the three with no pack to weigh him down, was likely to reach the plane first. In fact, he thought but did not say, he was beginning to doubt whether any of them would be able to reach it before it drifted hopelessly far away. He silently cursed himself for not taking the time to anchor it, but at the same time knew he had no time to waste. He kept pace with Maddy, not wanting to leave her too far behind lest she get into trouble and then he'd have to swim against the river of a current, something he didn't think was possible.

So he swam steadily, counting on Jayden to reach that plane and slow it down.

#

Aboard the Historica

Phillipo stood on the fantail and watched the massive wake ejecting plumes of whitewater behind them. Now en route back to Nassau, the Bahamian capital, where the ship would refuel before being readied for its next destination, he considered his options. As usual, his brother was clueless when it came to the actual day-to-day operations of Treasure, Inc. Surely all the employees could see that it was he who truly ran the show?

Find out where Atlantis is before Carter Hunt does…That's all, is it? Just find a city lost for millennia, those are my orders? Meanwhile, we've already found a gold pyramid under the Bimini Road. But that's not enough.

If he knew where Atlantis, or its fabled treasure was, he'd be there already, why couldn't his brother see that? But if getting there before Hunt was important, then that meant slowing Hunt down was important, too. And Phillipo knew of one way to do that, given his possible location in Cuba. He might not have gone that far south—it would have been a risky flight, pushing the boundaries of his fuel range—but Hunt had thus far proven unpredictable. Besides, Phillipo thought, removing a satellite phone from his pocket. It was but the matter of a simple phone call.

He used the ship's internet connection to look up a phone number, and then placed a call to the Cuban government.

#

Jayden reached the drifting seaplane and put a hand up on the slick pontoon. He felt a chill as the wind buffeted his back while pulling himself up out of the water. He flung open the rear door of the plane and glanced back before stepping inside. Hunt and Maddy still swam toward him, but they were losing ground as the wind blew the fuel-empty plane toward the Cuban mainland.

Jayden ducked inside the craft and began looking around for something to use as a sea anchor. The actual anchor had been cut by Daedalus' henchmen and left behind in the Bahamas, but another way to do it involved tying something bulky to the plane and letting it sit in the water to slow down the drift. But what?

Jayden rooted around the back of the plane but found nothing that would work. Then he moved up front to the cockpit and checked under the pilot seat. He felt a bag under the seat and pulled it out. He recognized it immediately from his Navy days as a parachute. Perfect, he thought. He hastily unpacked the 'chute while nervously eyeballing the rapidly approaching Cuban mainland through the windshield. Then he looked back to Maddy and Hunt and saw that they were falling even further behind.

Got to turn this 'chute into a sea anchor...a drogue, I think they're formally called, Jayden thought, recalling an old seafaring lecture. He bunched up the 'chute and took it out onto the plane's pontoon. He first unraveled the cord until he located the end, and then tied that to one of the metal struts that fastened the pontoon to the plane's fuselage. Then he heaved the parachute up and out, hoping to get it to unfurl some of it before it hit the water. It did, and then it spread open more while slowly sinking into the ocean.

Jayden smiled as the plane's drifting began to slow. The added drag of the submerged parachute swerved to slow the plane's drifting considerably. He turned back to Hunt and Maddy, who still swam toward the plane. But now at least they were making progress, Jayden could see. After a few more minutes, the pair caught up to the plane and Jayden helped first Maddy aboard, and then Hunt.

"Nice drogue," Hunt said with a smile.

"Yeah, that instructor we had for that class was hot, you remember her?" Jayden said with a smile.

Hunt nodded but When Maddy said, "Oh really?" he declined to comment further. "I'll pull in the sea anchor," he said, eager for an excuse to change the subject. While Jayden and Maddy got inside the plane to warm up after the swim, Hunt walked out along the pontoon and untied the paracord from the plane. He didn't exactly feel like hauling the heavy 'chute in, but decided to do it anyway since it was possible they might need it again. He also hated the thought of polluting the marine environment, and leaving something in the ocean to entangle sea life. So he hauled in the 'chute and pulled it aboard and bunched it up until it would fit in the backseat. That done, he climbed inside the cockpit, sitting in the pilot's seat even though the aircraft was now only an unpowered raft.

Hunt watched the Cuban coastline looming in the windshield. "Lucky for us it looks like the coastline is deserted here."

"Yeah, we don't need to get pulled over by the Cuban Coast Guard. I hear the jails aren't all that nice here."

"Probably not as accomodating as a good ol' Navy ship's brig, I'll give you that."

"That beach looks so inviting," Maddy said, "it makes me just want to lay out and dry off."

Hunt looked ahead as the float plane entered the outskirts of a wide-mouthed cove. "Looks like we're going to land up on the beach on the west side of the cove there, right before the point."

"Topless bathing is likely permitted here," Jayden said while Hunt picked up a pair binoculars and brought them to his eyes.

Maddy's acerbic reply was cut short by Hunt's warning from behind the binoculars. "Looks like we've got company. Fast boat coming around the point. Looks military. We've got to go."

Maddy bit her lip. "Shouldn't we wait to see if it's someone who might be able to help us?"

"No." This was said by both Hunt and Jayden in unison. "*Policia*," Hunt declared, dropping the optics.

"Do they have air patrols? How'd they find us so quick—there's nobody here!" Jayden wondered.

"Maddy, do you have the scroll?" was all Hunt had to say. She nodded, clutching at her backpack. "I do."

"Not that I don't respect the law," Hunt said, cinching his backpack straps tight, "but in this case it would behoove us to avoid all contact until we can sort things out."

"I had a teacher who used to say 'behoove us' a lot," Jayden felt the need to chime in with.

"I hope he or she also taught you how to listen," Hunt said, "because this is important: we're only going to get one chance at this." Hunt pointed at a palm tree-studded forest behind the beach as the whine of the police boat motor rang louder in their ears.

"One chance at what?" Maddy asked, fear etched into her every facial feature.

"At turning this plane into a glider so we can get out of here."

CHAPTER 33

Hunt could see that both Jayden and Maddy thought he was few sandwiches short of a picnic.

"The stress is finally getting to you, isn't old buddy?" Jayden cast a nervous glance back at the rapidly approaching Cuban police boat.

But Hunt's gaze was unwavering, his voice level. "No time to explain step by step, so first things first: It's a fast powerful boat, but with only two officers on it. We need to take control of that boat, hopefully without seriously hurting anyone, including ourselves."

Hunt allowed a precious second to tick by while his friends absorbed the verbal bombshell.

"You want us to hijack a Cuban police boat? I have to say, Carter, I know I said your idea of vacation was a little boring, but I take that all back now, okay? I take it back."

"It's our only chance, the way I see it," Hunt said. "We could try to run into that jungle there, but they'd probably shoot us before we even got across the beach. Not to mention…then what? We're on foot in the jungle with barely any gear, no food and water, hunted by the police?"

Their conversation was interrupted by the sound of a male voice through a loud-hailer speaking Spanish. Hunt recognized the word *alto* and *manos,* but that was more than enough to know what they wanted. But then, as if to remove all doubts, the message was repeated again, this time in perfect, although accented, English. "Attention: persons on aircraft, stop your vehicle and step out onto the pontoons with your hands up. Do it now!"

"Only two of us come out." Hunt hissed. "Jayden—you and Maddy step out with your hands up. Maddy, we need a distraction. Take your shirt off. You two act like lovebirds just having fun in the middle of nowhere caught with your proverbial pants down."

"Sounds good," Jayden said, winking at Maddy, who rolled her eyes.

"You two are my distraction," Hunt said, keeping things focused as the plane began to rock with the waves caused by the oncoming patrol vessel. "But as soon as I have control of the boat, I'll need your help."

The loud-hailer boomed again, and this time there was a warning shot fired into the air.

"Go!" Hunt said, staying low below the windows while Jayden emerged first with his hands up. Maddy already had her T-shirt off. She turned around, facing away from Hunt out of modesty before removing her bikini top. Then she stepped outside onto the same pontoon as Jayden, her hands also in the air.

The patrol boat slowed as it drew alongside the sea-plane, the driver allowing a distance of ten feet as a buffer, not knowing what to expect. The other man on board, a middle-aged Cuban in a police uniform but brandishing an automatic weapon, trained his firearm on Jayden and Maddy. Hunt watched from a concealed position in the back of the plane, peeking out from beneath the parachute. He saw the gunman smile upon seeing Maddy, and then turn back to say something along with a healthy dose of laughter to his associate in the driver's seat.

Seeing that it wasn't going to get much better than this, if at all, Hunt made his move. Coil of rope in hand, he crawled to the opposite door that Jayden and Maddy had exited from while hearing the police continue to bark through the loudspeaker about not moving and keeping their hands up while the boat was pulled into position alongside the plane, as Hunt was hoping.

No noise, no noise, he told himself as he took a deep breath and then slipped into the water head first without making so much as a ripple. He kept his eyes open despite the sting of the warm saltwater, because for this to work he would need to see, even if in blurred fashion. The former Navy man swam underneath the seaplane, deep enough not to break the surface between the two floats where the body was raised up from the water, but not so deep as to lose track of where he was.

He surfaced near the front of the floatplane, behind the prop. There, he looped one end of the rope around the starboard side support strut. Then, he very quietly stealth swam underneath the plane, between the pontoons. To the port side, which was where Jayden and Maddy stood on the pontoon, hence a risky place to be. He quickly wound the rope around that strut also, creating a crude harness, the same idea as a water-ski tow-rope. That done, he grabbed another deep breath and slipped once again below the water's surface.

Hunt swam toward the boat, utilizing a smooth breast stroke that propelled him through the water with a minimal amount of exertion and disturbance of the surrounding water. He glanced down and saw the silvery sparkle of a school of fish, the ocean bottom not visible to his blurry vision without a mask.

When he saw the underside of the patrol boat, he angled his body so that he swam deeper, knowing that all attention would be focused on this side of the plane, where Jayden and Maddy stood on the pontoon at automatic gunpoint. He passed beneath the hull of the police boat, glancing up as he passed under it to ensure he had sufficient clearance. By the time he reached the other side of the boat, the need to breathe was strong. But still he swam, maneuvering for the stern end of the boat, where he had noticed a boarding ladder earlier.

Easy breaking the surface, he reminded himself, aware that even a small splash would bring unwanted attention. He slowed his pace as he ascended, reaching a hand out of the water first to steady himself against the side of the boat. He knew that most boats had stainless steel hooks in the back made for towing or lifting them out of the water, and as he eyeballed the stern from the water he was relieved to see that this was in fact one of them.

Hunt could hear that the conversation between the police and Jayden, who was doing most of the talking, was starting to move past the wow-factor of Maddy's toplessness and into more serious business. He felt the plane rock a little and thought perhaps one of the policemen might have stepped on a pontoon to board it, but then heard Jayden say, "Okay, we'll get onto the boat, just don't shoot."

Hunt threaded the end of his rope through first one hook, and then the other, hiding behind the back of the boat as he did so. Then he tied a knot to secure the rope in place that was now passed through two points on the stern of the boat and two points on the front of the seaplane.

Step 1 complete, Hunt thought. *Now for the tricky part.*

He held onto the boat as it began to rock. Jayden and Maddy were stepping on board. He knew he would have to be very, very careful, that should he draw the attention of the police boat crew before he was ready, it would likely cost him his life, and possibly that of his friends. Never mind the law and due process, either, Hunt reminded himself—out here, on a lonely stretch of Cuban coast, the law *was* these two men who likely had a high degree of discretion when it came to what they reported back to the precinct.

"We ran out of gas," Jayden was saying in English. The word "visa" was used a few times by both law officers. Hunt eased smoothly along the back of the boat to the boarding ladder. He gripped the metal rungs and hung in place, listening to make sure both officers were talking, for if one was not, it could mean he was walking around the boat, and that would spell the end for Hunt if he came to the stern. But Jayden and Maddy together did a good job of keeping the talk going, of keeping both Cubans engaged in conversation, and so Hunt put his feet on the bottom rung of the ladder and hauled himself up a step, careful not to apply too much force and rock the boat as he did so.

"Miami," Jayden was saying, "we came from Miami but got lost, off course, and then we ran out of gas. We're sorry, it was an accident..."

Maddy also chimed in with corroborating words of her own, while Hunt crept up another step on the ladder. Only one more step to go, but that one would take him over the transom, making him easily visible to all on board. He had only one small trick up his sleeve to stack the deck in his favor just a little bit, and it was time to play that card.

Hunt extracted the emergency penlight he carried from the pocket of his boardshorts, wary of either making a noise while undoing the pocket catch or of dropping the item. Penlight in hand, he monitored the conversation, which was escalating in tension. Hunt figured his friends were perhaps thirty seconds to a minute from being taken into custody. Gripping the corner of the boat with one hand, he tossed the penlight up and over the stern of the boat, so that it landed in the water along the boat's port side.

Doing this meant he had to hope they didn't see where the throw originated, but this small bit of luck was on his side. Both Cubans spun and looked left upon hearing the small splash made by the flashlight hitting the water a few feet away. Jayden, not one to look a gift horse in the mouth, seized on the opportunity and sprung into action.

He flung himself into both men, one arm around each of them, while Hunt hauled himself up over the transom and into the boat. The blast of the AK was followed closely by the pop of a pistol. Hunt saw fiberglass shards spray into the air as the rounds chewed up the boat's deck and rails. Fortunately the officers had only been able to squeeze their triggers reflexively and had not been able to raise, much less actually aim, their weapons.

"Maddy, get in the plane!" Hunt didn't look to her for an answer, but instead landed on the two water patrolmen alongside Jayden, stripping the AK from the squat, burlier man who looked as though he would be at home on the offensive line of the Miami Dolphins. Jayden, meanwhile, was able to snatch the pistol from the taller, thinner officer. Hunt and Jayden trained their newly acquired weapons on the marine patrol team. Both Spanish-speaking men immediately put their hands in the air without a word.

"What's our plan, Carter?" Jayden side-mouthed to Hunt.

"Nobody gets hurt. We go our way, they go theirs."

But the sound of additional engines approaching made that prospect suddenly seem much less likely.

Hunt looked to his left along the coast in time to see two more Cuban *policia* patrol boats speeding towards them. Jayden moved to the steering console but Hunt told him not to start the boat.

"Why the heck not?"

"Because we'll just be in a boat chase, two against one. We'll lose."

"So what, you're giving up?" The look on Jayden's face was one of incomprehension, like he simply could not believe what he was hearing out of Hunt's mouth. But Hunt shook his head.

"Not giving, up, I just think we should leave a different way. Jayden, get in the plane. Take the pilot's seat. I need you to steer."

"Wha—what?" Jayden stammered. "Carter, the plane's out of gas, remember? Not even vapors left!"

"But the boat's not. I tied a tow line from the boat to the plane. We'll have our new friends here drive the boat at full throttle, and I think that'll be enough to get us airborne in the plane."

"You think?"

"Yeah." He eyed the rapidly approaching marine patrols and noticed that one of them had a mounted 50-caliber machine gun on its prow.

"But then what? Even if we get airborne, we've still got no gas!" Jayden eyed the boat's fuel fill cap, on the top of the transom. "If we had all the time in the world, we could siphon some out of this boat and then transfer it to the plane, but..." He pointed to the incoming patrol boats, which were now within seconds of reaching them. "...we don't."

"That's okay, the plane can go where the boats can't go." Hunted pointed to the jungle beyond the beach. "We can glide inland somewhere to escape the boats. We'll still be on the run and they'll see where we went and radio for help, but it'll buy us some time."

Jayden threw up the hand not holding the gun. "Better than what I've got, which is nothing. Let's rock."

"Get in the plane and keep the wheel steady once I get us underway. It'll tend to drift—keep the nose pointed at the stern of the boat."

"Nose to ass, got it."

"You would.

"Go."

"But wait—how will you—"

"Jayden, there's not time to explain. Just go. I'll handle it from here."

With a scowl toward the Cuban *polica*, Jayden swapped guns with Hunt, giving him the AK and taking the pistol with him back to the plane.

Hunt waved the barrel of the automatic rifle toward the Cuban who had been driving the boat earlier, and then toward the steering console. He looked at the other officer and pointed to the seat opposite the driver's, and that patrolman moved slowly to it and sat.

The boat's engine was already on and idling, so Hunt waited for Jayden to jump out of the boat, swim to the plane, and climb into the pilot's seat, which seemed to take forever. The incoming patrol boats were close enough for Hunt to see that one of them carried two officers, while the other carried three—with one on the mounted gun.

From his position in the rear of the patrol boat facing the front, Hunt shouted some Spanish words that meant 'go' to the boat driver, waving the gun muzzle at him when he turned around to look. The Cuban put the vessel into gear, slowly at first. The drag of the plane caused the boat to angle to one side, but then the driver compensated by adding more speed, and the floatplane's swings became less pronounced until it was being towed in a straight line behind the boat.

Hunt hated to turn his gaze away from the boat driver and his associate who was no doubt watching Hunt like a hawk, but when the 50-cal gun from the leading patrol boat in their wake began to crackle as it spit out rounds, he forced himself to turn around for a two-second look. And that look was all he needed to know that his plan had a very slim chance of succeeding indeed.

"*Mas rapido!*" Hunt pointed to the throttle and shook his AK menacingly. The driver responded by jamming the throttle up to full speed, which sent Hunt reeling backwards into the transom, where he cracked his elbow on the fiberglass edge. His grip on the automatic weapon faltered, and the seated officer started to get up before Hunt reasserted his hold on the long gun while falling to the deck and pointed it at the man.

He shook his head at him while centering the barrel of the deadly firearm at his midsection. The officer sat back down, bouncing up and down as he did so, as the boat was now travelling fast, the throttle jammed all the way up while the boat driver braced himself against the steering wheel, sea spray buffeting the windshield.

Hunt saw the seated Cuban's eyes grow wide as he looked past him, which prompted him to take a quick glance backwards as well. He had to push himself up to his feet, leaning against the transom in order to do so, but he managed it with a couple of more bumps and bruises along the way. When he looked back he saw the seaplane bouncing up and down, going airborne for a few seconds before skimming back along the wave tops. Meanwhile, as Hunt whipped his head back forward, he could see that the boat driver was showing no sign of letting up on the throttle, apparently deciding that a bumpy ride was preferable to getting shot with an automatic weapon. Or maybe he was hoping Hunt was going to either lose control of the AK or be seriously injured from bouncing around the boat. Either way, Hunt knew that he had only a few more seconds to put the final step of his plan into place...the most dangerous step.

Then he felt something dislodge from his pants and clatter to the deck. He spotted the pistol he'd found at the campsite. It landed halfway between him and the seated patrolman, who eyed the weapon longingly. Hunt shook his head at him while stepping forward and putting his right foot on the pistol. He slid it back to him and picked it up while holding the AK steady with one hand. Deciding it wasn't worth possibly losing control of it again and giving his adversaries a weapon, Hunt tossed the pistol overboard, now depending exclusively on the automatic weapon, and the two pistols Jayden had in his possession.

He turned his focus back to the plan. He needed an important implement to be able to carry it out. He shouted at the Cuban not driving the boat. "Knife," he said in English, not knowing the Spanish word, but making a pantomiming motion that hopefully explained it. He knew almost all boats would have some kind of knife in order to cut rigging in an emergency, or perhaps for a little fishing when not on active duty.

The Cuban looked perplexed but seemed to understand, as he nodded and pointed to the cubby space beneath the steering console. He tapped his own chest and pointed to it. Hunt nodded, giving permission to get up, but he kept his gun trained on the officer as he stepped quickly to the console. The driver looked at him in alarm, thinking a situation was developing, but Hunt moved along the side of the boat, bracing himself against the gunwale, letting him know that he was still very much in control.

The bullets ricocheting off the side of the boat told him that wouldn't be the case for long, though. The officer not driving grabbed a rusty bait knife and nervously handed it off to Hunt butt first.

Hunt took it with a nod of thanks before waving him back to his seat with the gun muzzle. Then he wobbled back to his spot at the transom, staying low to avoid the gunfire from the two chasing patrol boats, now right behind the plane. He caught a glimpse of Jayden white-knuckling the stick, shouting something at Hunt that he could only take to mean, 'Do something, we're about to go airborne!' even though he couldn't hear the words. The fact that the plane was still tethered to the boat was now treacherous, since it was bouncing higher and higher, its wings giving it the needed lift to go airborne, but then being jerked back down by the rope.

Hunt whipped his head around for one last check on the Cubans, then decided it was time. He eyeballed the seaplane's pontoons, waiting for the next time they lifted off the water. When he saw the air gap form between the water and the pontoons, he leaned over and cut the starboard-side rope, quickly standing up and turning around in time to see the Cuban sitting back down. They would still rush him if they could.

With the rope cut, it slid free from both of the boat hooks on the transom. Immediately the seaplane rose higher in the air. Hunt told himself not to let go of the rope, or else he'd be left behind on board the boat without the plane. He tossed the AK overboard, unable to do what he was about to while carrying it, but also not wishing to leave it behind for the

Cubans to use against him.

Hunt wound the cut end of the rope around his right wrist, knowing that the force he was about to endure would be significant. But he was not expecting what happened next. The seaplane suddenly caught an updraft and rose even higher in the air. Hunt stood up on the transom and jumped off, hoping to avoid the water and increased drag it would cause if at all possible. But the rope was long enough that he was dipped waist deep into the ocean before being lifted into the air. The plane dropped only slightly as a result, but Hunt gasped as he saw one of the patrol boats rocketing straight underneath the plane, occupying the water the plane had ridden on only seconds earlier.

He saw the mounted 50-cal spit fire as he raised his legs so that he was dangling by the rope straight down from the seaplane. He kicked the mounted gunner operator square in the head with both feet, sending the man reeling over the side of the boat. Hunt never got to see what happened to him, for the next thing he knew, he was lifted high above the fray by the seaplane, which was still on an upward trajectory. Hunt knew that this was good since they would need all the altitude they could get, without any fuel, to facilitate a long-distance glide. But that didn't make him feel any better at the moment, being dragged into the sky by tons of ascending metal, dangling at the end of a rope while being shot at from no less than three vessels below.

Hunt looked up and saw Maddy's horrified face looking down out the open door. Hunt knew that because of the way he had tied the rope to the plane—the only way he could while in the water, to the struts connecting the pontoon to the wing—that he wouldn't be able to be pulled all the way into the plane, He'd have to pull himself up to the pontoon and then climb in. So he began to raise himself up hand over hand, flashing back to his military training days, doing the same thing on a base while a drill sergeant yelled at him. He almost managed a smile as he concentrated on the memories instead of the reality. When he next looked up he was about halfway to the pontoon.

Below him he saw that one of the patrol boats was pulling alongside the one towing the plane, no doubt telling the driver to stop, while the third boat—the one with the mounted gun—sped away in order to get some distance from the plane so that they could fire at it.

Hunt mentally urged Jayden to turn left, to make themselves a more difficult target from the water, but still they continued in a straight line, jitterbugging up and down. Jayden was not a pilot, Hunt reminded himself, so he was doing well all things considered.

Keep climbing, soldier. Again, Hunt focused on putting one hand in front of the other, fingers burning with the effort as he ascended the moving rope while being dragged through the air at an angle.

Finally he reached the strut the rope was tied to and gripped the solid metal. He swung a leg up and over the pontoon, straddling it like a rodeo bull. As soon as he looked down, he saw a spark of orange six inches in front of his face as a bullet ricocheted off the strut his rope was tied to. He gripped the strut and forced himself to his feet, still holding onto the rope in case he lost his balance and fell.

He felt Maddy's hands on his shoulders and reached up to her, clutching the door frame. He hauled himself in and tumbled into the co-pilot's seat on top of Maddy.

"Shut the door!" Hunt bellowed. Maddy pulled it closed and then Hunt yelled to Jayden.

"Remind me to get you a pair of those pilot wings they hand out to kids on the commercial airliners. You did good," Hunt yelled.

"Flying's for the birds, you know that?" Jayden said, sliding out of the pilot's seat with a last adjustment to the control stick. He moved to the back seat and began firing a pistol from the window at the patrol boats, aiming for the engines, hoping to disable them without hurting anyone.

The first thing Hunt did was to glance at the altimeter: 500 feet. *Not bad!* Then he banked the plane left, toward the beach and the Cuban jungle beyond.

CHAPTER 34

Hunt found the seaplane to be eerily silent as he guided it through the air as an overweight, cumbersome glider. He couldn't help but glance back through his window as he passed over the empty beach and a thick stand of jungle. The patrol boats cut power as they entered the shallow water fronting the beach, with no way to pursue their prey. Hunt knew they had radios, though, and cursed himself for not at least incapacitating the one on board the boat they had taken over.

A question from Jayden interrupted his thoughts. "This is a pretty lonely stretch of coast. What are the chances those police just happened to come across us?"

Hunt pulled up slightly on the stick before answering. "I put them conservatively at slim to none."

"So Daedalus called the Cuban authorities?" Maddy asked from the back seat.

Hunt nodded. "I think so. They probably knew they could cause more trouble for us that way without having to do hardly anything themselves. But there's something else, something about Atlantis."

"There's always something about Atlantis, isn't there?" Jayden quipped.

Hunt went on. "Like Maddy showed us, this area does fit the raw physical description, when sea levels were lower. But there are no remnants of it left. So maybe Treasure, Inc. knew that already and that's why they didn't want to bother coming down here."

"That would put them a step ahead of us in the search, though," Maddy said, "and yet they didn't know about the Bimini Road pyramid."

"It's not a linear search," Maddy said. "It's more like a tangled web, with dead-ends and loops all interconnected in a sprawling maze."

Hunt eyed the jungle through the windshield, not seeing any break in the greenery. "Not to put a damper on the discussion, but this hunk of steel is not going to stay aloft forever with no gas, and so we need to figure out how to land this thing."

"Not liking the landing options," Jayden said, not mincing words as usual. Indeed, there was nothing but unbroken greenery in all directions except for behind them, where the ocean was rapidly receding from view.

"There's something else I don't like, even if we spotted a road we could land on."

"A road we could land on sounds pretty good to me right about now," Jayden said. "What wouldn't you like about that?"

"Attracts too much attention. A candy apple red seaplane landing on the street in some small town? They'd know exactly where we landed."

Jayden again turned to look out the window. "It's all just jungle, except for the ocean behind us. And in front of us, as you can see a couple of miles or so away, there's what I would call a big hill or a small mountain, also covered in jungle."

"Mountain…" Maddy said, trailing off as if in thought. Then she mumbled something unintelligible and took the rolled-up *Critias* scroll from her backpack, hastily removing it from its plastic bag and unfurling it. "Wait a minute…"

"We don't have a minute," Hunt said glancing at the altimeter. They now flew at 250 feet and were losing altitude. "We're losing the coastal updrafts that kept us aloft over the beach. I'm afraid it's all downhill from here."

Jayden looked out the window to his right, then behind them out Maddy's window, then back through the windshield. Then he turned around again and saw the crumpled up parachute lying on the floor. "Hey Carter, you think that 'chute will hold all three of us?"

Hunt pursed his lips in a grim line before replying, "Looks like it's going to have to since I left my wingsuit at home. Get it ready."

Jayden moved to the rear of the plane and began untangling the parachute. "Maddy, you gotta pack up your novel there, it's time to go."

"There should be another pyramid. That's what I was missing! *That's* what this is saying. Another big one." She looked ahead through the windshield while Jayden shook his head as he fumbled with the unwieldly parachute in the confines of the plane.

Hunt turned the plane sharply to the left to avoid the looming mountain now filling the plane's windshield. "150 feet and dropping," he called out, eyeing the tops of the jungle canopy below. He could see the occasional tall palm tree poking out of the more ubiquitous leafy trees that made up the bulk of the canopy. It was a thick, wild forest, with absolutely no gaps through which the ground was visible; there was no possibility of landing the plane here.

And yet gravity was taking it down. There was no avoiding that. It was like a bad dream, Hunt thought, where you kept hoping you would wake up, except that it was all too real.

"Need that parachute, Jayden!"

"I got it sorted as ready as it can be. It's going to be a little weird because I had to cut some of the cords to make the sea snchor, but it is what it is. We'll need to bail out this door back here."

"Is it ready?" Hunt glanced out the window at the treetops below, then to his altimeter: 100 feet. He pulled back on the stick and was relieved to see and feel the nose of the beleaguered aircraft incline slightly, buying them a bit more altitude. He was well aware that a parachute needed some height for it to be effective, and that it would be triple overloaded as it was.

"Ready!" Jayden called form the back.

"Maddy ready?" Hunt confirmed. He didn't want to leave the controls of the plane a second earlier than he had to. But when she replied in the affirmative, he knew it was time. He turned the plane slightly to the left, away from the base of the mountain so that it would coast as long as possible over the jungle, hopefully crashing some distance away from where they landed. Then he clicked out of his seatbelt and jumped into the back with the others.

Jayden was sitting next to the open door, trees visible rushing by outside of it. The 'chute was bunched up on the seat next to him, the paracord neatly laid out so as not to get tangled. He held the single harness in his hands and handed it off to Hunt. "You take the actual harness, and Maddy will hold on to you. I figure you two lovebirds would appreciate it."

"What, in case we don't make it!" Maddy nearly screamed, panic more than evident in her voice.

"We'll make it if we go now." Hunt fought to keep his voice level while gawking at the rapidly approaching forest outside the window. Jayden got into makeshift web of paracord fashioned into a crude harness while Hunt stepped into the original harness,

"I know it doesn't inspire confidence, but it's the best I could do for—"

"Great, let's go!" Hunt said, grabbing the bundle of cord. Then he pulled Maddy to him and wrapped her arms around his midsection. "Hold on to me, Maddy, hard. Squeeze." Then, to Jayden: "Go, go, go!"

Jayden dove head-long from the gliding airplane, keeping the parachute bundled until he cleared the wing. Then he let go of it and the fabric billowed out into shape, like a blooming flower in time-lapse. Hunt and Maddy bailed out next, with Hunt orienting his body to dive beneath the wing after Jayden. He was surprised to see himself falling below Jayden, and for a split second he wondered if the paracord harness Jayden had rigged had come loose, that he and Maddy were going to fall to their deaths.

But then he felt a sharp pain under his shoulders as the resistance of the open parachute took hold and he, the piggybacked Maddy and Jayden above them were jerked skyward with sudden and violent force. The entire jump was strangely silent since there was no airplane motor. The only sound was the wind through their ears, until Jayden started screaming, that is. No sooner did Hunt feel himself and Maddy begin to descend than he felt the treetops against his feet and ankles. *Barely enough time*, his inner voice screamed. Yet there was nothing more he could do about it now. He had played his hand and now it was time to see the results.

Hunt watched the seaplane crash into the jungle perhaps a half-mile away, watching as the left wingtip hit a tree branch stout enough to cause the plane to spin in a circle like an out of control boomerang. The cracking of branches was heard as the earthbound vehicle shattered tree limbs on its way to the ground.

And then they were in the sky alone. But not for long.

Maddy's screaming brought Hunt's attention back to his immediate plight: they were dropping through the jungle canopy, right now. He felt Maddy press her face into his chest, shielding it from the whipping leaves and branches as they plummeted at breakneck speed through the trees. It's a controlled fall, Hunt thought—the 'chute was producing drag—but it would be just barely enough. He tried not to think about how fast they were moving as they crashed through the understory.

Hunt saw dirt coming up from below and braced for the impact…

…but it never came. A few feet above him, Jayden swore like a sailor who just found out shore leave was cancelled. "The 'chute's hung up! Tangled up good."

Hunt looked up and saw Jayden dangling there with the parachute's white fabric snared across two or three trees a few feet higher. "We'll just have to cut ourselves free and drop."

"Easy for you to say, you're only ten feet over the ground. I'm more like twenty."

"Be glad it's only twenty. We Jumped from the plane around 100."

"Can't argue with that."

Hunt told Maddy to hold on while he untied part of the makeshift harness until he could slip out of it. "Three, two, one…drop!" The two of them landed on the forest floor in a heap, their fall thankfully cushioned by a bed of fallen leaves.

"Clear the drop zone," Jayden called down, and Hunt and Maddy pushed up to their feet and moved out of the way. Jayden faced a twenty-foot fall, but was able to dangle down from part of the rigging Hunt and

Maddy had left behind. Still, his fall was a potentially ankle-breaking fifteen feet, but realizing it wasn't going to get any more favorable, Jayden let himself drop.

He landed on his feet, but leaning too far backwards. To his credit, he transitioned into a smooth backward roll, ending up on his knees in an upright position.

"Wow, it's nice and cool in here, not so sunny. Great day for a nature walk!"

Hunt wasted no time. They had illegally entered a foreign country run by a communist dictator, and were already on the run from police after damaging at least one boat, and crashing a plane into the jungle. At least it hadn't started a fire, Hunt thought; that was the plus side of running out of gas, he supposed. He was also aware that none of them had any food or water, and barely any gear. He pointed toward the mountain.

"Let's get to that, climb up as high as we can—it didn't look all that steep—so we can get a view of what's down on the other side. Then we'll make a plan."

Jayden and Maddy agreed, and without further delay the trio set out across the forest. The ground was level and solid, with only the occasional rock or exposed tree root to watch out for. To take their minds off their predicament, Hunt engaged Maddy in conversation as they trekked. "So you were saying something about there being another pyramid?"

"That's right," Maddy said, falling into step with Hunt while Jayden walked point a few yards up ahead. "They refer to it in Plato's lost *Critias* pages as 'the distant pyramid'."

"How do we know that's not the one we already found under the Bimini Road that had nothing in it?" Hunt asked.

"Because it mentions the distant pyramid being in the 'southerly manifestation' of Atlantis, which, due to the mirror image similarities with the island of Crete, as well as topographic contours of the islands and surrounding seabed, I took to mean Cuba, even though Cuba is many times larger than Crete."

"But that would have been a plus for the Atlanteans, right?"

"Yes, more land, and it's an island protected by an ocean on all sides, with high mountains from which to observe approaching ships." She nodded up at the looming green mountain they were at the base of.

Hunt pointed up at the mountain, which sloped gradually upward for the first one-third of its height, but then became steeper. "It still looks to me like we can basically walk our way up to the summit without any climbing gear, which is a good thing, since we don't have any."

Jayden removed a balled up wad of paracord from a pocket. "I did manage to salvage this. Paracord always comes in handy. Hopefully we won't need it, though. I'm ready when you two are." He looked to Maddy as he said the last sentence.

"I'm ready, too."

Hunt nodded emphatically. "Up we go."

#

The going was easy enough until abut one-third of the way up the mountain, where the incline became substantially steeper. Hunt suggested they take a short break to rest, and the three of them sat on a grouping of boulders. Jayden found some water cupped in the bulb of a tropical plant, and drank from it. Assuring the others it was good, they also availed themselves of the hydration.

That done, the group continued their ascent. Although it was steeper, they could still walk on two feet most of the time, here and there needing to use their hands to maintain balance. The tall trees became less frequent and shorter, while the understory of ferns, mosses and other smaller plants became thicker. Jayden remained point man while Hunt and Maddy ascended side by side. Hunt remarked at one point that at least they had heard no aircraft in the area.

"I guess that means they're not pulling out all the stops to find our plane," Jayden said.

"Or they're looking in the wrong place," Hunt offered.

"Speaking of looking in the right place," Jayden said as he slipped on a mossy rock and regained his footing by gripping the trunk of a small tree, "when we get out of here, maybe we should get back to the Bimini Road before our friend Daedalus claims that golden pyramid for himself. Or just takes it apart to sell the gold."

"Definitely," Hunt returned. "When we get out of here."

They continued working their way up the mountain, which became wetter the higher up they progressed. About three-quarters of the way up it became even steeper still and Hunt had to stop frequently to assist Maddy when she slipped. He told her he would stay with her while Jayden made the rest of the ascent to check the view if she wanted, but she insisted she could make it and that they go on as a group.

On they went, their clothes now sticking to their skin with sweat, faces and hands scratched from passing through thick foliage. Numerous biting insects plagued them as well, but these became somewhat less in number the higher they went. Jayden remarked more than once that he was simply glad to be alive at all at this point, whatever happened from here on out.

Near the top of the mountain Hunt noticed a terraced formation, sort of like wide steps had been cut into it, like pictures he had seen of Asian rice paddies. He figured it was some sort of erosion pattern caused by rains sluicing down from the top of the mountain peak. Finally, Jayden reached the summit with a quiet whoop and a holler that he made sure wouldn't carry too far in case anyone could hear somewhere down below. But a few steps before Hunt and Maddy got to the apex with him, he said, "Bad news, guys. It's still forested as far as the eye can see."

Hunt and Maddy clawed their way the remainder of the distance to the summit, with Hunt giving Maddy a final shove to make sure she got there safely. Then Hunt stood and took a look around. Jayden was right. Behind them, in the direction from which they had come, they could see the jungle with the ocean in the distance. In front of them, a vast expanse of jungle extended to the horizon.

Jayden put a voice to Hunt's thoughts. "And to think I thought of Cuba like Havana, with city streets and '50s cars and nightclubs and stuff."

"Yep. Doesn't look that way from here, does it? On the bright side, there's a lot of police and military presence in Havana, so that's probably not a good place for us to be, either."

Maddy sat on the ground and put her head in her hands. Hunt was afraid she was going to cry. He was about to move to comfort her when an outcropping of rock a little ways down the opposite slope from the one they had ascended caught his eye. Without a word, he walked down to it. Again, he noticed the odd terraced layout to the ground, which he thought was strange since there was no reason to do any kind of agriculture way up here. As he stepped down the terraces, Maddy's prior words came to him: "There's another pyramid…" and then it hit him.

This mountain. The broad base and pointy top. The terracing. The proximity to the supposed southerly location of Atlantis mentioned in the lost *Critias* pages. Hunt's skin prickled with awareness.

We're standing on a pyramid!

Easy now, Hunt told himself, leaning on the rocky outcropping. *Just because it has some superficial characteristics of a pyramid doesn't mean it is one.* If it is a pyramid, though, he reasoned, that means there should be some way to get inside. He recalled no caves or anything like that at the base where they had walked up. Of course they hadn't walked all around the base of it. He eyed the way down the opposite face, noting that they would be able to walk down it easily enough. *Maybe we should look for entrances at the base on this side,* he thought. He was turning around to convey this line of reasoning to Jayden and Maddy when he spotted a cleft in the rocky outcropping.

A dark space lay between two rocks, itself shrouded by a clump of scraggly ferns. Hunt moved to it and parted the plant life to have a look. A rift wide enough to accommodate a man extended down into darkness.

He called up to Jayden and told him to bring Maddy down here. By the time they slid down to the opening, Hunt had already dropped inside. "Come on down. There's a vertical shaft here with cutouts in the rock we can use as ladder rungs."

Jayden and Maddy also entered the chute. "What is this, a cave?" Maddy asked, her voice echoing in the enclosed space.

"Not really. I think it's your missing pyramid."

CHAPTER 35

Hunt descended the vertical rock chute rung by rung. Looking down, darkness prevented him from seeing what lay below, but it was quiet except for the sounds of Jayden and Maddy's climbing, several rungs above him.

"Be a good guy and give me a head's up if you fall, Jayden, so I can brace myself."

"I was planning on taking you with me."

Then Maddy said, "Guys, I realize this is all fun and games for you military types, but I'm really nervous, okay? Please stay focused."

"Who's got a light?" Hunt asked, changing the subject. "I had to toss mine into the ocean when I hijacked the patrol boat." The darkness enveloped them a little more with each rung downward.

"Be glad I carry a tube of waterproof matches wherever I go," Jayden said. He flipped open a latch on his belt buckle, steadying himself against the rock wall with one hand, and then lit one. The sizzle was accompanied by a flame and then they heard a snapping noise as Jayden ripped a stalk from a plant that grew out of the wall. He set it on fire, pleased that it lit relatively easily, having been kept dry down in this vertical chamber.

"Grab some more sticks when you see them," he said, "because farther down there might not be anymore. Hunt and Maddy collected a few that they stashed in their waistbands, and then they continued on their way straight down. Since Jayden was the one carrying the torch, he had to go slower, but it also meant that he could see better. That's why Hunt was surprised when he heard Jayden call out that something was written on the walls.

"What, like graffiti?" Hunt called up, worried that he was about to have his hopes dashed that this was an ancient pyramid upon finding out the local gang members have left their mark down here. But it was Maddy, who was closer to Jayden on the wall than Hunt, who responded first

"Oh my God, these appear to be genuine works of art. There's a bull here, Carter. Bulls are symbols long associated with Atlantis!"

"Let's keep going." Hunt continued with his descent, now noticing that there were paintings on the walls in front of him. A naval scene, with longboats being rowed by dozens of warriors, shields in place. Another of a great city, a city built on a series of canals formed in…Hunt nearly gasped as he formed the words in his mind: …formed in concentric rings.

Atlantis!

"You're going to love this next one, Maddy. But don't lose your focus on the wall. Keep your footing."

Carter continued climbing down, and shortly after he heard Maddy gushing over the scenic rendering. "Amazing! It's got to be Atlantis! I can't even—"

"Something coming up here." Hunt's words put an end to Maddy's sentence. "Looks like it's the end of the ladder—it's opening up into a chamber of some sort."

But oddly enough the ladder didn't come to an end on the floor of the chamber, but about six feet up. Hunt waited for Jayden to come down lower with the torch, so that he could see the floor better, to make sure it was in fact a floor. When Jayden came to within a couple of rungs of him, he could see the flames casting his own shadow in wavering shapes on a floor that looked to be made of solid rock tiles.

"It looks solid to me, Jayden. I'm dropping down."

"Nice knowing you, buddy, if it turns out to be some weird illusion, or if the tiles are breakaway…"

Hunt dropped before Jayden finished his joking around. The thump of his feet hitting the stone reverberated throughout the mountain-shrouded pyramid. "I'm standing on solid ground, not to worry," Hunt reported. "Come on down."

Jayden dropped in first, his flaming torch flickering wildly as he fell, and then Maddy made the drop as well. The three of them stood in awe of their new surroundings. They had come to an antechamber of sorts, with the vertical chute emptying out into a polygonal room not seeming to be any standard shape. The ceiling was high and multi-faceted, and the walls were decorated with richly painted murals much more detailed than the ones in the chute on the way down. These, too, depicted scenes of a maritime city, of thriving commerce, culture and everyday life: oxen plowing fields, fishermen hauling in nets bursting with seafood, fish pens for aquaculture, musicians performing in front of socializing crowds, children playing in a field, and a pantheon of god-like figures, looking down on it all from sky-blue heavens above. Other than the artwork, the chamber was unadorned.

A stone stairwell led down from the edge of the floor.

"Let's see where this leads," Hunt said, wanting to keep things moving before Jayden's torch ran out. To be down here in the dark would be tantamount to a death sentence, he knew, but it was a fear he left unspoken for the sake of group morale. Hunt moved to the top of the stairs and peered down. "It's a long staircase," he observed.

"Beats the vertical ladder," Jayden pointed out. He and Maddy trailed Hunt down the stone steps, Jayden's torch casting flickering shadows on the walls, which bore no artwork here. After many steps down they came to a landing with a torch holder mounted on the wall, a stout piece of wood still in it.

"Is it petrified?" Maddy asked. Hunt pulled it down from the mount, hefting its weight.

"Nope, just a nice, solid piece of wood."

"That's what she said," Jayden quipped.

"Seriously, Jayden, is there ever a time when—"

"People, come on, this is not the time. "Hunt held the tip of the wooden staff to Jayden's flame and waited while it lit. It took a few minutes of careful lighting, but the flame took hold and then they had a powerful torch. "This should last a while," Hunt said, inwardly relieved. Jayden's torch didn't have that long to go.

The stairway continued down another flight in the opposite direction like a switchback trail. The three explorers took these down also, and by the time they reached another landing, Jayden's torch had been extinguished. Another stout piece of wood was wall mounted here, and so he collected that and lit it from Hunt's torch. "One more landing and I'll have one, too!" Maddy said.

They took yet another flight of stairs down, but there were no more landings. Instead, at the bottom of this flight was a short arched hallway. The trio followed it to its end, where it branched off both to the left and to the right, as well as offering yet another stairway leading down. Both side passages were longer than the one they had just traversed, but they could still see that both opened up into rooms or chambers of some sort.

"Right, left, down, or do we split up and go one in each direction?" Jayden asked.

"I don't want to be alone down here," Maddy stated.

"Let's all stick together for now," Hunt decided. "And I don't think we should go down yet. Let's check out the side passages first. Right or left, Jayden--your call."

"I'm closer to the right passage already, so…right it is, call me lazy."

Hunt laughed as he crossed to Jayden's side of the room, and then the three of them walked side by side through the right-hand passage. Murals decorated the walls here, depicting a theater of some type with an audience watching a play or show being performed. Another unlit torch was mounted in here and so Maddy took this one, lit it from Hunt's and the three carried on with a decent amount of light. The passage opened into a spacious chamber with high, vaulted ceilings.

Right away they could see that this room was different.

"Oh. My. God." Maddy whispered the words as the three of them stood just inside the entrance, awestruck.

"Is…is all this stuff real?" Jayden muttered, almost to himself.

The chamber was about the size of a large living room or great room. A series of stone pedestals placed throughout the space support a mind-boggling array of goods—piles and piles of gemstones, gold bars and ingots, silver and jade jewelry, statues made from precious metals, weapons fashioned from various materials including stone, metal and wood.

Treasure.

"I think we found it," Hunt declared. "But hold on—before we get lost in all these treasures and artifacts, I think we should check out what's in the other chamber, at the end of the other passage."

Neither Jayden nor Maddy responded, they could only stand there and marvel at the sheer spectacle of it all.

"Guys?" Hunt prompted. He'd been in too many pyramids by now not to question what was in all parts of them.

"Okay, let's make sure we didn't set off some kind of booby-trap by coming in here, is that what's on your mind?"

"Sort of, yeah. It seems to me like they disguised this pyramid as a living mountain, like that was the strategy, but who knows what it looked like 11,000 years ago?"

"Sea level was lower," Maddy said, turning away from the heaps of incredible riches in order to leave. "This would have been the peak of a once truly massive island. The parts that are underwater now would have been dry land. This mountain would have been an extremely high peak."

They exited the treasure chamber and walked back through the passage until they reached the intersection. This time, they took the left-hand passage. The same length as the other, it opened up into a chamber the same size and layout as the other.

And with the same amount of treasures. More gold, so much of it that the entire chamber was cast in a yellow light. There were also wondrous biological items here—massive ivory tusks, most likely from wooly mammoths. Huge shark jaws, even larger than what would be found in a great white shark. Massive hunks of amber, large pelts from various big cats, bears, otters and other unknown species. Peppered throughout, laying on the floor, were strings of pearls, gold coins, and necklaces made of various precious metals and strung with beads comprised of exotic gems. It was all so dazzling to look at that Maddy actually sat down on the floor, still holding her torch.

"My *God*, you guys! All my life, I've worked to uncover finds that shed some light on humanity's past, but this...But this..." she trailed off, spellbound by the sheer magnitude of their discovery.

But Hunt had questions that overrode the grandiosity. He walked a few steps and bent down to pick up a gold coin. "Did Atlanteans have their own money?" he proffered.

"No one knows for sure," Maddy said.

"I think we do now." Hunt tossed her the coin. It featured a bust on one side of a man whom she did not recognize, with writing that was unknown to her. The reverse side featured a seaside scene similar to those depicted in the murals they had seen, presumably Atlantis itself, in its heyday.

Hunt continued to walk around the room, examining artifacts, picking things up now and then from the floor. Jayden did the same, and after she regained her composure, Maddy got back on her feet and also perused the astounding finds. While there was some variation in the types of things stockpiled and preserved here for the millennia, it was essentially more of the same—a hidden room full of mass riches.

After some time spent examining it all, Jayden walked over to Hunt and Maddy. "There's all the money in the world in here, but there's no food. Also, these treasures are great, but they're not Cuban cigars, or even coffee. So we better work on getting out of here."

Maddy was unable to look away from a group of golden bowls, but Hunt agreed. "We've seen all we need to here. It's time to make sure we can get out of here alive so that we can tell the world that Atlantis was real. Come on, Maddy, let's go. We still need to find a way out of here."

She looked up from the sensational artifacts. "What do you mean, find a way out? Won't we just go back the same way we came in?"

Hunt and Jayden exchanged knowing looks. Jayden said, "I think you're forgetting about that ten foot drop from the rock ladder down to the first chamber. How would we get back up to the ladder?"

A few moments of silence passed while Maddy digested this. "I suppose you're right. Unless we piled up stacks of mammoth tusks and stood on top of them or something silly like that..."

"Besides," Hunt broke in, "We still haven't seen what else is in this pyramid. If it takes up the entire mountain we climbed up outside to get here, then we can't be all the way back down yet. It's hard to judge, to be sure, but I'm guessing we're at least half but not more than three-quarters of the way down."

Maddy tore her gaze from the artifacts. "Okay. You're right. Let's go. This chamber appears to be constructed exactly the same as the other one, so I recommend starting in the middle space where the left and right passages branched off."

Reluctantly, they exited the treasure-filled chamber and retreated back down the passage back to the central corridor that had led them to the pair of branching halls with the staircase leading down off the end of the straightaway. Hunt stood at the top of it, eyeing the way down. "Looks okay. Down we go."

The stepped down in a single file line, Hunt in the lead and Maddy in the middle. The walls here were featureless slabs of stone, with no artwork. Down they went for what seemed like a very long time. Hunt was about to comment about an endless stairway when he saw a new space beckoning below at the bottom of the steps.

"Almost there." He picked up his pace a little, his torch bouncing around as he descended the final steps.

Jayden and Maddy heard his voice before they reached the bottom. "Huh. That's disappointing."

"What is?" Maddy asked.

"Oh, wow! It's not another treasure room. But You guys are going to love this!

CHAPTER 36

Jayden and Maddy stood with Hunt in a smaller chamber that was empty except for one recognizable feature.

"It's the same kind of door lock mechanism as was on the Bimini Road pyramid!" Jayden bent down to inspect it, then looked back to Hunt. "Shall we?"

Hunt nodded. "You do the honors."

But Maddy was scared. "Wait! What if it lets water in?"

Hunt shook his head. "Unless it's a very specially constructed trap like in the Giza pyramid, I don't see how that could happen. We're several hundred feet above sea level. The Bimini Road pyramid was already underwater so that's why the airlock. And you notice there is no airlock here, only the door lock mechanism. They're only using that part of the overall construct."

She still appeared less than one hundred percent convinced, but acquiesced. "I guess we have to take a chance if we want to get out of here."

"That's the spirit!" Jayden said. Then he pressed down on the top of the hexagonal mechanism like they had done to the one in Bimini. The mechanism clicked into place and he lifted the middle section of the chamber out.

"Let's see if there's anything inside this one." Hunt took the internal portion of the hexagonal mechanism from Jayden.

"Probably not," Maddy guessed. "Because the last one had a clue that led here. Now that we're here, with the mother lode, so to speak, I'm thinking there's no need for a clue. But I'll have a look while you two check out the door."

Hunt and Jayden angled their torches to be able to peer into the new opening while Maddy examined the removed artifact. She shook it and held it at different angles while examining all sides of it. "I really hate to do this," she concluded, "but…" Then she dropped the item on the stone floor, where it shattered into pieces.

The three of them looked at the wreckage. Maddy bent down and sifted through it. "Nothing here. This is it!" She waved an arm up toward the treasure chambers. "The treasure of Atlantis."

"And I'm guessing this is our way out," Hunt said, indicating the new opening.

Jayden climbed up on top of the portal. "We've got another vertical, four-sided chute with a set of rungs carved out of the stone walls. I'll go first."

Jayden dropped his torch all the way down the chute. "Let's get an idea of how far we have to go. Still have two more torches…." The three of them crowded their heads together to watch the torch fall. The orange light receded until it was no longer visible.

"Long way down," Hunt said.

"Hopefully it just blew out on the way down rather than falling into water," Maddy said.

"I'll go first, but I'm in the dark without you guys, so stay close." With that, Jayden climbed into the vertical tunnel. He set his feet on the rungs hewn out of the stone wall, checked his purchase on the handholds, knowing that a fall was fatal given how far the torch fell, and then he began the descent. He proceeded very slowly since he was in the dark the farther away he got from Hunt.

Hunt started to climb into the chute, but then stood back down and said to Maddy, "I don't think you should bring your torch. It's a long climb and you saw what happens if you fall."

"But then we'll only have one torch."

"I won't drop it. I don't want to risk your safety for the sake of having one more light."

"You two lovebirds decide you want to stay in the Grand Treasure Room for the night or what?" Jayden called from down below on the wall.

"Coming…" Hunt experimented with tucking the torch into his waistband but the flame burned him so he abandoned that tactic. "Hey Jayden, still have some of that paracord you got form the parachute?"

"Yeah."

"I need it."

Jayden's exasperated sigh wafted up from below. "Be right there." Jayden's head popped up out of the chute and he gripped the rim with one hand while digging into his pocket with the other. Then he handed Hunt a wad of paracord before climbing back down. Hunt wound the cord around the middle of the torch, away from the flame, and then unraveled enough slack so that the torch hung down a safe distance below his feet.

"Just don't singe my awesome hairdo with that thing, okay?" Jayden warned from below.

"Not into the Lost City look, I guess. Fine, here goes nothing." Hunt climbed into the chute and began his own descent, waiting for Maddy when he was a sufficient number of rungs down. She climbed in, got her hand- and footholds set, and announced she was ready.

The three of the began climbing down as a group, proceeding slowly and carefully. Hunt's tied torch rig turned out to be effective, allowing him to have both hands free to climb with minimal interference while still providing light for the group. Down they went, keeping communication to a minimum while each of them focused on their next rung, knowing that a fall from anyone above would likely take out all those below as well.

None of them knew how much time passed; even though Hunt wore his Omega watch, he kept his focus on the climbing, his thoughts free of anything but where the next rung is. They had one scare when a swarm of spiders crawled up the wall past them, causing Maddy to shriek, but Hunt told her to freeze in place. "Calm down, let them pass, they won't hurt us!"

"They're crawling on me!"

"It's okay, Maddy, they don't want you, let them pass, they crawled over me, too."

"I think I ate one," Jayden said. "Not too bad, really. Protein snack. You should try one if you're hungry."

After a minute during which Hunt tensed, ready to try and catch Maddy if she fell, the onslaught of arachnids ceased and Maddy settled down. "We good to go again?" Hunt asked.

She said she was, and so the trio continued on their downward journey, now more wary of creatures that might inhabit the vertical tunnel. The going was smooth, though, and after an indeterminate amount of climbing later, the shadows emanating from Hunt's torch began to change and shift. The floor was getting closer. Jayden warned the others that they were approaching the bottom.

"Floor is solid stone," Jayden yelled, his voice echoing all over the vertical chamber. "Stepping off…I'm on solid ground!"

Hunt and Maddy continued climbing down the last few steps until they, too, stood on the stone tile floor with Jayden. On the floor was Jayden's torch that he had dropped from above, now extinguished. Hunt picked it up and lit again from his own, then handed it back to Jayden.

In front of them, a corridor with an arched ceiling beckoned into the horizontal distance. It represented the only avenue out of the small room they were in, so they ventured n that direction. Before long they came to a bend in the corridor, and when they rounded it they saw a track of sorts laid out down a long passage, as far as they could see.

"What do we have here?" Hunt wondered aloud.

Jayden ran up ahead to where a boxy object sat on top of twin metal rails made of pure gold.

"Ancient rail car system! The tracks are gold, the car looks like bronze, but who knows?"

The three of them took in the unusual sight: a bucket of a rail car, perhaps six feet long and three wide, with wheels that looked like they were made out of a silver alloy, aligned on the track. The sides were about four feet high, and a push handle was the only feature inside the car.

Hunt and Maddy joined Jayden at the car. Hunt inspected it briefly including underneath. "Looks sound to me. I'm thinking that if there's a rail car, the track probably goes for a pretty long way."

Jayden pumped the handle up and down, activating a piston that moved the car forward along the rails. "Or it could mean they had heavy loads to haul."

"Only one way to find out." Hunt climbed up and into the cart, standing by the push handle. He leaned his torch in the corner of the vehicle and began to pump the handle. It creaked at first with some resistance, but the action became smoother as Hunt continued to pump…and the rail car began to roll.

"Hop in guys. Next stop… unknown!"

Maddy and Jayden trotted along after the cart. "Just so you know, I'm not in the habit of jumping onto trains with men headed to unknown destinations," Maddy said, as Hunt pulled her by the hand up and into the rail car.

"I am. Reminds me of my hobo days, riding the rails," Jayden said, easily hopping inside the moving cart. "Let me give you a hand here, Mr. Engineer." Jayden took a position on the backwards-facing end of the push handle, while Hunt stayed where he was on the opposite side facing forward. Together, they operated the pump in classic seesaw fashion, moving the piston up and down to roll the car's wheels forward along the track. The ride was surprisingly smooth for such an antique construct, which Maddy commented on.

"Certainly it's an example of the advanced technology the Atlanteans were rumored to have possessed. I cannot wait to write about this miraculous find in the journals…if I get that chance." She finished on a darker note, a reminder that their fate was still very much up in the air, traversing unknown territory riding a rail car beneath a Cuban mountain.

"You'll get your chance, Maddy. We are riding the Atlantis Railroad right on out of here. Just hold tight!" Hunt began to pump faster, with Jayden following suit, and soon they had the car coasting along on the rails at a good clip. The two torches, now held by Maddy, flickered in the breeze created by their forward motion. After a time they noticed that the track was set on a slight decline, which added to their speed, and Jayden let out a whoop and a holler as they sped along underground.

"Driving that train…" he began to sing the well-known Grateful Dead song, eliciting groans from Hunt and Maddy that were lost to the creak of the pump and rattle of the car over the rail system. The pumped along the rails, enjoying the gentle downhill slope, until at one point they heard a fluttering noise and suddenly the air above them was filled will dark shapes zig-zagging about in hectic, unpredictable fashion.

"Bats!" Jayden called out.

"Duck!" Hunt shouted. He and Jayden stopped pumping while they crouched with Maddy at the bottom of the cart while the winged rodents wheeled and collided just above them. Hunt felt one bump into his head, but it was gone as soon as it happened. The rail car's momentum carried them through the swarm of bats and before long they were able to stand again and resume pumping the cart along its way.

"The fact that there are bats down here means that there is a way out somewhere," Jayden pointed out.

"But that could be the same way we came in," Hunt said.

"The glass is always half-empty with you, isn't it Carter?"

"I just have a feeling that we have a ways to go on this rail trip."

The three of them settled in for the ride, Hunt and Jayden taking breaks from pumping to coast through downhill sections while Maddy did her best to observe their surroundings with the torches. The walls of the tunnel became narrower, such that they could reach out and touch them while still inside the cart. Comprised of natural rock, they were unembellished with anything other than the occasional structural support created out of stone pillars or buttresses.

After a while the terrain became more flat, and they had to pump more to keep up the same speed. Hunt glanced as his dive watch. "We've been travelling long enough now that there's no way we could still be under the pyramid mountain."

"I was think that, too," said Jayden.

"So then where are we?" Maddy wondered.

Hunt answered her. "I think we must be underneath the forest, in between the mountain and the beach."

"Where does it let out, though? I didn't notice anywhere on the beach that looked like it could be used for that."

"Me neither," Jayden said.

"Just settle down and enjoy the ride," Hunt said, continuing to work the handle. "We'll find out where it leads soon enough."

#

Hunt let go of the hand pump and leaned against the side of the cart, watching the monotonous tunnel walls pass by. Checking his watch by the torch light, he shook his head. "It's been about eight hours. I'm starting to think this track is going around in a loop even though we think we're going straight."

"Please don't say that," Maddy said. "You're scaring me. I don't want to be lost down here…wherever *here* is."

Jayden, who had been staring behind the cart at the walls as they receded into the distance, shook his head. "No way, this isn't a loop. We're going more or less in a straight line. Look at that weird crack in the ceiling right there, for example." He pointed to a specific spot on the tunnel ceiling as the cart plowed on.

"True, I don't remember seeing anything like that. There are other irregularities like that, too. I think we're just going a long way in one direction, and with a downhill slope at first that has since leveled out."

Maddy appeared confused. "But…if we've been travelling at an average of say, even five miles per hour, for the last eight hours, that means we've gone about…." She trailed off, as if stunned by the implications of her own conclusion.

Jayden completed the sentence for her. "...forty miles. Which would put us somewhere in—or should I say *under*—the Florida Straits."

"About halfway between Cuba and Florida," Hunt concurred. The trio rode along in silence for a few seconds while they contemplated the significance of their estimated position. Hunt broke the silence by adding, "We must be in a tunnel beneath the seabed." He tried not to imagine the countless tons of water above their heads.

Maddy appeared impressed. "Imagine the engineering knowledge required to build a train tunnel from Cuba to Florida!"

"And the manpower they must have used. I'm thinking the people of Atlantis had slaves."

Hunt picked up the handle of the cart again. "Could be. All I know is, if what we've been talking about is correct, then we have a long way to go. We'd better buckle down and get to work."

Jayden got back on the pump again, too, and Maddy resumed her post as lookout up front. The scenery seemed unchanging and never-ending. Hunt remarked after a time that it was night now, and so it was dark outside.

"Not that it makes a difference in here," Jayden said.

"About eight more hours until we reach the U.S. mainland of Florida. More if this is going to the Bahamas."

"The Bahamas? You think this could go all the way back to the Bimini Road area?" Maddy sounded incredulous.

Hunt spoke over the steady creaking of the hand pump and the rumble of wheels over rails. "It's possible, I mean the two sites are connected and this railway system goes a very long way regardless of where it takes us; they probably could have built it to go there if they'd wanted to."

"I guess we're going to find out," Maddy said.

Hunt nodded as they rode on into the darkness beneath the ocean floor.

CHAPTER 37

Seven hours later

Hunt had torn away part of his T-shirt to wrap around his hands in order to prevent blisters from pumping the cart. Jayden had done the same thing, except using paracord. In the front of the rail car, Maddy used what was left the single remaining torch—the one Hunt had used had burned all the way down hours ago—to eyeball the tracks ahead in case she needed to tell them to slow down because of a broken rail section or some other obstacle. So far, they had come across no such inconveniences, but she knew they couldn't afford to take chances by assuming that everything would be perfect the whole way. After hours of this activity, her eyes were strained and tearing up, and yet, like a ship's crewmember on night watch, she knew she had to stay alert to let Hunt and Jayden know what might lie ahead. They were physically exhausted from powering the cart, while she was mentally fatigued.

That's why she thought she might be hallucinating when she saw the track coming to an end up ahead. A rock wall blocked the way and the track ended without ceremony; it simply butted up to the limestone wall and ended there. She held a hand up behind her and said, "Stop the cart!"

The rail car had no actual brake, but whether by design or accident, the slope of the tracks inclined for the last hundred feet or so, acting as a natural gravity-powered break, like an incline road at the bottom of a long highway slope for runaway trucks. Hunt and Jayden were all too happy to let go of the cart pump. They moved to the front of the car alongside Maddy, who showed them the fast-approaching dead-end.

"End of the line," Jayden called out as they began rolling uphill.

"Don't say that," Maddy said.

"I mean for the tracks, not for us, geez!"

"Still freaks me out."

"Let's jump out before it starts rolling back downhill, okay?" Hunt said. As the cart slowed, they jumped up onto the edge, Hunt taking the single remaining torch. They paused until the cart stopped at the apex of its uphill coast, and then jumped off onto the limestone ground. The cart rolled away from them back downhill, slowly at first, but then gathering more momentum until it coasted away on the flat track.

"Here we are," Hunt said, looking around. "Looks like there's only one way to go." Indeed, a small vestibule area lay in front of them.

"I sure hope it goes somewhere," Jayden said," because I'm sure not looking forward to pumping that thing all the way back to where we came from."

Hunt walked forward while holding his torch out in front of him. "Let's see…" He entered the small-looking area and immediately saw faint light coming from the right. Looking in that direction, he saw another small room, but this one was flooded with…

"Daylight! Not a whole lot, but I definitely see daylight!"

While Maddy and Jayden's excited footsteps caught up with him, Hunt examined his new surroundings. There wasn't much to see. It was a small enclosed space with a coral floor. So he looked up to where rays of filtered light came from, and saw a now familiar sight: a vertical chute with holds chiseled out of the wall on one side.

"It's another ladder chute! We're getting out of here."

Maddy and Jayden's celebratory hollering reverberated around the chamber while Hunt continued to assess their way out. "It's high, though, maybe a hundred feet."

"I'd climb a ten story building to get out of here right about now," Jayden said, entering the vertical chute room.

Hunt dropped his torch, which had burned ninety percent away, on the floor, leaving it to burn out since they now had enough daylight streaming in from above. Barely enough, but it was sufficient and was better than climbing with the torch which was on its last legs.

Without further adieu, Hunt positioned his hands and feet in the hewn rungs and started to climb for the outside world. Soon Maddy, and then Jayden, joined him on the upward journey. Aside from being extra-careful with their footing and handholds once they were higher up than they'd like to fall, there wasn't much to think about, except for...

I wonder what's up there?

#

Hunt stopped climbing a few feet below the edge of the chute. He could see now why only scant rays of light made it down to the bottom: the top of the vertical space was set so that it angled slightly up and away from the main chute, and the opening was narrow, barely big enough to fit his body through. The top of this was grown over with vegetation. He listened for clues as to the new environment they were about to enter. He could hear seagulls calling, and a breeze blowing. His leg was shaking with the effort of the climb without having eaten much, and he knew it must be even harder on Maddy, so he didn't linger quite as long as he would have liked.

"Going up and out," Hunt called down to Jayden and Maddy. Then he wriggled through the angled portion of the chute and pulled himself out of the ground into the daylight outside. Looking back at where he had just climbed out of, he was amazed that he would never have known it was there, so grown over with plant life the narrow opening was.

His first reaction was one of disappointment, as he dropped onto yet another low-lying, hardscrabble, sunbaked piece of piece of coral that was little more than a glorified sandbar. There was nothing here. He stepped away from the chute exit to make way for Maddy and Jayden, and then took a short walk around. But there was little need for exploring. The island itself was featureless and flat, and not very large. But it was what lay beyond it that attracted Hunt's attention.

Another island, a short distance away. Except that this one was not a deserted little clump of coral. Hunt caught his breath as he watched a massive ferry boat dock at a long pier where crowds of people waited to board. Looking closer at the island itself, Hunt could make out a large structure made of brown brick that extended along the island's perimeter for a long ways.

Jayden and Maddy walked up next to him, still winded from the climb out of the chute.

"Looks like some kind of tourist site," Jayden said.

"Where are we?" Maddy asked, getting right to the point.

"I'm not exactly sure yet." Hunt tried to make out the lettering on the ferry but found it a little too far away to read. "But wherever it is, we need to get over there, and that means a swim."

Maddy groaned at the thought of having to exert herself yet again in order to get out of a jam.

"Come on," Jayden said, walking toward the water, "you know they've got a bar on that ferry."

"I guess one more swim won't kill me," Maddy said.

"Not if I can help it," Hunt returned. Then he cautioned Maddy and Jayden, "Let's stay out of the ferry line, and try to swim up away from all the people so we don't get too many questions. Then we'll try to blend in and figure out where we are."

The weary trio of explorers ventured into the sea once more, this time not even knowing for certain what sea it was. The water was still warm, Hunt noticed, perhaps a touch cooler than it had been in Cuba. They waded in until they were waist deep and then began to swim toward the other island. Fortunately, the ocean was calm and currents were mild, enabling them to make relatively good time. At one point, Hunt felt a sharp stinging sensation on his calf. He lifted it out of the water to get a look at it and saw that it was covered in red, striped welts.

"Jellyfish!" he warned the others, but it was too late—they had wandered into a swarm of them. Treading water, Hunt looked around and saw hundreds of the clear, gelatinous forms drifting around. He knew there was nothing they could do but to keep swimming and hope that they would emerge from the swarm. Jayden sustained a sting also, but then they were in clear waters once more.

And closer to the island, too, Hunt noticed, hearing the ferry's loudspeaker announcing that it was now time to board for the return trip to Key West.

Key West, Florida! Suddenly Hunt knew where they were. The brown brick building on the island—he could see now that it was built as a polygonal ring that bordered the entire island—was an old Civil War era fort, Fort Jefferson, which was located in islands about seventy miles south of Key West known as the Dry Tortugas.

"Welcome to the Dry Tortugas, guys! Let's get to shore."

"Sweet, we're going to Key West! Duval Street pub crawl, here I come!" Jayden started to swim for the island with renewed vigor. Hunt and Maddy moved along after him, and once again, they settled into a rhythm.

#

The sound of the ferry's loudspeaker with a crewmember announcing last boarding call reached Hunt's ears as he, Jayden and Maddy trotted up onto the white sandy beach. They rejoiced in the feel of the hot sand beneath their feet. Dry land again!

"What do you say we try to get on that ferry," Hunt suggested, but Jayden and Maddy were already walking up the beach toward the ferry dock. "I'll take that as a 'yes'," Hunt said, jogging across the sand to catch up with them. They walked on the beach until it ended at a grassy field where many tourists were enjoying a picnic lunch. The ferry began blasting its horn, a signal that it was leaving.

"Come on!" Hunt jogged across the grass until he reached the boarding pier, a wooden affair that jutted out into deep enough water to support the huge ferries that transported thousands of people per year to the national park in the Dry Tortugas.

"I forgot my wallet, so I hope they don't ask us to buy a ticket," Jayden said, slowing back to a walk as they got further onto the crowded pier.

"I'm thinking you buy your ticket in Key West and it's round trip only," Hunt said. "With any luck, they won't even check for tickets since there's only one way to get here."

"But we know there's more than one way to get here," Maddy said with a sly smile.

The trio mingled in with the other stragglers who were also boarding the ferry at the last minute. Jayden held up a finger as if he had come up with a great idea. "If they ask, we'll just tell them we came from Atlantis. They'll think we're a taco short of a combination plate and transport us to the mainland immediately for evaluation. Then we can break out of the loony bin…"

"This way, let's go, right this way…" An employee was standing at the entrance to the gangway ramp that led onto the ferry, his hand on the clip of a rope barrier that he was about to barricade across a set of poles. "You three—you together?" he asked Hunt, Jayden and Maddy, who were all equally soaked, although this wasn't out of place since it was a beach destination.

Hunt nodded, but froze, mind already spinning with what he would say. But the man waved them through. "You're the last ones." Hunt, Jayden and Maddy hurried through onto the gangway, and the employee clipped the rope off behind them. Then he signaled the ferry captain that all passengers were on board. The horn blasted again, the dock lines were cast off, and the triple decker boat rumbled away from the pier, packed with tourists.

"Looks like we have a beautiful ninety minute ride back," the captain intoned over the PA system, so feel free to move about the ship and enjoy some food and cocktails. Next stop, Key West."

"Either of you have any money?" Jayden asked Hunt and Maddy. "Wallet went down with the seaplane, I'm afraid."

"Mine too," lamented Maddy. "But believe me, I'm not complaining, considering how everything could have turned out."

Jayden raised an eyebrow and then fished around in the pocket of his wet shorts. Then he held something up to Hunt, something that glinted silver in the sunlight.

"Maybe this silver ingot will buy us some food and drinks." He smiled mischievously. Hunt shot him a questioning glance. "You know that's not really ours, right?"

Jayden nodded slowly. "I know it, but I also feel like the people of Atlantis owe us a debt of gratitude for re-discovering their lost city and culture, and for the work we're about to do of making sure it gets into the right hands to be enjoyed by everyone and not only rich private collectors. Are we on the same page now, Carter?"

Hunt was taken aback by the degree to which Jayden had read him. He could only nod and add, "If it was a coin, I'd be against it, because they're too identifiable, but that's just a hunk of silver, so if you can open a tab with it, more power to you. If not, I'll have to make some calls when we get to Key West in order to get some funds my way."

"We'll be on the upper deck, enjoying the view," Maddy said, taking Hunt by the hand and leading him up a short flight of stairs. But Jayden had already vanished through a door into the boat's salon where the bar service was doing a brisk business.

A few minutes later, as Maddy and Hunt stood at the rail of the upper deck, watching the Dry Tortugas fade into the distance behind the ferry's churning wake, Jayden walked up with a tray of drinks and food.

"How does a margarita along with a cheeseburger in paradise sound?"

Maddy's smile was one of overwhelming thanks as she took both the food and the drink, along with a cup of ice water, while Hunt shook his head. "Given what you paid for it, it sounds like the most expensive meal I've ever had. Not that I'm complaining at this point, mind you. But leave it to you to trade a priceless artifact for some burgers."

Jayden handed Hunt the tray while removing a burger and drink for himself. "Oh, I think we all know it has a price, all right. And we already paid it."

Hunt looked out across the ocean toward the little island with the hidden Atlantean tunnel entrance, and raised his drink. They clinked glasses while the ferry chugged on toward Florida.

"To Atlantis."

EPILOGUE

Four months later
New York City, American Museum of Natural History

"And with that, ladies and gentlemen, please—enjoy our museum's most spectacular exhibit to date—Atlantis Found!" The proud museum curator stepped down from a podium as a sea of flashbulbs exploded from a gaggle of media cameras. Behind him, an entire large hall beckoned with an astounding display of treasures, artifacts and antiquities that were meticulously arranged in various tamper-proof display cases. Interpretive signage and interactive modules informed visitors as to what they were looking at. Actual video of the sites Hunt, Jayden and Maddy had discovered played on massive plasma screens around the room.

In the weeks that followed their amazing finds, Hunt, Jayden and Maddy had met with countless archaeological, anthropological, historical, and even geological experts the world over who had corroborated their story as well as shed new light on certain details. The net result of this discourse was that the treasures and artifacts located were deemed to be credible, meaning that the very existence of Atlantis itself was found to be credible, rewriting human history in the process. The original sites found by Hunt were now under international guard by neutral parties, including the United Nations, among others. The exact locations were closely guarded and kept under wraps, but the treasures uncovered were now on long-term display for public enjoyment, enlightenment and edification, and would be moved from major museum to museum around the world. Following this debut exhibit in New York, it would travel to London, then to Paris, then Munich, Moscow, Tokyo, Shanghai, and others.

The three explorers, now dressed in formal evening attire, stepped aside to allow the visitors to enter the exhibit first. They'd been consulted extensively in its construction, and had already been privy to the final exhibit design.

Jayden grinned at Hunt. "One helluva vacation we had, right?"

Hunt nodded, turning serious. "Fun enough that I think I've found my next career after the service, Jayden: Treasure hunting. Returning artifacts thought to be lost to the ages to the public at large. Righting past wrongs. I have the funds thanks to the inheritance from my grandfather. And now I have the reputation thanks to our little vacation. But I need experienced partners I can trust with my life. You've more than proven yourself. Are you in?" Jayden nodded, his expression, for once, one of complete seriousness.

"What are you going to call it, your treasure hunting company? Since Treasure, Inc. is already taken, I mean."

Hunt grimaced at the mention of Deadalus' outfit. "I was thinking of calling it 'Omega'."

Jayden pointed to Hunt's timepiece. "What, after your fancy watch? Although I admit it did come in handy during our dives."

Hunt nodded, acknowledging that fact. "No, I was thinking more along the lines of how, in physics and electrical engineering, omega is a unit of resistance. My group will be a unit of resistance against those who would deny others the privilege of experiencing the riches of human history."

Jayden plucked a truffle from the tray of a passing server and popped it into his mouth. "Works for me."

Then Hunt turned to Maddy, who had watched the conversation with interest. "How about you, are you in?"

She glanced down at the floor for a second before meeting Hunt's gaze. "I'd like to be, Carter, and I certainly commend you for your vision. But I need my career--my own work--it's important to me. But let's just say that I'll be your number one consultant."

Hunt beamed. "I think I have something I may need to consult you on tonight."

As the audience *oohed* and *ahhed* over the golden, glittering finds on display, Jayden chatted with an attractive female server offering pomegranate martinis while Hunt and Maddy strolled through the grand entrance of the museum toward the exit that led out to the street. It was crowded, and although Hunt did his best to lead Maddy smoothly through the crowd, he nevertheless bumped into a tall, dark-haired man with a swarthy complexion who was on his way into the exhibit.

"Pardon me, I'm so sorry," the man said, causing Hunt to look over at him. He was about to say excuse me, when he saw that the man was Daedalus, dressed sharply in a tuxedo and bow tie. Maddy was looking away from him, and Hunt continued walking, for he had nothing to say to the man.

"How was the exhibit, I can't wait to see it myself!" Daedalus said, pretending to make innocuous conversation with a stranger. Hunt ignored him and led Maddy out. They walked out into the crisp New York night and hailed a taxi. The two of them got in and Hunt told the driver to take them to the Ritz Carlton.

"You have good taste, Mr. Hunt, I'll say that," Maddy said.

In spite of the kaleidoscopic array of sights outside the cab window, Hunt maintained direct eye contact with her.

"Thank you, Dr. Chambers. The Ritz might not be as fancy as Atlantis, but it'll have to do for tonight."

Sign up for Rick Chesler's mailing list to be informed of new releases: **www.rickchesler.com/contact**

If you enjoyed ATLANTIS GOLD: An Omega Files Adventure, you might also enjoy the following novels by Rick Chesler:

TWO PRIMITIVE TRIBES LIVING HALF A WORLD APART.
ONE GUARDED REVELATION THAT WAS NEVER MEANT
TO BE SEEN.

AND A CALAMITY ABOUT TO BE UNLEASHED.

During a terrifying break-in at a marine laboratory, a European-North African terror group makes off with a large quantity of deadly nerve agent. Demands are made and large-scale attacks are launched in the United States from coast to coast.

When the President of the United States becomes a target of the terror group while hosting a party on his yacht, OUTCAST is hell-bent on showing America that their way isn't the best way--it's the only way.

Made in the USA
Las Vegas, NV
12 March 2021